SERVING TIME

He stroked Fern's well spanked arse. 'Let's get you lying across your doggie basket, sweetheart, with your little legs wide open.'

Oblivious to everything except her soaking heat-heavy crotch, Fern obeyed. The stranger holding her leash now, she crawled over to the wicker canine bed and knelt before it. The man tugged gently at her collar, urging her forward till her soft belly settled in the central hollow, her arms and legs stretched out on either side. He put his hand between her legs.

'Such a hot little bitch,' he murmured. Further heat rushed to her groin. Fern whimpered. 'Beg nicely for my fingers,' he said softly.

A NEXUS CLASSIC

SERVING TIME

Sarah Veitch

This book is a work of fiction.
In real life, make sure you practise safe, sane and consensual sex.

First published in 1995 by
Nexus
Thames Wharf Studios
Rainville Road
London W6 9HA

This Nexus Classic edition 2004

www.nexus-books.co.uk

Typeset by TW Typesetting, Plymouth, Devon

Printed and bound by Clays Ltd, St Ives PLC

ISBN 0 352 33509 2

One

'Tell me about your crime, and I'll offer you an alternative mode of punishment,' the police psychiatrist murmured.

Fern Terris stared at the man who had just taken up residence in her lounge. He had introduced himself at the door as Dr Brett Marshall. He had said he was here to discuss her trial which was to take place the next day.

Fern hesitated. 'But you already *know* what happened from the police reports!'

The neatly bearded stranger stared: 'I want to hear it in your own words, Miss Terris.'

But you'll hate me! Fern curled her legs more firmly under her haunches, and bit back the thought. All she'd ever wanted was to be loved, but she couldn't show weakness. Couldn't show this unsmiling dark-haired authority that she was lonely and scared.

'Well, I was piss . . . I mean inebriated when I committed the offence,' she said, fiddling with the silver Cupid on her charm bracelet. 'Went shopping in *Poise* the department store.'

'You're often drunk during the day?'

Only on champagne to help ease the emptiness! The words danced through her head, but she kept them safely imprisoned there.

'No, I . . . I'd been to a wine bar for lunch after looking round a new art gallery,' Fern continued. 'Then I went on to *Poise* and ended up on the ground floor behind some nightdress rails. I felt tired, sat down to have a reviving smoke, and fell asleep.'

'Go on.'

'You know the rest!' Fern started to shrug, then she

1

looked more closely at Dr Marshall and thought better of it. That well-tailored black suit and the buffed leather shoes showed that he wasn't the type of man to appreciate the offhand approach. 'Well, as I slept they closed up the store for the night. I was completely concealed by the racks of lingerie. I must have dropped my cigarette, which set some silky basques and baby doll nighties alight.'

'Continue,' the man ordered, leaning back in the reclining chair. Fern swallowed. In the weeks since her arrest she'd tried hard not to remember.

'Well, the flames spread through the shop floor and set fire to the curtains. When I came to, I staggered upstairs to safety but . . .' she sucked in her breath. 'But the store's security guard wasn't so lucky. He was trapped in his little office till the fire brigade arrived.'

'And now the authorities will lock you away for a long, long time,' said the man quietly, his gaze raking her taut breasts and buttock curves, outlined by the cream cotton jumpsuit.

'You don't know that! I mean, it's not as if he's *dead*.'

'He suffered from smoke inhalation and could have been seriously burned,' Dr Marshall said testily.

Fern grimaced: 'But he'll be compensated by the store.' She twisted the ruby cluster round her middle finger till she saw him frowning.

His tone was cold yet even: 'Miss Terris, can money really compensate for physical injury?'

'I . . . guess not.' She had to say what he wanted to hear. She had to get him on her side. She was good at making men like her. At least they liked her for as long as she was a novelty in their beds.

'I see your own background's been extremely opulent. It'll be strange for you, living in such discomfort,' the psychiatrist added.

Fern turned her fidgeting fingers to her choker-style necklace. 'What . . . what do you mean?'

'Life in prison, of course,' Dr Marshall said.

'That's not a foregone conclusion!'

'For committing arson and endangering life, then assaulting a police officer? I see from your case file that you also resisted arrest!'

'The drink was responsible!'

She'd never tell them *why* she'd really gone to *Poise* – or with who. It was too shameful.

'Then prison will dry you out, my dear. Mark my words, that's where that pretty flesh of yours is going. Britain sends more people to jail than any other country in Europe today.'

Fern resisted the urge to nibble her long manicured nails. She cleared her throat. 'You said you'd come to tell me about an alternative penalty.' She didn't like to use the word *punishment*. Not when she'd been physically pampered all her life!

'I did indeed.' The man smiled in her presence for the very first time. 'A group of us have set up an experimental reformatory on the Scottish coastline to re-educate serious offenders like yourself.'

Fern shifted her slim hips in her chair: 'And how does it differ from prison?'

'In most ways!' the police psychiatrist answered. 'You get to cook your own meals with quality ingredients. You can watch any television programme, order books.'

'Such excitement!' Fern muttered.

'Believe me, my girl, you'll miss these numerous little freedoms when they are taken away.'

He looked round the centrally heated and wool-carpeted room. 'Want to know what prison is like? Well, imagine spending most of your life in a cell with up to three others. You'll be known as the *new meat* there. The moment the officers lock you in for the night some butch momma will be pushing her pussy up against your face and instructing you to get that lazy tongue out and lick.'

'There's no need to be so crude!'

Brett Marshall shook his head. 'You want crude? Crude's cleaning out your own commode. Crude's eating whatever's set in front of you or going hungry.'

'All right! All right! Let's assume I opt for your reformatory with its nicer regime,' Fern cut in nervously. 'What's the catch?'

3

'You sign a contract in which you promise to submit to appropriate discipline.'

'You mean . . .' No he couldn't mean that! Fern forced back the thought.

The man smiled coldly. 'I mean you agree to accept whatever chastisements we decide to apply.'

'Going to cane me, are you?' Fern snorted.

'If that's what it takes.'

This was the 1990s, so she couldn't quite believe him. 'Sounds like I'd be better off in jail!' she muttered sarcastically, beginning to pleat the ends of her waist-length chestnut hair.

'Well, we go to court tomorrow,' the police psychiatrist said. 'It's up to you.' He reached for his briefcase, stood up and moved towards the door. 'You can instruct your lawyer to say that you're willing to serve time in our reformatory for an indefinite period. In truth, you'll probably only serve a few months. Or you can keep quiet and go to prison for at least a decade. Some arsonists get life.' He looked tellingly at her young, high breasts and her firm waistline. 'If you spend ten years locked up in jail, Miss Terris, you'll be thirty-four when you get out.'

The reformatory it was! The next day Fern had her lawyer opt for the softer-sounding option. Then she was taken to the cells below the courts to await the transport to her new punitive abode. Not that she planned to be under anyone's thumb for long. She was pretty, she was bright – she could make friends and influence people. It would just take a caressing hand on some prison officer's thigh.

Fern looked up as a key grated in the iron door of her cell. It swung slowly inward.

'Right, let's teach you some discipline,' said a familiar voice.

She looked beyond the court officer and saw Dr Marshall standing there. He held out a pair of handcuffs.

'Surely that's not necessary?' Fern said, quickly putting her arms behind her back. She was much too classy for this!

4

'Only till we get you in the van,' the police psychiatrist replied.

'As you wish.' She'd make him do what *she* wished in time. Men were suckers for sexual satisfaction! She'd press her breasts against his side as they sat in the back of the vehicle. She'd move her stocking-clad thigh next to his.

'Hands in front. Good girl, that's it.'

She winced as he clicked the cold grey cuffs into place.

Carefully maintaining her balance, she followed the officer and the psychiatrist to the van. She was helped in by two solicitous hands on her elbows and seated on the long low bench that ran the length of one wall.

'Good luck, Miss,' the officer said, beginning to shut the doors. Fern hoped she wouldn't need it. Dr Marshall sat down next to her and she held out her cuffed slim wrists.

'Please, take them off.' She tried to make it sound as if she were talking about her panties or her lace blouse rather than the handcuffs. She seductively parted her full pink lips.

She watched Dr Marshall's hands as they slid the small key into the lock and freed her. He had large hands, authoritative hands. Hands which could explore each soft centimetre of her skin, undress her. The van turned a corner sharply, giving her the excuse she required to seduce the doctor. Quickly she fell against him, letting her nearest hand land half over his inner thigh and partway over his cock.

'Whoops!' she said breathlessly. She made as if to take her palm away and let her eyes widen, holding his gaze. 'Mmm, feels as if you're pleased to meet me!' She felt the primeval knowledge and power quicken within her as his manhood twitched then lengthened through his suit trousers under her hand. She looked up at him through mascara-dark lashes, smiled, and waited. Waited for him to take her in his arms.

Instead, in one movement that left her confused and breathless, he pulled her over his knee, so that her arms and legs were lying stretched along the van's hard seat, fully supported. 'You're about to receive your first reformatory spanking,' he said.

5

'But I haven't done anything!' Fern protested, trying to scrabble back.

The man held her firmly by the waist, keeping her helplessly in position. 'Attempting to seduce an official for personal gain is a moral offence in our punishment book.'

'I haven't read your bloody book!' Fern muttered.

'And you won't,' the police psychiatrist continued. 'It's a series of unwritten rules, a mixture of common sense and basic courtesy. In time the guidelines will exist inside your head. That's what being a good citizen is all about.'

'All right, so I should have taken my hand away from your crotch sooner,' Fern admitted awkwardly, twisting her head back to look at him.

'Shouldn't have had it there in the first place,' corrected the man. She squirmed as he stroked her buttocks through her skirt. 'The case notes we have, suggested you'd try to use your sexuality for non-sexual purposes.'

'I'm sorry! Okay?'

Maybe if she appeased him he'd let her get up from his lap. Lying here like this was *so* humiliating.

'Let's lift this skirt up before I spank you,' Dr Marshall murmured, starting to peel away the smooth black linen from her nether cheeks.

'Spank me? You can't!' Fern muttered, reaching a hand back to swipe his away.

She opened her mouth in surprise as he grabbed hold of that same wrist and clipped the handcuff on, then brought the other wrist down before her and did likewise. Now her hands were fastened in front of her and she couldn't protect her poor bum.

'Time for a long sore lesson,' Dr Marshall continued. Fern stared at the seat of the vehicle as she felt him pushing up the lined fabric of her skirt until he tucked the hem under her armpits. She felt the cool air on the naked stretch of thigh above each stocking top.

'As it's your first offence since being sentenced to serving time, I'll just spank you over your pretty pants,' the police psychiatrist said.

'Gee, thanks,' Fern mumbled, anxious as ever to pretend

6

she wasn't grateful or intimidated. She wouldn't give the bastard the satisfaction of knowing she was out of her depth.

Dr Marshall stroked her buttocks through their thin cotton coating until she wriggled with fear and anticipation. 'You'll be punished shortly for that unnecessary piece of insolence,' he said.

He pushed the button on the wall leading to the driver's cab, and the glass panel immediately wound down. 'Rab, one spanking over her pants to be recorded in the punishment book.'

Fern shivered and closed her eyes, hating the fact that the driver might hear her taking her thrashing. He could watch in the cabin's mirror as she got a toasted rear end.

'And a second smacking on the bare backside for being rude to me.' Dr Marshall added in a conversational tone.

Fern squirmed in his lap. She felt hugely aware of her small high buttocks and was glad that her panties were waist to thigh white cotton. At least he wasn't yet contemplating the secret dark crease of her arse!

She tried to steady her breathing, aware that the inscrutable doctor was still staring down at her helpless buttocks. What would this correction be like? She had never been spanked before. 'You aren't really going to do this?' she said, but it came out as a question rather than a determined statement.

'Oh trust me – I certainly am,' the tall dark doctor replied.

She closed her eyes as he fondled her waiting globes. Shameful new heat thrilled through her pubis. If he was this good in a van, he'd be absolutely incredible in bed! But he wasn't here to pleasure her: instead he wanted to punish her poor raised bottom.

'Use sex only for satisfaction,' he reminded. Then he lifted his hand.

Fern sensed rather than saw the movement; felt the air currents change then winced as the first downward slap made contact with her taut right cheek. As a warm glow spread through its smooth centre, her tormentor spanked

the flesh above it, then below it. 'Ouch, that hur . . .' Fern
started, the words changing to an indignant squeal as he
turned his attention to the other buttock and doled out
three equally stinging slaps. Then her tormentor smacked
the bare flesh at the top of her thighs till the cool flesh felt
hot and tender.

'Girls hate a tops-of-leg spanking, but it makes them behave much better,' he murmured, before smacking the
backs of her thighs all over again.

After that, he settled into a painful pattern. Spanking
first one pantied buttock then the other. Fern wriggled
about defencelessly as he used her bottom like a drum on
which he beat out a one-handed tattoo. His right hand was
big, his right arm was strong, her small rump was soft and
supple.

'Shouldn't have tried to seduce you. Won't do it again!'
she gasped, wincing and squirming across his lap.

The doctor spanked the lower portion of both tender
cheeks: 'You won't if a hot sore bum reminds you of the
error of your ways.'

Fern writhed across his knees as he continued with his
relentless hand-heavy rhythm. Her nipples rubbed against
the van seat. Her pubic mound pushed against his lap as
she tensed and untensed her major leg muscles. Her main
attention, though, was concentrated on her poor disarmed
bottom, still receiving slap after slap.

At last he stopped. Fern cautiously opened her eyes. The
van looked brighter than before, as if filled with extra sunshine. She could see that Rab the driver had left his glass
partition fully wound down. Damn it, he'd have heard her
apologise, heard her little gasps and moans and squeals,
her breathless entreaties. She'd never be able to look him
squarely in the face again!

What was a woman to say or do after a man had spanked her for being devious? Fern's mind raced with possible
humorous and dramatic one-liners, each of which she instantly sent away. Her backside was still beneath the police
psychiatrist's palms, so she didn't want to enrage him further. She just wanted to be allowed to sit on the side of her

hip and pretend this had never happened and continue the journey to the reformatory in sore-bummed peace.

'Does your bottom hurt?'

She winced as the bearded man stroked her hot cheeks again and again. Of course it bloody hurt – it had been well-roasted!

'Yes sir,' she murmured with fake obsequiousness.

'But you understand *why* you were punished?' the man prompted.

Fern lay over his lap like a glowing offering: 'For trying to seduce you so that I'd be better treated at the reformatory?'

'Mm hmm.' Dr Marshall stroked on and on and on. Fern whimpered at the sudden surge of blood to her pubis. Suddenly she felt very aroused and accepting and open, her sex just crying out to be completely filled. 'As long as you behave in the way civilised humans were meant to behave you'll be well treated at *Compulsion*,' the psychiatrist continued smoothly.

'*Compulsion*?' She kept her nose pressed against the van seat, no longer wanting to look at his knowing face.

'Mmm, that's the reformatory's unofficial name. You see, you're *compelled* to follow our dictates until you incorporate them into your psyche and they become *your* dictates. Thereafter, you can leave.'

She'd probably be out in a week, Fern thought, cheering up a little. After all, Dr Marshall had just told the magistrates' court that she had an above-average IQ and was exceptionally creative. It should be easy to earn good behaviour points by saying what they wanted her to say, doing what they wanted her to do. She'd soon be back in her pretty bungalow to resume her shop-till-you-drop and party-animal life.

If only she was at such a party now, and could find someone who'd slake the throbbing between her legs caused by all this buttock-based attention. Driven by some inner wanting, Fern rubbed her mound against the psychiatrist's hard thighs.

She heard the taunting tone in the man's smooth voice: 'Did that spanking excite you, Fern?'

Now what? If she said it had he would probably repeat it. But if she said it hadn't and he knew that she'd lied . . .

'Not because of . . . just because it brought heat to the whole area,' she stammered, closing her eyes with new embarrassment.

'Then I'll leave the cuffs on for a while to make sure that you don't play with yourself.'

Worse and worse! 'I wouldn't!' Fern lied. She'd always loved the quick hard relief brought by her own middle fingers.

'Only you have to learn self-control at *Compulsion*,' Dr Marshall continued. As he spoke he caressed both cheeks of her pantied bum. 'We've found that offenders such as yourself are often instant gratification types, impulsively in pursuit of the next wad of money or love affair or desired mood change. We teach you self-restraint, how to wait.'

That was all she needed, Fern thought sulkily.

'Sulking won't do any good,' Dr Marshall added.

Damn him, he seemed to know everything! 'Can I sit up now, sir?' she asked humbly.

'Only when Rab finds a lay-by,' the psychiatrist said.

'We're stopping for a break this soon?' Her watch showed that it was only three quarters of an hour since they'd left the court's busy car park.

The man hoisted her higher upon his knee: 'We're stopping so that Rab can warm your arse for your earlier rude words.'

'But I was rude to you, not him!' This time Fern risked a reproachful look back at the man – she had to do *something*!

'True, but I'm delegating the task.' He fondled her writhing posterior. 'My arm's a little tired, whereas his will be painfully alert. And he does so enjoy chastising a new offender – especially when it's a pretty woman!' He rested a palm on each of her buttocks as if savouring their obviously well-spanked warmth. 'I usually keep a close eye on him after he's bared a bad girl's bottom to make sure he doesn't get carried away.'

It was awful to lie here knowing that her bum was going

to be toasted again, Fern thought. She'd better keep quiet though – at least until they reached *Compulsion*. Hopefully there would be some wimpish social worker there to whom she could make an official complaint. She'd get Dr Marshall and Rab fired. She'd get herself sympathy and cups of tea. She'd work at getting an early date with the parole board. She'd beat the system yet!

But for now it was going to beat – or at least *spank* – her. Fern trembled as she heard and felt the van nosing its way into the side of the road. She nibbled at the insides of her cheeks as the engine was switched off and she heard Rab's cabin door opening and closing.

'Let it be noted that the offender walked to the punishment site,' Dr Marshall said as the double doors of the van opened and Rab pulled his way up and in.

'It's noted, Guv,' said Rab.

Christ, he sounded like a relic from the fifties! She was glad that her head was facing away so that she didn't have to look at him, but she hated the realisation that he was staring down at her pantied little bum.

'Let's get some cool air on that hot bottom,' Dr Marshall said conversationally.

Anxious to be freed from her humiliating position, Fern used her cuffed wrists and spread knees to lever herself up to a kneeling position on the long low seat. She started to sink back on her haunches, then thought better of it. It would be foolish to put any kind of pressure on her stinging rump.

She got to her feet quickly as Rab reached for her right arm.

'Seems I've got to warm your arse for you, darling.'

Fern turned to face him, looking up into the eyes of an angry and uneducated man.

'Please,' she whispered to Dr Marshall. 'I can't bear him to . . . Can't *you* spank me again instead?'

'I could but I won't. It wouldn't be as hard or as shaming. And the object is for you to feel shame now. After all, your response to my letting you keep on your pants was a particularly ungrateful one.'

11

'I was grateful really,' Fern lied as Dr Marshall turned her towards the van's open doors. She saw Rab's gloating gaze contemplating the rotundities beneath her raised linen skirt, and decided to say nothing further. The driver was obviously enjoying her ignominy. She'd do her very best not to wriggle or squeal.

'Right, darling, let's get you down,' Rab said, jumping onto the grass at the side of the road, then turning and holding out his hands towards her.

'I'll manage myself,' Fern said primly, then put her feet together and jumped. Both soles of her shoes hit the grass at roughly the same time, but the surface was wet and her cuffed arms had taken away some of her balance. Her heart lurched as both feet slid from under her and she sprawled on her belly on the grass.

What if a car came along now? What if a farmer was inspecting his fields? Hugely aware of her cuffed wrists and pulled back skirt, Fern got clumsily to her feet and backed away from the lumberjack-shirted driver. Rab smiled without warmth.

'You'll be grateful for my help in time.' He slapped his large right hand against his loose denims, and stared at her. Fern looked helplessly towards the psychiatrist.

'Know when to have the good grace to accept another's aid,' Dr Marshall said, levering himself down from the van to stand beside her. 'You've already got a sore bum coming to you so we won't punish you for not taking Rab's hand today.'

Fern knew better than to mutter 'Gee, thanks' this time! She kept looking nervously at Dr Marshall as he scanned the landscape.

'Want to tie her to that tree over there?' he asked Rab.

'Nah, I like a bent-over bum. There's a fence round that big tattie field down there,' the driver answered.

'It's just a *spanking* this time, remember, Rab,' the psychiatrist cautioned.

'Aye aye, boss. Worse luck!' Rab said.

'What . . . what else do you do?' Fern whispered, registering the phrase just a spanking *this time*.

12

'At *Compulsion*?' Dr Marshall replied. 'Depends on the crime and the culprit. If you change your wicked ways you may never have to find out.'

'I'm not wicked!' Fern said as Rab put a hand on her shoulder and began to walk her towards the distant fence. Her calves felt tremulous.

'But the arson attack, your lack of real remorse and refusal to respect authority have been reprehensible,' Dr Marshall said.

'And now I'll take it out on your bad wee bum,' Rab added in a gloating voice.

Fern wished she could get free of the cuffs in order to slap his ugly face and push him away from her. But she'd have to run for cover, then, and where could she go? She'd arranged for a tenant to rent the bungalow her parents had bought for her, so she couldn't go back there until her sentence was over. And she hadn't held down a job since leaving college. Daddy had given her a weekly allowance for the past few years. Fern sighed as she continued walking towards the site of her punishment. Now that he'd disowned her because of her crime she was very much alone.

Well, not quite alone. There was Wanda, of course, but she couldn't risk leading the authorities to Wanda. Fern's jumbled thoughts were forced into further fragments at Rab's next exultant words.

'Almost there, darling. Ever been bound over to keep the peace before? Makes your arse stick out nice and high for me to toast with my hand.'

Don't look at him. Don't think about what's happening next!

She stared at the recently mown grass a few feet in front of her. Though she tried to slow her steps, they were taking her closer and closer to the dreaded fence. If only she hadn't been rude to Dr Marshall! If only she hadn't set fire to the store! If only she'd ... Fern's mind raced with if onlys, but her bum already knew it was too late.

They reached the gate and Rab pointed to a smooth new piece of fencing along from it: 'Put your belly against that, my bonny angel.'

Fern looked weakly at Dr Marshall, who nodded. 'Rab's to give you a five minute spanking across a fence for your earlier impertinence.' He smiled down at her. 'Whilst it's going on, you'll only be able to think of the heat in your poor bottom, how sore it is. But afterwards think of the lesson – reflect on how nice you could have been to me, or to anyone else you interact with.'

'Yes sir,' Fern muttered.

Rab reached for her elbow, but she stepped swiftly sideways to avoid his touch. She was resigned to this spanking but she could at least spoil some of his enjoyment by getting onto the fence by herself! Inhaling hard, she placed her cuffed wrists against the top rung and her feet on the lowest one. Then she levered herself up with her wrists, bent her body reluctantly forward and let her bound arms hang down as low as they were able.

'I'll just make sure you stay there,' Rab said tauntingly. Fern trembled as she felt him fumbling at her ankles and wrists.

When he moved back, she looked down. Damn him – he'd used restraints to put her totally at his mercy. The bastard had fastened one end of his belt around one of her ankles then tied the free end to the chain between the cuffs. Now her bottom was a raised and tempting target, and she couldn't move her flesh enough to evade even one single spank.

The men had warned her to keep her skirt up around her armpits throughout the punishment walk, so now the only protection Fern had was her cotton panties. And Rab had made it clear that they were coming off!

'Right, get this wee bum nice and bare for your Uncle Rab,' he said now.

Not if she had anything to do with it! Fern pushed her belly closer to the fence in a bid to hold her knickers in place.

'Don't get on the wrong side o' me, girlie,' he added, fingers moving against her thighs as he pulled at the legs of her pants. 'I've a really hard hand.'

'He does,' Dr Marshall added. Though he was presumably standing close to her back, his voice seemed to come from very far away. 'There's bigger girls than you have pleaded to be spared a thrashing from our Rab.'

Fern tensed her eyes and her mouth. Her belly felt glued to the fence. This was much too shameful. She inhaled and held as the van driver took hold of the back of her waistband and tore her panties away. She felt the cool breeze brushing over her helpless bottom and the flesh above her stocking tops. There was a silence in which she could tell that both men were contemplating her newly bared bum.

'Quite a pink rump already, isn't it, Dr M?'

She heard Dr Marshall's quiet assent: 'I gave her quite a spanking over her panties for pawing at my crotch, Rab.'

'Nothing to what she'll have had by the time I've finished teaching her manners,' Rab added with relish in his voice.

She sensed him moving closer, and felt the first two-palmed fondling of her twitching arse cheeks. His hands were rough, and mercilessly thorough. She tensed her thighs together as he stroked and squeezed each inch of skin.

'Not nearly as hot as it's going to be,' he added, rubbing what felt like a thumb or stocky finger down the furrow between her buttocks. 'I'll have it baking!'

Hate you, hate you, hate you, Fern shrieked inside her head.

'Don't waste time blaming Rab or anyone else,' said Dr Marshall's smooth calm voice, 'that's the approach of losers. Just concentrate on how much you hate this humiliation, and what you can do to redeem yourself.'

'I've said I'm sorry!' Fern muttered. She felt a sudden pain, and heard the accompanying loud slapping sound. 'Aaah! Ouch!' Both spanks brought back some of the heat of her earlier punishment.

'Give me a minute and I'll really give you something to cry about,' Rab said.

Obviously in search of greater leverage, he put one hand on the side of her back, and started to spank her more firmly. His hand toasted first one taut globe then the next. Fern jerked and writhed, vaguely aware of little squealing

15

sounds. It took her a few seconds to realise that they were coming from herself.

Christ, the man knew how to spank! Bound as she was, Fern couldn't see how far he was lifting his hand back, but she could feel each flesh-on-flesh explosion, hear each resounding crack. 'Getting nice and toasty, now,' Rab gloated, stopping for a second to rest his hands against her extremities.

'Two more minutes,' Dr Marshall said.

Which meant she was just over halfway through her second-ever chastisement. Who'd have thought a grown woman could feel such shame? Shame and much as she'd mentally hated Rab's degrading words, she'd felt an unwanted creeping physical pleasure. Now that he was caressing her bottom cheeks, she registered a heavy arousal-led heat between her legs.

'Let's see if we can make this arse the colour o' the poppies over there,' Rab said, and Fern knew without opening her eyes that the poppies would be the deepest red.

'A thrashing hurts more after a wee rest,' he continued, fondling her already-sore orbs. She tensed as his palm left her bum, then yelled as it made contact again with renewed energy. He spanked the full swell of her cheeks, walloped hard at the top, then the sides and the jiggling underswell.

'I'll not leave your bonny legs out,' he continued in his horribly exultant voice. 'They'll come up real pink with the right treatment.' He started to heat the tender backs of her thighs with every fourth or fifth smack.

'Ah! Ah! Ah!' Fern grunted in an accompanying rhythm. Her pubis rubbed against the fence as each new slap enlivened her quivering cheeks.

'Enough,' said Dr Marshall's voice. Fern tensed her buttocks, expecting Rab to fit in a few more spanks. There was no further movement. Silence. 'Miss Terris, would you like a few moments to compose yourself?' Dr Marshall said, 'or do you want to be unbound straight away?'

'Unbound,' Fern muttered, then hastily added, 'Please, sir.' Much as she loathed the idea of Rab seeing her flushed shamed face, it was preferable to him continuing to stare at her naked and sore backside.

16

'You get the engine started,' she heard Dr Marshall say, obviously speaking to the driver. Fern relaxed a little as one set of footsteps moved away.

She flexed her ankles as the psychiatrist freed them from the belt. 'I'm going to uncuff your wrists,' he said. 'I'll leave them unfastened for the remainder of the journey if you promise to behave yourself.'

'I'll behave, sir!' Fern muttered, blushing. She was going to make sure she couldn't go wrong by not uttering a single word. After all, a hastily blurted insult or a lie could earn her another thrashing and she couldn't stand the thought of baring her poor hot bottom again. Dr Marshall put his arms around her waist to help her down, and she leaned gratefully against him. She felt a sense of loss as he broke the contact by setting her firmly on her feet on the grassy ground.

'You can smooth your skirt down if you like,' he murmured. Fern did so right away, wincing as the linen rubbed against her tenderised bottom. 'We'll buy you new pants to replace the ones Rab ripped off,' Dr Marshall said. 'He was out of line.'

Would he be spanked for it, Fern wondered sourly. She decided not to ask – it would probably be construed as impudence!

'You're probably wondering if he'll be penalised for it,' Dr Marshall continued. 'Yes, he will.'

They trod back up the field. 'Don't you want to know how we'll chastise him?' the psychiatrist continued.

'Only if you want to tell me, sir.'

'Of course. That's only fair.' The doctor smiled. 'He loves punishing young girls – therefore we won't let him chasten any of the recalcitrant inmates for a fortnight. Two weeks frustrated denial for a pair of torn panties, you understand.'

'Yes, sir.'

Dr Marshall put a hand on her arm. Fern closed her eyes. God, not another spanking!

'Fern – we're not trying to turn our offenders into submissive robots. We simply want to teach you a fair way to behave.'

17

But the teaching hurt so much! She hesitated, then spoke: 'So I can ask questions?'

The man smiled indulgently. 'Of course you can ask questions!'

Fern pushed further. 'I can disagree with what you say?'

'Yes – just as you would in the outside world, the world we're trying to equip you for,' the psychiatrist elaborated. 'We only ask that you give new ideas a trial period; learn to live in a different way.'

Their steps took them closer to the road and the van.

'Let's recap, Miss Terris. What did I spank you for?'

'Using my sexuality for non-sexual purposes,' Fern said.

'And why did I have Rab spank you?' the doctor continued.

'For being rude instead of grateful when you offered to leave my wrists uncuffed, sir,' Fern explained.

'Ultimate lessons learned?' the man enquired.

Be more subtle when being vamplike and keep your big mouth shut! Fern thought sarcastically. Her brain searched for a more politically correct reply.

'I've learned that I should be honest and respect others, Dr Marshall.'

'You've done well,' her new mentor said.

Fern felt the strange half-physical, half-spiritual expansion she got in her chest whenever anyone was kind to her. Mummy and daddy had always been too busy making money to dole out praise. Fearful of spoiling the moment of closeness with the enigmatic doctor, she looked at the sweet mown grass in front of her as she walked, and said nothing more.

They reached the van. Dr Marshall circled his arms around her waist and lifted her into the back. Fern started to sit down then looked round wincingly for a cushion.

'Here,' Dr Marshall said, 'have my coat.'

Taking it off, he folded it into a smooth plump square and set it down on the long seat. Fern lowered her sore bottom onto it with relief.

'Thank you, sir,' she said.

Dr Marshall spoke to the back of the driver's head:

'We're ready for off, Rab.' He pressed the button and the panel rose back up. 'He'll be feeling sorry for himself all the rest of the way back now because he can no longer listen to our conversation. He loves to know what the offenders are doing and saying next!'

'Does he often drive offenders who've just been tried?' Fern asked.

'Uh huh – and those who've been found guilty in one of our numerous internal trials!' He looked at her more closely. 'We had a case like that only last week.'

'Oh?' Fern queried. She figured she'd better know what was coming next, what sentencing at an internal trial could earn you. She hoped it didn't involve a cruelly bared bum!

'We let one of the inmates out on a day-release course,' the psychiatrist said. 'The silly little madam attempted to run away. Between you and me, she left so many clues that I suspect she secretly wanted her bottom warmed!' He shrugged. 'Anyway, we caught up with her as she tried to thumb a lift, took her into the back of the van for a thorough caning. When it was over she kicked Rab in the shins.'

'Awful,' Fern said in a small voice. She remembered her own urge to slap Rab's face and push him over.

'Don't get me wrong,' said Dr Marshall, 'you can hit a man who's unfairly hitting you. We're all equal in this life. But the girl had involved us in a lot of expense and potential problems with the authorities. She'd brought this caning on herself so should have taken it with good grace.' He smiled coolly. 'Anyway, the lesson we then had to teach her was to accept due punishment without retaliating or the ultimate outcome is much worse.'

'What did you do?' Fern whispered, feeling curious yet afraid of the answer.

'We left her jeans at her knees and made her kneel up on the passenger seat of Rab's cabin after we'd caned her. We buckled two thongs round her waist and tethered her to the back of the seat.'

Fern ran the tip of her tongue over her suddenly dry lips: 'Didn't she damn you to hell?'

The doctor shook his head. 'She knew she'd done wrong.

As I say, I believe she was testing her own limits. We warned her to keep her hands flat on the top of her head as we drove, or she'd get an extra thrashing. We also reminded her that every vehicle coming in the opposite direction could see her reddened arse.'

'And no one told the police?' Fern asked, the shameful yet exciting vision filling her brain.

'Hell, the police aren't above giving out a hiding if it's required!' the unruffled doctor replied. 'But no one called them. A couple of lorry drivers even gave us the thumbs up sign.' He looked at her more seriously as the van speeded up. 'And of course she signed the same disclaimer as you, giving us the right to warm her bum for her if necessary.'

Fern licked her lips. 'I hadn't realised you meant corporal punishment! And I'd no idea how much it would hurt!'

'Your little rump needn't suffer much – not if you become resocialised immediately,' the psychiatrist said.

Fern widened her hazel eyes and looked up at her new mentor. 'If you could give me a list of what counts as doing wrong . . .'

'That would be pointless when you are released into the community.' He looked into her still-flushed face. 'No, you have to genuinely become a more thoughtful citizen. And if that means you learn by us whipping your more tender charms then so be it.

She'd been spanked twice already, but now Dr Marshall was talking about *caning* and *whipping*! Who would lay on the rod, and for how long? How much harder would the chastisement get? Would they bind her wrists each time and always strip off her protective panties? As the van grew ever closer to *Compulsion*, Fern wondered what was in store for her helpless bum.

Two

Waves crashed into ungiving rocks. Fern tuned in to the sound, then peered through a blackness darker than you ever found in the city. As Dr Marshall helped her from the van, she breathed in the ozone air.

'How long was I askeep, sir?' she asked, careful to add the sir.

The doctor checked his luminous watch. 'Oh, a couple of hours.'

'And this is *Compulsion*?' Her eyes followed the winding path down, down, down to a large rectangular building half-hidden by conifer trees.

'Half of it,' Dr Marshall admitted, sounding thoughtful. 'Let's hope for your sake that you never get transferred to the other half!'

She was allowed to ask questions, but her brain felt sugar-starved, dull.

'Will they let me have something to eat?' she asked the psychiatrist.

'Whatever you want, my dear! And a bath, and a long rest.'

'A bath sounds brilliant!' She wondered if they'd let her use her favourite tangerine bathing oil.

'I'll soap your tits if you ask nicely,' Rab taunted. 'And scrub your wee pink pussy lips.'

Damn! She hadn't heard him leave the cab, but now he was breathing down her neck and doubtlessly grinning.

'Don't worry. No one will interfere with you unless you do something to deserve it,' Dr Marshall intervened.

Fern, dressed in her sensible skirt and blouse, Dr Marshall, in his single-breasted slate grey suit and Rab in his checked shirt and denims, made their mismatched way down the path towards the far-off gates.

'Looks like they've all gone to bed,' Fern said, looking in vain for welcoming window lights.

'Ms Lenn, the admissions officer, knows that we're arriving. She'll be waiting up for us,' the police psychiatrist said.

'You phoned on ahead?' Fern murmured.

'As always. Casual visitors aren't tolerated here.'

She wouldn't have any visitors anyway. No one but Wanda cared enough to make the journey, and Wanda wouldn't dare, because . . . Fern forced back the memories of the past, of Wanda's softly curving lips and Wanda's unusually large hands and Wanda's strong thighs in their fringed cut-off Levis. She had to forget about what had happened and what might yet happen. She had to concentrate on getting through the little that remained of today.

At last they reached the arched locked door. Dr Marshall pressed a buzzer, waited, then said his name into the answering intercom.

'I've brought prisoner Terris,' he said.

After a few moments a slightly plump brunette in her forties answered the door. Fern stared at her light grey uniform of short-sleeved top and trousers. The woman seemed to be assessing Fern's own black skirt and equally sensible white blouse.

'Welcome!' she said at last. 'We've run you a bubble bath and prepared you a meal.' She ushered them all in to a firelit reception area.

'This,' said Dr Marshall, smiling, 'is our admissions officer, Ms Lenn.'

How many offenders did they admit, for God's sake? Or did this woman have other tasks? Did she take off that thick grey belt round her waist if you were disobedient? Fern shivered and kept her palms protectively near her bare bottom, wishing that Rab hadn't torn off her shielding cotton pants.

But the woman merely served her up an exquisitely prepared Spanish omelette, then left her to enjoy a herbal bath before showing her to a large, cream-wallpapered room.

'See you first thing tomorrow, dear,' were the woman's parting words.

Tomorrow would be her chance to exploit some silly social worker! Moments after curling under the duck feather duvet, Fern floated off to sleep.

'This is your wake up call.'

The strange voice came from near the top of her bed. Fern jumped into wakefulness, pulled the duvet over her naked breasts and sleep-warmed nipples, then sat up and twisted her head round. She saw that the words had crackled from the cream-painted intercom above the headboard. They might have warned her of its role! The clock showed that it was 8 a.m. She never rose much before midday at the bungalow and always had a leisurely brunch before heading off to the shops.

She'd just have ten more minutes. She turned over on her sleepy side, and pulled the duvet over her head to block out the increasing sunshine. When she next surfaced it was 11 a.m.

Slowly Fern got out of bed and shrugged into the white knee-length dressing gown that had been left on the chair for her. She switched on the electric kettle beside the television and made herself a decaffeinated tea. A quick scan of the room showed a mini-fridge which contained skimmed milk and butter, and wholemeal bread and muesli in the cupboard immediately above. Relaxing, *Compulsion*'s newest inmate ate and drank and watched a programme about reflexology. She was idly massaging her own feet in the hope of stimulating new energy, when there was a knock at the door.

As Fern crossed the room, Dr Marshall walked in. This time his suit was a midnight blue one. He looked so strong and tall and self-possessed that she immediately felt afraid.

'Why didn't you get up with the alarm, Fern?' he asked.

'Dr Marshall! I . . . I'm not an early riser.'

'Didn't *used* to be an early riser. A healthy body requires a set routine,' the psychiatrist said.

'Right! Well, I'll know next time,' she muttered, pulling the terry towelling robe more closely against her.

'But you'll have to be punished this time,' the authoritative mind-doctor replied. He spoke into the intercom. 'She's ready for you now, Ms Lenn.' He turned back to Fern. 'The woman was scheduled to show you round the building at 9 a.m., so you've inconvenienced her with your laziness. That gives her the right to thrash you till you learn to obey.'

Fern stretched her arms into an unworried yawn. From what she'd seen of Ms Lenn so far, the woman was the mumsy rather than the sadistic type. She'd probably slap Fern's thighs a few times or let her off with a warning. As the psychiatrist left her bedroom Fern lay back down on her bed.

A few moments later Ms Lenn walked smartly through the door.

'Sorry about this,' said Fern. 'I'll get up with the alarm tomorrow.'

'It's a polite but effective alarm, isn't it, Miss Terris? In prison they'd just have banged on the iron doors to wake you up.'

'I guess so. I didn't think . . .' Fern responded, surprised at the woman's firm tone.

'You'd have eaten a tasteless breakfast in a canteen with thousands of other foul-breathed inmates,' Ms Lenn continued.

Fern winced as she pictured the grey hopeless scene. 'I . . . yes.'

'Yet this is how you repay our hospitality,' Ms Lenn said, and her face bore none of the softness of last night. 'We want you to learn to appreciate the finer things in life that you currently take for granted, Fern. And the psychological profiling we did while you were on remand shows that these lessons can best be learned through the repeated warming of your bare backside.'

Taking hold of the girl's dressing gown collar, she began to march her out of the room and down a wide white corridor. 'We always introduce a new girl or boy at our assembly. In your case the others are going to meet your naked bottom before they get to greet your face!'

24

They wouldn't. They couldn't. Public birchings had been repealed years ago, hadn't they? Even caning was normally done in the corridor or the privacy of the headmaster's study. To have an audience of strangers contemplating her uncovered bum.

'I'll get up at dawn tomorrow!' she said haltingly as they reached a thick red curtain with a gap that showed a small stage and outlying assembly room.

'That's a kneejerk reaction,' Ms Lenn said blandly. 'We just want you to develop a wholesome framework.'

'I'll develop one – honest!' Fern was hugely aware of her vulnerable small bottom under the concealing dressing gown.

'Once a misdemeanour has been noted a naughty boy or girl can't evade correction,' the admissions officer said.

Taking hold of Fern's nervous shoulders, she gently manoeuvred her through the curtain so that she faced into the assembly hall. Upwards of a hundred male and female inmates in their late teens, twenties and thirties sat in padded cherrywood seats, staring hopefully at the stage. Its polished pine floor held a large sloping stool that seemed fastened down to the centre stage. Unwilling to speculate about its uses, Fern looked away.

'She's new,' someone whispered from the front row. Fern started to raise her right hand in an uncertain greeting.

'Save the salutations for later. We're about to introduce them to that delectable wicked bottom,' Ms Lenn said.

Fern felt the hotness flooding her face and neck at the woman's taunting. She wished that she could put back the clock, could rise and shine.

'Bend over that whipping stool,' the woman said. 'No, no – bum facing the audience so that they can see its pretty pinkening.'

Reminding herself that she'd agreed to this reformatory regime, Fern obeyed.

'Grip the stool's legs,' Ms Lenn continued. 'If you let go we'll have to fasten you over. And if you protect your well-thrashed cheeks with your hands we'll have to repeat that particular stroke again.'

My God, could this really be happening? Was she really going to be punished in front of this gloating criminal crowd?

'Yes, Ma'am.'

Determined not to anger the woman further, Fern put her palms on the stool, stepped closer and lowered herself onto it. Then she took hold of its stout lower legs, and stared down at the thick wooden mounts which held it securely to the floor.

'Now we bare the buttocks so that they're ready for punishment,' the older woman said.

Fern wondered if they'd ever be ready. She could still remember how she'd writhed under Dr Marshall's and Rab's aching spanks. But she'd agreed to serve a short sentence here rather than endure a much longer one in prison, she reminded herself fearfully. She had to accept whatever the admissions officer wanted her to take.

The twenty-four-year-old held her breath as she felt cool fingers on the backs of her thighs. Suddenly she felt very young, small and defenceless. She gripped the stool legs more tightly as the terry towelling dressing gown was edged up inch by hellish inch. The material seemed to drag against her thighs, as if trying to protect her tender bum, unwilling to be lifted. But at last she felt Ms Lenn denuding her buttocks and lower back of the camouflaging robe.

A man in the audience laughed loud and long. Another whistled.

'Fancy warming that one, do you, Tom?' a woman yelled as each inmate surveyed Fern's naked little rump. It wriggled a little despite itself and someone shouted, 'Keep it moving, sweetheart!'

'It'll move with a vengeance in a moment,' Ms Lenn said into the mike.

Fern stared down at the ground as the admissions officer told the others of her poor rump's fate.

'Miss Terris decided to ignore this morning's alarm, so we're going to wake up her bare bottom with the paddle. I'll use it till I decide her nether regions have had enough.'

Fern was vaguely aware of a man in his twenties entering

26

from the side of the stage and handing something to the woman. He walked out again and Ms Lenn approached Fern's miserable face.

'Have you seen a punishment paddle before, Fern?'

'No, Ma'am.' She wasn't sure that she ever wanted to see one.

'It's very effective. Imparts a throbbing all-over glow.' She squatted down before the girl. 'Look at it. See its nice hard polished veneer?'

'Yes, Ma'am,' Fern whispered with trepidation.

Ms Lenn smiled coldly: 'It's going to give you the most scarlet bum.'

Despite herself, Fern tensed the aforementioned bum.

'We can still see your crack!' a male voice shouted with crude enthusiasm. Fern squirmed on her belly against the stool in an agony of shame and anticipation. She'd never sleep late again in her entire life!

'I'm sure that you're really a good girl and that you'll soon be willing to prove it,' the admissions officer said. She stepped back.

Fern felt the currents of air around her change, then the implement struck her bent-over cheeks and she cried out into the atmosphere.

'If you'd been this alert at 8 a.m. we wouldn't have had to thrash you,' her superior said.

Again the paddle contacted with her taut pale globes. Again Fern jerked her hips as if to pull them away from the painful source, and groaned her anguish. 'Please,' she whispered, mindful of the woman's threat to tie her down if she didn't stay in place. 'Not again!'

'Oh yes – again and again and again,' the officer replied, a pitiless glee in her voice.

Fern flinched then howled as the paddle roasted first one hot cheek then the other. She no longer cared what the watchful audience might think.

After a final whack the woman set down the polished implement. 'Keep gripping the stool's legs, Miss Terris, and think about why you're here, and what you're learning.'

'Yes, Ma'am. Whatever you say, Ma'am,' Fern muttered, wishing she could cup her blazing buttocks. According to the prison officials she was here to learn to live a healthy balanced life.

'Don't tell me your findings,' Ms Lenn continued. 'Dr Marshall will hear your conclusions at your first analysis session. He'll be seeing you once a week.' Fern sensed her moving closer, breathing faster. 'You took your chastisement well, so you can now have a sexual reward.'

The girl moaned as knowing fingers stroked her dripping labial lips. God, that was exquisite!

'You're very wet, aren't you, Miss Terris? Our psychological profile was obviously right.'

What could she say? The new prisoner closed her eyes and opened her legs widely. She'd never felt this aroused before – never ever. She had never felt such a heavy need in her achingly distended mound.

Beyond clear thought, she pushed down against the woman's hand, silently begging these same fondling digits to enter her. If they'd only thrust up hard and thickly like a man's erect rod.

'Make the bitch plead for it!' shouted one of the men from the crowd.

Fern suddenly became aware of herself, of her body and her remaining pride. 'Ma'am, please,' she said. 'Please don't!'

'As you wish,' said the officer.

Immediately the source of pleasure was withdrawn, leaving her quim longing for satiation.

'Dr Marshall's already warned you that you have to *earn* the right to touch yourself, girl?' she continued, walking round the girl and slapping her right hand against her grey skirt suit.

'Yes, I just don't feel like it,' Fern lied. She closed her thighs on the shameful slick rush of genital juice, trying hard to rebuild her dignity.

Ms Lenn patted her sore cheeks affectionately: 'Fine. Let's get you back to your room where you can put cream on your sore bottom and have a little rest.'

Knowing that she wanted to put cream on her *clitoris*, Fern pushed herself tremulously from the stool and stood up, holding weakly to its wooden surface. Ms Lenn reached, smiling, for her right arm but conscious of further lesbian comments from the audience, Fern backed away. She couldn't let a woman touch her. At least, not a strange woman. Not when others could see.

'Really, I can walk unaided. I'm fine.' She looked at the admissions officer for permission to smooth her dressing gown down, and the older woman nodded.

'Once a wrongdoing has been paid for,' she explained, 'we don't prolong the ordeal.'

Ms Lenn leading the way, they walked silently back to a cream-painted door with a nameplate saying FERN in embossed golden letters. 'You'll have noticed that your room's been decorated in the neutral shade of cream.' She smiled amicably. 'Offenders can change them as they wish, with paint and posters. You can buy most things at the store or order them from the outside world. You'll get money for the work you do here every week.'

'I see, Ma'am. Thank you, Ma'am.' For once she didn't care about colour co-ordination and commercial possessions. Fern could only think of her pulsing clit. Would she get the chance to bring herself off somewhere soon? It would just take a dozen sure strokes with her fingers. Somehow that thrashing had given her a swollen and needful crotch.

'In you go,' the admissions officer said. 'There's cold cream in your bedside cabinet. I'll be back for you in thirty minutes.'

'What about clothes? I . . .'

'Providing you're a good girl you can wear your own.'

Fern pushed open the door and immediately saw the three suitcases that she'd initially filled with her belongings and taken to the court building. She'd been made to leave them with an official. Now she was relieved to see that the safety labels she'd stuck over the zips looked untouched.

'Providing you follow our dictates you can keep your personal possessions,' Ms Lenn added before taking her

29

leave of her. 'Be dressed and ready for the guided tour in half an hour.' She left.

Walking gingerly, Fern approached the cabinet and pulled it open. Both shelves held various lotions and oils. Gratefully she removed the largest tub of soft white emulsion, took the lid off and lay down on her belly on the bed.

How she relished the opportunity to cool her hot backside! Fern scooped out two palmfuls of the balm and applied it quickly to her flaming rump cheeks. Sighing with relief and the beginnings of a new pleasure, she circled her fingerpads round and round and round. Her digits traced the tender crease above the well-paddled backs of her thighs, and she trailed the thrill-sparked tissues a second time and then a third.

God, but her labia were wet! Aware of her sex lips damply cleaving to the bed, Fern reached her right hand down and touched the pink leaves gently. That paddling had been far from soft, yet it had somehow made more than her bottom ache. Her hollow had started to yearn for a stiff phallus or several thrusting fingers; it was still begging for relief.

It made no sense. God knows, she'd hated each merciless whack at the time. She had cried out and wriggled with shame and tropical torment. She had ached to undo her wrongs and avoid this bum-baking ordeal.

What the hell. It was time to go with the flow! Aware that the admissions officer would soon be back, Fern turned carefully over onto her small punished buttocks. Then she spread her thighs as far apart as they would go. She usually aroused herself this way, finding the feel of her hugely stretched-apart legs very exciting, as if some lust-mad lover had staked her out in order to have full access to her defenceless lush core.

Closing her eyes, Fern put the middle finger of her right hand above her clit. New sensation immediately frisked through her. Slowly she started the beloved familiar journey towards bliss. She could imagine herself being displayed on a stage, a group of male strippers selecting her from a grinning audience. Each stripper was determined to prove Fern was at the mercy of her throbbing sex. They'd tie her spreadeagle-style to a four poster and stroke her warm tummy then dole out tiny teasing licks . . .

'Uh.' Fern heard herself give the little half-human grunt she made as orgasm grew closer. She increased the circular incitement of her hand. Any moment now she'd surge over into the sweetest ecstasy.

'*What the hell do you think you're doing?*' said an angry male voice.

Fern thrust her hand away. She sat up, dazed, and stared towards the open door at the glaring man. She hadn't heard him enter! Shakily she reached for her dressing gown, which had fallen to the floor.

'You'll not be wearing that for long when I tell Ms Lenn what you've been up to,' the officer said.

He was wearing the standard grey *compulsion* officer uniform. He was in his mid-thirties. A tall man, with large strong limbs and mid brown hair that was slightly longer than fashion dictates. He looked as though he'd taken care of himself, Fern thought weakly. More alarmingly, he looked more than capable of taking care of her already-painful bare rump.

'Do you have to tell Ms Lenn what I was doing, sir?' she muttered, using the terry towelling garment to cover her sex-slicked pubis and hard-nippled breasts.

The officer quirked a thick dark eyebrow: 'Why shouldn't I?'

'We could . . . just have fun together.' She had to avoid further whipping and she needed to come so much.

'Let's have you over that coffee table, then.'

Fern followed his gaze to the low marble-topped table. 'Looks cold,' she half-joked, trying to make him smile at her.

'Your hot arse will soon warm it up.'

He knew about that, then. Fern swallowed hard. Had he been one of the men who'd made comments from the audience? There would be no dignity in this after-punishment sexual act. But her quim was pleading for release, for any kind of satisfaction. And he wasn't going to allow her to touch herself.

31

Avoiding the man's mocking gaze, Fern got up from the bed and walked slowly to the low-slung piece of furniture, hugely aware of her nakedness. Then she lowered herself down onto her recently creamed bottom, and put her hands behind her head.

'On seconds thoughts I'll have you on your tummy,' the man continued.

'Oh, right.' Clumsily Fern got up again then faced the table and eased herself, belly down, on its marble surface. Her swollen nipples rubbed against the smooth hard top.

Driven by her desires, she pushed her pubis into the table's edge.

'Hold it,' said the man. 'You'll wait until *I* decide to dole out the pleasure.'

'Yes, sir.' At least he wasn't going to report her to Ms Lenn!

Fern pushed her head over the end of the marble as she heard him cross the room. Waiting, she stared down at the cream-coloured carpet. Her tummy felt stuck to the coffee table. She was hugely aware of her throbbing scarlet bum.

'Nice,' said the man.

She sensed he was staring down at her rear, and squirmed a little.

'Still quite red,' he added, fondling each tender globe. Fern winced, then was glad that he couldn't see the gesture. If he was anything like the hateful Rab then he'd be getting off on her helplessness and shame!

She wanted him to fill her quim rather than feel her rump. When he'd walked in she'd been seconds away from orgasm. Now, as he stroked and squeezed her tormented bottom, she raised it lewdly from the table, and pushed back.

'Christ, you need it!' the officer muttered.

She relaxed slightly as she heard his zip go down, then tensed anew at the unaccustomed largeness of his prick head. The few boys she'd been with after all-night raves hadn't been nearly as swollen as this.

'Spread your legs further,' ordered the man. He administered several hard little smacks to both her inner thighs.

Fern squealed and quickly obeyed him. Anxious to avoid further punishment, she tilted her bum so that the back way into her sex was even more fully on display.

'Keep yourself this open as I fuck you,' the officer continued.

Flexing her ankles, Fern concentrated on keeping her calves and thighs as well-splayed as he ordered. She fought against the urge to close her legs hungrily against the sudden thrusting hardness of his prick.

How he filled her up, stimulating her inner vaginal rim and nudging exquisitely at her cervix. How his belly slapped against her already soundly thrashed bare bum. His tummy was spanking her cheeks like a human paddle. Once again, Fern felt the deep sensual signals that said she was about to come.

The officer got there first. He strained, exhaling hard, against her and his fingers pumped convulsively at her breast spheres.

'Don't stop, I beg of you,' Fern whispered as his thrusting momentarily spasmed to a halt.

'You'll get your share,' the man muttered, starting to move more slowly inside her. 'I'm up for a second session most nights.'

Did he fuck most of the offenders, then? Was that an officer's perk? There was so much she didn't know about this place – and she sensed it might make painful learning. But for now this powerful shaft was moving deliciously inside her soaking quim. 'God, yes,' she gasped as the skilful phallus moved to a deeper, faster rhythm. 'That's exquisite. That's . . .'

'*That's against the rules.*'

Body freezing into position, Fern turned her eyes towards the voice. Ms Lenn stood impassively in the doorway. Looking more closely, the girl could see the admissions officer holding a long curve-handled cane.

'This is called a rattan. It makes bad girls beg. If I had my way I'd use it on your arse right now until you howled for forgiveness.' The woman ran the slender whippy rod through her hands. 'But as you've committed more than one crime in the same day, Miss Terris, you have to go before the much more formal Internal Court.'

Walking over to the sex-linked bodies, she flexed the rattan then let it rise and fall six times on the man's defenceless buttocks. The officer groaned and pushed forward into Fern as if trying to evade each swish.

'Ah! Ah!' Fern cried out as her quim was stirred by the thrusting. 'Please let me come, Ms Lenn,' she whispered, beyond shame.

'I was just walking past her room. I heard her groan! She was wanking, and I put a stop to it,' the officer cried in anguish, his shaft deflating inside Fern by the second.

'Miss Terris was asked if she wanted to climax after her paddling. She gave an unequivocal no,' Ms Lenn replied.

The admissions officer moved towards the head of the heavily breathing man. 'Get up, Davy. Go back to your room. Report to my study at nine tonight wearing nothing but an apology.'

The man pulled his half-hard prick from Fern's body and she cried out and pushed her mons back as if to seek its thick promise again.

'Save your excitement for someone more honest than that one,' the woman added, as Davy slunk out of the room, pulling his trousers up over his pink-striped bottom. 'He's duped fellow offenders by pretending to be an officer before.'

'You mean he's ... ?' Fern pushed herself slowly back from the marble surface and reached for her dressing gown again.

'He's an offender, yes. A recidivist, in fact. This is his last chance to give up a life of holiday timeshare fraud. He'll get a long prison sentence if he reoffends after this.'

Fern pulled on the terry towelling robe and knotted it firmly around her. 'If fraud is his misdemeanour then he hasn't *physically* hurt others. Is it right that he should be caned?'

'Losing their hard-won cash and being taken for fools does physically hurt others,' Ms Lenn said. 'Davy knows of the stomach upsets and migraines he causes, but he thinks he wants to be a ruthless property tycoon.'

34

'Thinks he does?' Fern echoed, figuring she might as well find out what constituted cane-worthy behaviour here.

'Mm, the people who adopted him wanted a high-flyer for a son, so Davy goes all out to do the dominant lord of the manor bit with his big cigars and small slim mistresses,' the admissions officer continued. 'Deep down though, he'd be happy in a nursing capacity, wants to serve.'

He could service her any day! Fern pushed her thighs together, feeling the wetness on both smooth surfaces. Her labia throbbed in desperation. Ms Lenn took hold of her arm.

'There's an internal court case already in session, Miss Terris. It'll be over in a few minutes, which means that the panel can decide your own painful sentence. They may even administer it right away.'

Mahogany panels ran from ceiling to floor. The floor itself was of dark-stained pine. The dock looked equally foreboding.

'Will offender Terris please step forward,' the judge said, banging his gavel. He wore a formal wig and gown.

Feeling silly in her towelling dressing gown and squelching crotch, Fern obeyed. She approached the bench, then put her arms behind her back, the fingers of one hand linking to the other. She tried to look guileless and defenceless, hoping that the near-orgasmic heat in her face would soon abate.

'You were told last night by Dr Marshall and again today by Admissions Officer Lenn that it was an offence to touch your private parts without permission,' the man said, looking at her sternly.

'Yes sir.' Now she genuinely wished she hadn't disobeyed.

'Have you anything to say in your own defence? Any mitigating circumstances?' the judge prompted.

'Yes! I always thought masturbation was okay!'

'It is. It's wonderful,' said the judge, with the first glimmer of humour in his eyes. 'It brings physical relief and a measure of emotional satisfaction. But you have to have something special to look forward to here at *Compulsion* whilst you're learning to be a better person. By limiting the times when you can orgasm we offer you the carrot as well as the stick.'

Fern toed awkwardly at the carpet: 'I just got so excited. I . . .'

'Ms Lenn saw that. She wants the inmates to be happy here. She was kind enough to offer you a climax,' the judiciary replied.

'I know, but . . . well, other people would have seen us in action.' Fern risked a quick look at the man. 'It wouldn't be right.'

'Miss Terris – get over here and lie across my knee as I explain cause and effect to you,' the judge said.

Could she bear such further debasement? Fern looked wildly at Ms Lenn.

'Go on,' the admissions officer urged. 'If you thwart him he's liable to dole out the hardest whipping.'

Dipping her head, Fern dragged her bare feet across the floor.

When she reached the elevated area where the judge sat, she looked up. He nodded to two of the officials: 'Put that recliner on the little stage. I'll come down to her level.' He walked down the steps till he was facing Fern. 'This way the others get to see your bad, bared bum.'

Fern trembled as he took a seat on the recliner. He patted his lap and stared at her with demanding eyes. Fern stepped nearer to her fate. 'Don't dally, girl. You'll just make it worse for your bottom.'

Wincing, she laid her dressing-gowned belly over his formal black robes.

'Let's get this housecoat lifted nice and high.'

She felt his fingernails scrape her legs as he lifted the garment; felt the courtroom's centrally heated air on her warm pink bottom.

'Obviously that paddling didn't teach you obedience,' the judge said coolly, running a considering palm over both heaving flanks.

Fern cringed at his shaming words.

'Anyway, Miss Terris, I was going to explain why you're to be disciplined for turning down Ms Lenn's offer of fulfilment and then fondling your lovebud in secret.' He squeezed both buttocks. 'Do you know how much crime is caused by men and women who can't even admit their desires to themselves?'

'No, M'Lord.' Fern squirmed ashamedly. She was sure she was about to find out!

'Day after day at *Compulsion* we admit people for various transgressions. Many have sexual fetishes and predilections that they've never dared explore.' He stroked Fern's soft smooth globes till she thought she'd scream with disgrace or desire. 'Let's look at a typical scenario.'

'Yes, M'Lord.'

'An eighteen-year-old youth fantasises about wearing women's panties. If he was honest with himself he'd simply buy a pretty pair and relieve himself with them wrapped around his manhood. But he feels ashamed to go into a shop for such an item – so he steals some from his neighbour's washing line. Then he finds the very act of thieving gives him an adrenalin buzz.'

The judge shifted his knees slightly so that Fern's poor bottom was even more obscenely raised. 'He keeps stealing. He gets caught by the police and fined. He does it again and this time hits a man who tries to stop him. He ends up in prison for theft and assault, which means he loses his job, perhaps even his home.'

The man placed his palms flat on Fern's bared buttocks. 'What's the moral, Miss Terris?'

This was the easy part! Fern took a deep breath: 'He should have admitted his desires in the first place, sir. And I should have admitted mine and let Ms Lenn excite my private parts.'

'Your *private parts*!' the judge mocked. 'Such a coy term for such a wanton little girl. We know that you've brought youths back after all-night raves and had sex with them in your bungalow, Miss Terris. We draw up background reports on potential inmates before inviting them to serve their sore-bummed sentences here.'

'I'm sorry, M'Lord. I shouldn't have been promiscuous, M'Lord.' Fern continued, inwardly hating the fact that they knew about her past life.

'I suspect you're just saying certain things to please us,' the man said sadly. He palmed both her taut wriggling hemispheres. 'You shouldn't settle for fewer sexual partners just because you think that's what some outer authority wants.'

'No, M'Lord,' Fern muttered. She wished he'd cover up her helpless bum, or at least stop fondling and pressing it. She wished the officials would stop grinning and staring at her writhing cheeks.

The judge fingered the tops of her thighs as if he were selecting merchandise in a grocery store: 'What we hope, Fern, is that you'll eventually choose fewer casual sexual partners because you've learned to respect and value yourself.'

Some chance of respecting herself when her bottom was the entertainment of the day! Fern bit back the words. They probably had some psychological reason for exposing her posterior.

'For now, though, I have to pass sentence on you for the crime of not owning up to your carnal appetite, my dear,' the judge said. He ran a knowing thumb down each genital lip. 'We have exquisitely refined devices here, Miss Terris, as your . . . er *private parts* will learn in a moment. You're about to become acquainted with the real meaning of unsatisfied desire.'

'Yes, M'Lord. Thank you, M'Lord,' Fern murmured obsequiously, staring down at the ground and inwardly urging him to smooth down her upturned dressing gown.

'Take your clothes off, then, my dear,' he murmured, 'and face the others in the room.' So saying, he pushed her gently from his lap. Fern slid to her knees. She wished fervently that she could stay there. 'Don't be shy, girl – you're hardly a virgin,' the man prompted. 'Get that garment off and show the officers your unsated little breasts and bum.'

Slowly Fern got to her feet. She cast a pleading glance at Ms Lenn, but the woman simply tapped her stick against her own leg and raised a warning eyebrow. The last thing she wanted was that hard rod warming her poor soft rump. Fern unknotted her dressing gown cord with trembling fingers and looked nervously at the judge.

'Good girl. All the way off. Hand it to the gentleman in the peaked cap. You won't be needing it.' The judge sounded slightly impatient and slightly amused. Was he also lustful? The man now taking the dressing gown from her certainly was. Fern avoided making eye contact, but was hugely conscious of all four grinning male officers and the inscrutable Ms Lenn. When she'd been an obedient inmate the older woman had been nurturing and even motherly. But since Fern had slept late and lied about being aroused after her thrashing, the admissions officer seemed indifferent to her fate.

'Let's have a twirl,' the judge continued. 'No – much more slowly if you please, Miss Terris. And raise your arms high above your head like a would-be ballet dancer.'

Aware of her pouting pink nipples and slightly jiggling bottom, Fern did as she was told. After all, a refusal would doubtless earn her further chastisement. And they had already hinted that her next correction would soon be under way.

'Now show the court what a horny girl's pussy looks like,' the judge continued matter-of-factly.

Fern blinked: 'But they wouldn't do this if I'd been sent to a proper prison!'

'The other prisoners would do more than just look. They'd have you licking out their menstrual blood like it was your favourite entrée,' the judge said. 'They'd have you suckling like a baby at their breasts.'

'But you're the *staff*, not the *prisoners*,' Fern muttered, playing for time.

'Prison staff turn a blind eye to lots of enforced pleasures and outright punishments. Believe me, they're just as culpable. Haven't you even heard of the Chicken Run?'

'The . . . ? No.' Fern shook her head. She wanted to cover her bare breasts with her hands, but was afraid of drawing further attention to her nakedness.

'It's when prisoners single out a new inmate they don't like. They hold him down and shove a slim roll of paper up his arsehole. Then they light the far end of it.' He shook his head, obviously amazed at man's inhumanity before continuing with his graphic story. 'The prisoner has to run up and down making chicken noises and flapping his arms till the flames singe his naked backside.' The judge walked up to Fern and turned her around to face him: 'We wouldn't do that here – it's genuinely barbaric. It can cause lasting pain and leave physical scars.' He pushed her hair back tenderly from her face. 'And you know what? It doesn't change the sufferer's behaviour for the better. He just feels scared.'

He let his hands drop to his sides. 'What we're attempting with you is totally different, Miss Terris. Yes, you'll feel humiliated when we make you expose yourself to stranger after stranger. And you'll scream and beg for mercy when you taste the rod and the whip.' He smiled gently. 'But afterwards you'll connect the incident with whatever you did wrong, and you'll want to do right to earn climax rather than correction. You'll become better behaved.'

At least on the outside she would! Fern nodded and tried to look suitably contrite. If she could get out of here in a few months she could go back to being a party animal.

'Now I'm going to put this chair in front of you, and you're going to bend slightly at the waist to grip the back of it, then spread your legs,' the judiciary said.

Fern swallowed and cast her gaze down to the floor. She was aware of the man dragging the wooden seat closer to where she stood. This was hateful!

'Do it now,' he said. 'Let the officers see your hungry little hole.'

'And if I don't, you'll . . . ?'

'I'll encourage your bottom to reconsider.' The man indicated a long hard cat-o'-nine-tails on the overhead wall.

The wood of the chair back was surprisingly smooth under her fingers as she gripped it tightly. Her breath sounded ragged in her ears.

'Push those legs further apart. Further. Further.'

40

Just when she thought her thigh muscles would give way, he allowed her to stop.

'Now, Ken,' he said addressing an official that Fern couldn't see. Nor did she want to. 'Pry open her tender wet pussy lips.'

Could the watchers see her earlier wet-look lust, then? She'd become aroused when that awful paddling took place, and had become even more liquid when she fondled her own swollen clitoris. Then Davy had fucked her over that cool marble table top, and each thrust had brought the fluid flowing to her pubic hill.

'We're just going to open you up a bit, darling,' Ken said in a far-from-endearing voice.

Fern gripped more tightly at the chair. She cried out as his thick fingers peeled her labial leaves away from cleaving to each other. The man stroked them for a moment, so that she shivered with loathing and lust.

'Don't fight it, sweetheart,' he murmured, his voice taunting. Then he inserted his thumb all the way. 'Soaking inside and out,' he confirmed to the watching men and rod-wielding Ms Lenn.

Fern was glad that she was facing away, but hated the fact that they were being given a view of her exposed dark anus and paddle-pinked bottom.

'Bet you want to stick more than your thumb up there, eh, Ken?' one of the officers snorted. Fern just knew Ken would answer that with a wink or grin.

'He may eventually get the chance,' the judge added, coming to stand at Fern's head. 'So far Miss Terris has been very disobedient. At a later date she may end up being fucked by a man without being allowed to come.' He smiled. 'You're about to taste a version of that now, my sweet – only it's by mechanical means rather than by man-power. Ken, take her to the dining room and introduce her throbbing pussy to our Deferred Gratification Machine.'

41

Three

A deferred gratification machine sounded devilishly effective! As Fern walked, naked, along the corridor in front of Ken she wondered what they'd do to her pussy; what she was about to endure. Would they make her ride some battery-operated phallus that would keep her groaning on the edge of a climax for a squirmingly long time?

'In here, angel. That's right. Push the door open wide.'

Fern found herself looking into a canteen filled with a dozen trestle tables. Eight men and two women sat at some of them with cups of tea and coffee in their hands.

'Miss Terris refused to admit to her sexual appetites,' Ken said, putting a hand on Fern's bare bum and prompting her to the front of the room with its yawning canteen hatch. 'So the Judge thought it only fitting that she be teased into lust in our very own dining room.'

Fern stared dully at the diners as she reached the top of the canteen. This simply wouldn't happen in a normal prison! But in prison she'd lack interesting food, cosy private quarters and all of the other luxuries she could see were available here by right. Moreover, if she did what they wanted here at *Compulsion* she'd be free to go in a few short months.

Ignore their stares, she told herself, letting her hands fall to her sides. Still, it was awful having others gaze at her breasts and pubic patch and tremulous belly. *Just do what they ask of you*. Ken was already binding her ankles to hoops set near the foot of the wall.

'I'm not the first woman you've done this to, am I?' she whispered, as he raised her hands above her head and used

43

the rope round his waist to tie her wrists to a hoop high above her.

'God no, sweetheart. There's dozens have begged for mercy in this very spot during the past few years.'

Compulsion was well established, then. Presumably it had funding from somewhere. Surely some government body hadn't permitted this? Fern shuddered. They were about to use some hellish device that would make her plead for forgiveness, yet there was no one she could tell.

'Ready, angel?'

Fern stared dumbly at the man. She'd never be ready.

'Cat got your tongue?' he said, kneeling to strap something around her naked waist.

With her arms tied high above her head and her legs stretched out in a taut A-line, Fern's movements were limited. Desperate to see what Ken was doing, she craned her head.

She could see a broad brown leather band shackled to her waist. A free-swinging pouch on more slender straps seemed to be attached to it. As she strained, Ken pulled the thin straps under her pubic patch and brought them up behind, where he attached them to the band at the back. Now the pouch was held tightly over her Venusian mound and labial leaves and hood-hidden clitoris.

Ken stood back to review his handiwork. 'Very nice,' he said. 'Very effective indeed.'

'What are you going to do to me?' Fern croaked.

'I'm about to switch on this little machine. It'll vibrate exquisitely through your pretty pubes. You'll writhe and buck like crazy. Just as you're about to orgasm, the appliance will stop.'

'How will it know?' Fern queried.

'It's programmed to detect the electrical skin changes that show climax is near. It also reacts to your body heat.' He smiled mockingly. 'This little beauty is extremely sensitive.'

Fern feared her clit was too. As she stared, blushing, at the occupants of the trestle tables, Ken flicked on a switch near one of the ankle hoops. Was this thing also remote controlled? They had computer chips nowadays, so anything was possible. The vibrations thrilled through her labia, the familiar expanding excitement started in her lower belly, and Fern gave up on technological thought.

What a fiendishly effective machine! Its pulsations were light yet focused. As her arousal built rapidly, Fern closed her eyes and breathed fast and hard.

'You can't see us but we can still see you,' Ken taunted. 'See the wetness on your thighs, see your pussy trying to rub against the deferred gratifier.'

'See that your nipples are begging for a sucking,' shouted one of the guys.

All Fern could think about was the increasing pleasure above her labial lips. She groaned, uttering sounds more animal than human. Her voice always went deep and staccato as she was about to come. She felt the pre-orgasmic nearly-there signal in her brain, and pushed against the source of satisfaction. It promptly stopped.

For a moment Fern kept moving her hips despite the taut harsh pull of her bonds, then she opened her eyes: 'Why . . . ?' she gasped.

Ken grinned: 'You were getting too excited, darling.'

'But I need to . . .'

'No, you *want* to come, but the judge says you've got to be kept on the edge for an hour.'

An hour was an achingly long time to be deprived when you were as swollen-sexed as she was. Fern stared dully at the nonchalant Ken. 'I don't think I can take it,' she said miserably.

'Dearest,' the guard crooned, 'you don't have an option. The machine will take you to the limit then automatically stop every time.'

'How do you know when it's safe to switch it on again?' Fern asked, feeling her desire receding slowly.

'It knows itself, does a sort of vaginal thermometer test.' He smiled. 'You should hear some of those girlies groaning when it restarts its fiendish buzzing. Their hot little pussies can hardly bear another vibrating tease.'

'And no one has ever come before the machine has stopped?' Fern queried.

'No, sweetheart. Not ever.' Ken's eyes brightened with power or amusement. 'Gratification is *always* deferred.'

Fern stood, whimpering with loss as the main rush of distended desire flowed away from her clitoris. I'll just think about non-sexual things next time, she promised herself. I can outwit this. Then the hellish machine switched itself on again and the hot vaginal hunger started anew, then stopped, then started again.

When she was reduced to sobbing with unquenched lust, the judge walked in. He held a large silver stopwatch. 'Only another five minutes of squirming in this position, young lady, then we go back to court for the second part of your trial to see if you deserve another hot sore bum.'

'Anything!' Fern moaned, trying to push her aching pubes harder against the gently pulsing taunter. 'I'll taste the paddle if you'll override this machine and let me come!'

'Four and three quarter minutes to go. You can bear that, you wicked little girl! Just think about how you could have enjoyed being finger fucked by our skilful admissions officer,' the judiciary chided, 'if only you'd been honest about what your quim really needs.'

'All right! All right! I wanted her fingers up me!'

'Don't just *want*, dearest,' the man murmured. '*Beg*.'

Fern moaned anew. She'd never felt so ashamed.

'I may let you climax if you say the right words,' the judge continued thoughtfully.

'I beg to be finger fucked by my admissions officer!' Fern gasped raggedly, getting close to nirvana again under the throbbing power of the machine.

'You'd hold your pussy open for her, wouldn't you, my dear?'

'Yes M'Lord!'

The judge nodded: 'And you'd ask her to use the paddle on you again to teach you proper obedience?'

'Anything, sir! I'd bend over the chair for an hour and take the lash . . .'

'I don't think you're really trying,' said the judge. 'I

46

don't hear the unmistakable note of genuine humility, so we'll just watch whilst you squirm your way through the rest of this deferred gratification hour.'

Three minutes later his stopwatch buzzed. In that time the machine had switched off to let her cool down for a moment, then had started to tease her clit again with renewed fervour.

'Unstrap the machine, boy,' the judiciary said.

Ken knelt and started to undo the various straps and buckles from the implement between Fern's legs, his movements were reluctant.

'Then untie her wrists and ankles, and help her over to the service hatch,' he said, staring at the sheen of sex-juice now coating the insides of her lust-weakened thighs.

Fern looked away. She flexed her limbs as they were freed from their bonds. She stared at the canteen lino, aware of the diners whispering. Ken put his hands on the cheeks of her arse to move her towards the nearby hatch.

'Ken, stop pawing her or you'll get a thrashing of your own!' the judge ordered.

'Yes, M'Lord,' Ken muttered, sliding his palms up to encircle Fern's small waist. He held her firmly.

'Miss Terris, face into the serving hatch and lean your belly against it,' the judiciary said evenly.

Swallowing, Fern did as she was told.

'Good girl. Now stick your arse out further, and slide one hand between your legs, and start to fondle your pussy,' he added with obvious enjoyment.

Fern twisted her head round to look at him blankly: 'What?'

'We're going to watch you come. And hear you also, no doubt! You've been squirming for so long I'm sure you'll want a chance to reach satisfaction.'

'Yes, but . . .'

The judge warningly shook his head: 'But you don't like admitting your needs to other people. Don't say we're going to go through all that again!'

As she bent over the hatch, he unfastened his belt and slowly doubled it. Fern kept her head turned around and her naked bum facing him.

47

'Admit that you want relief.' He flicked the belt four times against her defenceless bottom. Fern cried out as the movement sent new sparks of pain and a perverse resonating pleasure to her loins.

'I want to come, M'Lord,' she whispered, blushing.

'Then get those fingers on your hot clit now, girl, before I decide to fasten them higher above your head.'

Breathing fast, Fern put her right hand between her swamped legs, and circled the juice-logged circumference of her orgasmic bud.

'Twist your head around again. Look at us as you touch yourself,' the judge ordered. 'We want to see your mouth tighten or enlarge as you get close to climax. We want to watch your eyelids going all fluttery, and see your face go nice and red.'

Worse and worse! Yet she was so close . . . Trying to filter out their winks and knowing grins, Fern obediently turned her face towards the assorted amused diners. Her fingers traced the desperate tissues round and round and round. Going, going.

'Can we watch her being soundly thrashed after the second part of her court case?' shouted a man.

'Depends on the judge who sentences her,' the judge with the stopwatch said evenly. 'I'm occupied with giving reports to our parole board for the rest of today.'

A new judge with the right to strip her and stroke her. A sound thrashing. The words flooded Fern's brain, and she pushed more strongly against her caressing fingers as her climax began. The pleasure started – as it always did – at some undefinable point of her sensual centre. It spread out, in expanding echoing waves of ecstatic exhilaration that made every other thought momentarily recede.

'Mh . . . aaaaaaaaaaaaah!' she half-cried, half-moaned, her voice-timbre alien and alarming. Her fingers worked and worked to help the prolonged sexual sweetness through.

On and on and on. How long could an orgasm last? She pushed her fingerpads harder against her clitoris as if hoping to speed the process, as if her body and brain couldn't quite cope with this much rapture. Still the enchantment swelled and held and peaked.

At last the contractions which signalled the end of that particular Eden began to throb through her. Aware of a sudden empty ache, Fern slid two comforting fingers inside herself.

'Need a hand, angel?' a girl in dungarees laughed, and three others sniggered dutifully.

Fern focused on the other diners as if for the very first time. God, they'd just watched her stimulating the parts her mother used to call her front bottom! Fern removed her desire-dewed digits, glad that neither parents or friends could see her now. They wouldn't recognise the former late night raver and serious shopper. Wouldn't believe that her slightly bored drawl had become a desperate wailing plea to be allowed to come.

'Time for a shower and some sustenance, then it's back to court for you, my girl,' the judge said kindly.

'As you wish, M'Lord,' Fern murmured. She stared at the ground as Ken marched her naked body from the room.

Warm water. Wild strawberry shower gel. A pot of Earl Grey tea and wholegrain salmon sandwiches. Three quarters of an hour after she finished her bathing, dressing and repast, Fern heard an authoritative knock at her door.

A man in his sixties stood there. His hair was iron grey, his body strong but slightly stocky. He was dressed in a navy blue boiler suit.

'Come to take you for your trial, young Miss.'

'Oh? You're officer . . . ?' she waited for him to supply his surname.

'Officer nothing! I'm one of the inmates, the same as you.'

'Then I'm staying here!' Fern said, stepping back into her room. She'd already made the mistake of pandering to another fellow inmate, the thrusting Davy.

The man grimaced: 'Don't be awkward, lassie, or it'll be worse for your arse.'

49

Fern stalled for time, pawing the ground with one leather shoe. The last thing she wanted was to earn herself a further whipping. On the other hand, she might have her nether cheeks warmed if she wrongly followed this man.

'I'm Bill Stark, the head gardener,' the man continued in an inappropriately angry voice. 'Dr Marshall's decided you should work for me. The timetable originally said I had to collect you from your room to take you to the vegetable plots.'

'But I've to go to court now!' Fern said, hoping to shake him off.

'Lassie, don't patronise your elders and betters,' the gardener said. He looked as if he hated her, or just hated women. 'I already know all that!'

He gazed dourly at the newly donned full-length pinafore which reached to her ankles. 'When the work placement officer drew up your itinerary, he didn't expect you'd need your pussy and bum cheeks punished this early,' he said staring in the direction of that self-same quim. 'Anyway, someone's scored out the part that says I've to take you to the gardens and written that I've to take you to court first for sentencing instead.'

So he knew of her recent thrashing, then! Fern pretended a sudden interest in her hand-crafted shoes with their Grecian urn motif. She'd always loved their unique leather artwork.

'Doubt if they'll be letting you keep that dress on,' said the man with obvious satisfaction. 'Way I hear it, you bribed some poor bastard to fuck you when you knew it was against the rules.'

'I've told them I won't do it again,' Fern muttered. Her words sounded phony and inadequate.

Bill Stark stared at her contemptuously. 'So, are you coming with me or not?'

'I . . . no, I'll wait for official confirmation!' After a moment's hesitation, Fern gently closed the door in the man's face. She walked over to the bed and sat down, then stood up and walked to the window. She gazed out at the stretching clumps of evergreen trees. Behind the forest ran the road that had brought her here, a road back to a life without shame.

And a life without such spectacular orgasms. She blinked as the thought invaded her mind. How strange that she'd honed in on that rather than feeling angry about the thrashings! Outside she'd had a life where she didn't have to submit to the paddle or the cane, a life where people just wandered about as they pleased. Here she had to think about each issue, deciding if it was right or wrong, for her own good or for the benefit of equally deserving others. She could no longer act without trying to work out the result.

She'd just turned away a strange man from her door. Had she acted responsibly, or ought she have been more trusting? As a second knock resounded through the cream-coloured room, Fern jumped and tugged nervously at the folds of her pinafore dress, glad that it covered her pantied bum. 'Who is it?' she shouted.

'Ms Lenn.'

Gratefully she rushed to let the other woman in.

'This man Bill Stark came! He said I was to go with him. I didn't go, but not out of badness but because I wasn't sure . . .'

'Hey, it's all right. Slow down!' Ms Lenn looked approachable again, unlike the watchful grim-mouthed woman who had stood at the back of the courtroom. 'Was he carrying a clipboard?'

'He wasn't carrying anything.' Fern shook her head.

'Then he's the one at fault. He should have had a schedule showing your work duties and working allegiance to him,' the admissions officer reassured her.

'Just working? I don't have to . . . ?'

The older woman stared: 'Don't be coy, girl. Say the words!'

'Don't have to . . .' This was so hard. 'Satisfy him sexually?'

Ms Lenn raised her expressive eyes ceilingwards. 'God, no!' She put a gentle hand on Fern's arm. 'Bill lives here permanently. He's a first class worker, but he's a voyeur

51

and indulges himself whenever he's let loose in the world outside *Compulsion*. He gets to look at the girls here whilst they're being punished. That's his main erotic treat.'

Fern thought this through. 'And none of them . . . touch him?'

'Oh, some of them do. The ones who've been denied sexual release for a few weeks will impale themselves on anything vaguely rodlike! But if they haven't been given permission, they take a good hiding from the officers for breaking the rules.'

'Assuming you catch them,' Fern added thoughtfully.

Ms Lenn smiled: 'I'll admit all these trees make things difficult! But we have our ways.'

'He doesn't like me,' muttered Fern as they walked towards her second trial.

The admissions officer nodded her agreement. 'Bill doesn't like anyone who doesn't let him fuck them. Makes him a hard taskmaster – but means he gets work-based results.'

'And he won't try anything on?' Fern queried.

'No, we'd have his pants down in seconds if he did. We'd leather him till he squealed and begged for mercy.'

'And he knows all this, Ms Lenn?'

'Oh yes, he learned by trial and error. His buttocks know!'

At least a reformatory where the men were disciplined as much as the girls sounded egalitarian and fair. Fern walked more lightly towards the courtroom doors, then hesitated before them.

'Am I likely to be punished further?' she asked the admissions officer.

The older woman's gaze was resolute. 'I'm afraid so. Yes.'

This time the courtroom was even busier.

'Many inmates come here during their coffee breaks,' Ms Lenn explained.

'I thought they've just had their time out in the dining room,' Fern said.

'No, breaks are staggered.' The admissions officer smiled

wryly. 'Means there's always someone working, someone resting and someone getting whipped!'

Whipped. Fern shivered, her heartbeat quickening at the sudden rush of lust to her quim. What on earth had made that particular sexual frisson happen? She must have been subconsciously thinking of that orgasm she'd had with her fingers after they'd stopped tormenting her with the deferred gratification machine. As she mused, a stranger in a judge's wig and gown took his place at the front of the suddenly hushed courtroom, and her second trial began.

'The accused, Miss Fern Terris, will approach the bench.'

Grateful that they'd allowed her to wear clothes and shoes this time, Fern walked tremulously forward. The judge stared down at her, his mouth neutral.

'I understand that you have already appeared before this court today?'

'Yes, M'Lord, for relieving myself manually after pretending I wasn't aroused, M'Lord. When it comes to masturbation I've learned my lesson,' Fern said quickly.

The judge frowned. 'Yet you're here to be taught another one!'

'Yes, Your Honour.' Fern searched for words that would make her actions sound less lewd. 'I was . . . pleasuring myself when a man came in. He told me he was an officer and that he'd see that I was punished for my actions. I tried to bribe him with my body not to tell.'

'Tried to bribe him with your body? You mean you spread your legs and begged him to fuck you?' the judiciary confirmed.

Fern felt her throat tense and she stammered, 'Y-yes.'

'You've certainly been doing your own thing since you arrived here,' the judge said, stroking his chin. 'Indeed, I understand you even offered yourself in the *Compulsion* van to our very own Dr Marshall.' He looked at the leather-bound red tome on the table. 'The spanking you received for that doesn't seem to have done much good.'

'It really hurt, sir,' Fern whispered obsequiously, hoping that the others wouldn't hear.

'Of course it hurt. That's the whole point, girl,' the judge said snappishly, 'but it hasn't hurt enough to make you better. Since then you've slept late, played with your clit and seduced another inmate in your room.'

Fern cleared her throat and stared numbly at the floor. 'I didn't mean to. That is, I'm sorry. Yes!'

'At least you're starting to take responsibility for what you do,' the judge continued, 'though that won't save your arse from whipping.' He smiled as Fern shuddered. 'That's just a term of speech. I haven't passed sentence yet.' He stared harder at her. 'Let's have a look at that bum. If it's already glowing macintosh red I'll be merciful. If not . . .'

Fern stared at him and licked her lips. She'd been so glad to be wearing clothes again but now he was going to lift her pinafore!

'Come on, young lady. You've been found guilty of playing with yourself and of shafting strangers, so this is no time to play the blushing virgin,' the judiciary said. 'Turn your back to me and edge up your dress,' he continued more firmly.

Fern shuffled her feet round. Her eyes momentarily met Ms Lenn's. Ashamed, Fern looked quickly away and concentrated on a mahogany panel in the distance. Bending at the knees, she gripped her calico hem and started to pull it up.

'Keep going. This court has seen numerous pretty panties!'
But not mine, thought Fern in anguish, *not mine*.

When the .pinafore had reached her waist, she held it there with one hand.

'Now pull your knickers down,' the man said.

Awkwardly Fern obeyed him. She left the silk pants at her ankles, hoping that she might soon be allowed to edge them back up again.

'I'll just make a formal inspection of this rump,' the judge said from his seat behind Fern. She gazed fixedly at the wall in front of her as she heard his measured footsteps approaching. Her bottom felt its nakedness keenly. She flexed her fingers against the bunched-up calico round her waist again and again.

A large male hand squeezed one cheek, then a second knowing hand compressed the other. 'This bum's at a boringly normal temperature,' the judge's voice continued. 'When was it last taught to behave?'

'At . . . at around midday. I got paddled for ignoring my alarm call, Your Honour.'

She sensed the man nodding. 'The records show you've had a cold cream soothe, a cool shower and a long-deferred orgasm since then.'

'Yes, M'Lord.' And sustenance and a rest. In many ways they were taking care of her beautifully.

The judge stroked her bum cheeks more firmly: 'So the flesh has had time to go back to its natural colour.' He toyed with Fern's unclothed nether regions some more. 'Do you know what I want to do when I see two disobedient creamy curves, Miss Terris?'

'No, M'Lord.'

'I want to put stinging red stripes upon them.'

'I see, M'Lord,' Fern whispered. Her mouth felt dry.

'No, you won't *see* – but you'll certainly *feel*,' continued the man. 'We'll soon have you squirming!'

She sensed him walk away from her and heard something scrape against the woodwork.

'I'm recording in the punishment book that you've been sentenced to six of the best.'

'Thank you, M'Lord.' At least she'd try to win points for being polite!

'Take her to the basement chamber now. Use restraints if necessary,' the judiciary ordered.

'I . . . I can walk there, Sir,' Fern mumbled, not daring to turn round and face the man.

His voice was coolly amused. 'I mean they can tie you down once you reach the basement if you try to evade the cane.'

'I can bear it, M'Lord,' Fern said more strongly now. She'd seen Ms Lenn's rattan, and it looked ineffectually thin and dried-out. How much could a slender whippy rod hurt a girl's bum?

'Brave words, Miss Terris,' the judiciary continued, and

his voice held a knowing, slightly gloating note. 'Follow the officer on your right,' he said.

Fern glanced towards the towering bearded man. Not another stranger! The official jerked his head at her and started walking towards the court doors. Fern reached to pull up her silken pants.

'The prisoner is to keep her pants at her ankles,' the judge said. Fern looked round at him pleadingly. 'Off you go, girl,' he added. 'If you take lots of nice small steps you won't trip.'

Fern put her fingers to her dress, hoping to edge it down.

'No, leave it there, sweetheart, so your pretty bum is easily visible to everyone in the corridors. Mm, like that!'

He walked back and stood in front of her, tilting her head till her reluctant eyes met his. 'You weren't as cowed by the threat of the cane as we'd anticipated, my dear.'

Fern drew in her breath: 'I . . . that's because I recognise that I did wrong. I accept my punishment, Your Honour.' *Like hell*, she thought inwardly, but she'd do what they said if it meant an early parole.

The judge's voice hardened slightly: 'But we want you to connect this wrongdoing with a memory that brings you mental and physical suffering. I suspect we're failing to do that. Yet it's the only way your impulsive criminal behaviour will ultimately change.'

Unable to keep looking into his eyes, Fern let her lids flutter down. His finger remained tilting her chin. He seemed to be reaching into her mind. She hated his calm awareness. 'So, to increase the punishment, you're going to speak to every person you meet on your way to the basement chamber,' the man said.

'Yes, M'Lord,' Fern muttered. She hated this part – the strangers smirking, making lewd comments, staring.

'You're going to say, "I've been a very bad girl and now I'm about to get my bottom severely caned".'

'I can't . . . Oh God, please don't make me say that!' Fern gasped. She opened her eyes wide and tried to make a pleading connection with those of the man. But his own gaze was merciless.

'Sorry, it's not negotiable,' he said.

'And if I don't?' Fern queried.

'The officer will leave you tethered after your six strokes of the rattan, and he'll report back to me. I'll sentence you *in absentia* to up to a dozen more.'

She'd have to say what he wanted, then. The alternative was just too prolonged and painful. Six of the best was one thing – eighteen would set her poor bottom on fire! 'I'll do what you command, M'Lord,' she said tremulously.

'Follow the officer, then,' the judiciary repeated, and let go of her chin.

Each footstep a considered, shuffling thing, Fern started to make her way slowly up the stairs towards the doors of the courtroom. The men and women seated in the middle and back rows stared at her naked tummy and exposed pubis and curvy thighs. After she'd passed them, she was aware of each turning to see her denuded bottom. This bunched-up dress was somehow worse than being fully naked, the clothed half of her body drawing more attention to the stripped and vulnerable part.

At last the officer reached the doors and pushed one open for her. 'After you,' he said, with a taunting smile. Fern preceded him out into the corridor. 'Walk on in front,' he continued, 'I'll tell you when to take a right or left turn.'

'Yes sir,' Fern muttered. She figured she'd best be respectful. After all, he might soon be the one wielding the rattan!

Trying not to think about her knickers round her ankles or her poor exposed bum cheeks, she shuffled on. She felt her heartbeat quicken as footsteps approached them.

'Remember to speak nicely to each stranger!' snorted the officer.

A youth of around nineteen came strolling round the corner. He was pushing a trolley containing a hundred or more red carnations, each bound to a single fern. 'One for each room,' he explained cheerfully, following Fern's startled gaze.

'All the inmates receive a fresh flower every week,' the

officer added, 'to remind them of the simple beauties of the outside world – the world they've temporarily forfeited. You'll find one in that slender crystal vase on your dressing table, my dear.'

'Nice,' Fern muttered. She realised that the youth was now staring at her bare tummy and triangular pubic patch, his pupils widening.

'Haven't you something to say to the man?' the officer prompted, nudging her gently in the small of her back.

Fern looked back at him beseechingly: 'Oh please!'

'You'll be saying a lot more than please if your disobedience earns you eighteen of the cane, girl!' he warned.

Fern's buttocks tightened involuntarily at the prospect, and she fought to bring the hateful words to her lips.

'I've . . . been a bad girl who's about to get her bottom caned. Would you like to come and see?'

'Reckon he'll come all right!' the officer laughed. Fern looked shamefacedly at the youth's jean-clad groin. The material outlined his hardening phallus. Did everyone here get off on sexually stimulating or debasing her, then?

'I've to deliver those to the rooming maid,' the boy said to the official. 'It'll take about five minutes.'

'This bottom will be more than happy to wait,' the officer said. He stroked Fern's twitching bared bum as he spoke. 'We'll be disciplining her in the basement chamber. It seems a stint over Dr Marshall's lap and a paddling on the assembly stage did no good.'

'The chamber! Rather you than me!' the boy said, looking at Fern before whistling through his teeth.

'You mean you've been caned?' she asked.

'Christ, yes! They used this long willow rod that's been soaked in vinegar . . .'

'You'll be feeling it again if you don't get these carnations delivered on time,' the officer broke in.

'Sorry, sir. See you in five minutes, sir,' the youth said in a rush, and briskly wheeled his trolley away.

Fern shuffled on, the officer walking a couple of feet behind her.

'Felt the cane before, have you Missy?' he murmured.

'N . . . no.' She swallowed. 'But it looks nice and thin.'

'Therein lies its strength. It stings much more than a hand or a paddle,' the man answered. 'The rattan can really stripe you hard!'

A women in her thirties came walking towards Fern. She had thick wavy fair hair above a plump cheerful face. She was wearing a leisure suit and looked matronly. She blushed when she saw Fern's state of undress.

'Invite the nice lady to your chastisement, Miss Terris,' the officer said.

'I've been . . . wicked,' Fern mumbled, looking somewhere over the other woman's right shoulder. 'Would you like to come and see me taste the cane?'

She held her breath. Having the youth watch her would be bad enough. She couldn't bear for this motherly woman to see her take her thrashing. Surely the stranger would refuse to observe such a session? Surely she wasn't the sadistic type?

Fern looked up, and was shocked to see the gleam of excitement in the other inmate's eyes.

'It's for your own good,' the woman said softly. 'Really – it'll set you on the path away from crime.'

'But I don't want you to watch!' Fern gasped.

'You never will, the woman said, 'yet you'll thank *Compulsion* for this one day, dearie.'

Sure, and I suppose I'll even beg for extra thrashings, Fern thought, clenching her hands into fists.

'I was just on my way to watch the court cases. I'll come and see you take your caning now,' added the plump inmate.

Fern started to move slowly forward. Now both the officer and her new-found audience were walking behind. 'What are you in for?' she asked over her shoulder to the woman.

'Business deception,' she replied.

Fern kept putting one knicker-bound foot before the other as the woman continued with her explanation.

'I used to sell mail order diet pills – they were really just vitamin tablets. By the time the police caught up with me I'd made thousands of pounds.'

59

'And now?' Fern prompted.

The woman sighed: 'I used to think that I was just robbing the gullible of twenty quid or so, that they'd get over it. *Compulsion*'s made me see that I was treading on people's dreams.'

'I dream of taking this caning without you watching!' Fern muttered.

'That's not the same thing,' the older inmate said.

'Since when were you the oracle?' Fern jeered. They'd said she could ask questions, so she was going to ask awkward ones of this know-it-all inmate.

'The judge obviously recognises you need to feel shamed by this thrashing. That's why he's making it a public one,' the heavier woman confirmed.

'And you're just tagging along for my sake?' Fern continued.

She heard the woman swallow, then mutter: 'No.'

'Why be my audience then?'

'I . . . like watching too!' the inmate admitted.

Fern tensed. 'You like watching someone being punished?'

Again the indrawn breath and agonised hesitation: 'Yes.'

'That's really sick!' Fern muttered, still stumbling forward in her confining knicker bonds.

'You haven't been here long,' said the woman. It was a statement rather than a question.

Fern sighed heavily. 'No.'

'Haven't seen someone else being birched on the behind?' the inmate continued.

'Well, no.' Fern had felt Davy flinch as he took six strokes of Ms Lenn's rattan on his naked buttocks. But she hadn't been able to see him take his caning, as he'd been lying on top of her with his cock buried inside. 'But what does that prove?' she enquired.

'Proves that you don't yet know what you're talking about,' the older woman said with feeling.

'Turn left,' the officer said. 'You've stairs to go down soon so get ready to bunny hop!'

Bunny hop indeed. They were adding to her ignominy

with every second. Fern grimaced, but forced herself not to look back and glare.

'Watching someone else tasting the rod or the whip can be very exciting,' the fair-haired woman continued. 'Yes, you feel ashamed for them and for yourself, and for the human race's darker more primitive side. But it still . . .'

'Gives you something to do when the weather's bad?' Fern interrupted sarcastically.

The woman sounded resigned to her own behaviour. 'It makes a lot of us excited even though it isn't politically correct.'

'I hate violence!' Fern muttered.

'Me, too. But carefully meted-out corporal punishment isn't the same as mindless violence. CP's a thought-about and sophisticated thing.'

'I can live without such sophistication!' Fern said over her shoulder.

'You've lived without it so far,' said the officer, 'and have been functioning as an empty-headed bimbo. We're hoping to discipline you into becoming more than that.'

The man was an arrogant malicious sod! Fern let her hatred for him fuel her on. When she reached the stairs she held onto the bannister and made feet-together-and-knees-bent jumping movements. When she reached the carpetted and centrally heated basement she found herself facing a large polished oak door.

'Welcome to the chamber where our more demanding miscreants are punished,' said the officer. 'Prepare to have the sorest and reddest hide.'

Four

So this was what a punishment chamber looked like! Dress still bunched above her waist and her panties at her ankles, Fern made her way apprehensively into the massive rectangular room. Her leather shoes nestled into the soft wool carpet. She breathed in the jasmine fragranced air. Curiously, she walked to the facing wall and gazed up at the whips and rods and paddles. 'Your poor bottom will taste them all if you don't become a worthwhile citizen during the next few months,' the guard said.

Fern opened her mouth to reply, then a strange male voice gave a low moan of pleasure. Following the sound, she turned and started to hobble towards a shadowy alcove forty feet away. When she reached the recess she saw a female officer kneeling beside a young man who was tied, face upwards, to a couch-sized, cushioned rack.

'Easy,' whispered the woman teasingly. She was a handsome navy-suited officer in her forties. He looked to be at most twenty-three.

'I beg to be allowed to come, ma'am,' he pleaded hoarsely, then moaned again.

The woman looked over her shoulder and saw Fern. 'Step closer if you like. We'll be out of here soon. I can see you've got your dress lifted, ready for punishment.'

'Y-yes,' Fern muttered reluctantly, 'I'm here for six of the cane.'

The officer grimaced in sympathy. 'Young Eamon here has just been subjected to half an hour of moving against my hand with his very stiff phallus. Each time he's nearing peak pleasure I take my fingers away.' She kept her right palm lightly wrapped round the boy's straining tumescence as she spoke.

'What did he do wrong?' Fern whispered, looking at the boy's flushed face.

'He played with himself without permission during the night.' She ran her thumb pad over the glistening purplish glans and the youth groaned loudly. 'But we found crusty stains on your sheets, didn't we, Eamon? And you looked so guilty when we held them under your nose!'

'Yes, ma'am. I'm so sorry, ma'am,' the youth gasped pitifully, and pulled at his four thick bonds.

Fern could see that the straps holding his wrists and ankles to the rack were of the purest lambswool. 'So that he doesn't hurt himself when he tries to get free,' the woman explained, following Fern's gaze.

Fern frowned, not quite following their logic: 'You'd use those if you were whipping him too?'

'Yes.' The guard seemed to understand her confusion. 'We're out to impart a strong lesson to one part of the inmate's anatomy – usually their genitals, breasts or luckless bottom. But we don't want to drive their wrists and ankles half mad with discomfort and pain.'

'Very thoughtful, I'm sure,' Fern muttered awkwardly.

'You'll be glad of such thoughtfulness when you're the one who's being made to whimper,' the older woman continued. She looked down at the unfortunate youth. 'All right, Eamon – let's have you rubbing against madam's hand with more vigour.' She tightened the long slender fingers she already had in place, 'Perhaps I'll be generous and won't pull away this time.'

The boy lifted his hips as best he could in his tied-down state, which enabled him to thrust forward about a centimetre. He repeated the sensation enhancing gesture again and again. Droplets of perspiration beaded his forehead. Two of them trickled down his face. His wet lips parted. 'Ma'am – I beg. Oh, mercy! I'm so hard. I can't bear it if you deny me again!'

'Keep rubbing while I think about it.'

The boy tilted his small round hips. The woman shook her head and tutted. 'If I think you're not really trying I'll take my hand away.'

64

'No. Trying. I plead!' the youth gasped. The official seemed to tighten her grip on his shaft and he closed his eyes in relief and an almost-there anguish. Thrust and thrust and thrust and thrust and thrust.

'Is this better than playing with yourself, young Eamon?'

'Yes, ma'am. Oh yes!'

'So you'll follow the rules next time and wait for me to give your prick this much pleasure?' the officer continued.

'Do what you want ma'am. Anything. I beg!'

More and more fluid was leaking from the boy's straining rod. His scrotum seemed to swell of its own accord as his phallus grew thicker. The woman doled out a moderate up-down-up friction and he cried out and creamy fluid squirted from his manhood's open eye.

'Good boy. You held off well.'

'Thank you, ma'am,' the youth murmured, his face softening with long awaited relief and obvious exhaustion.

Fern noted that his eyes held something akin to love – at least the kind of love she'd seen portrayed in the movies or on TV. Sadness hollowed at her chest: she'd never *been* in love; wasn't even sure if she'd ever loved someone. And she suspected she'd never been loved in return.

Momentarily envious of the boy's relationship with the woman, Fern turned away. She found her own officer and the tracksuited woman close behind her, their eyes as large as her own from staring at the sexual scene. All three of them watched as the navy-suited official untied the youth, helped him shrug on his clothes and led him away.

'You can touch yourself for the next four nights as a reward for containing yourself for so long there,' his tormentor was saying to him as they moved towards the door.

'All right for some!' Fern said with a shaky laugh, trying to lighten the atmosphere. She looked at her own officer and at the curly-headed observer but neither of them smiled back. Fern had made light of the caning she was due, but now that it was nearing her bottom felt vulnerable and frantic. She longed to cover it with her pinafore dress which was still bunched around her waist.

65

'Right, Miss Terris, let's get you into the punishment position then wait for the flower boy,' the officer said.

Fern backed away as he approached her: 'Hey, if we're about to get this close shouldn't I get to know your name?'

'It's Mr Arramerci – but just call me Merciless,' said the man with a sardonic sneer. 'I am when I'm facing a girl's bare bottom and I'm wielding the cane!'

'He's just trying to worry you,' whispered the matronly woman.

Fern gulped: he was certainly succeeding.

'So what's your name?' she whispered back to the sympathetic woman, as the officer strode towards a sloping piece of leather furniture further up the massive room.

'You can call me Lydia,' the other inmate said, with an uncertain smile.

'Miss Terris – meet *Compulsion's* version of the punishment trestle,' Officer Arramerci cut in, tapping the nearest section of the piece of equipment.

Fern noticed that it had thick strips of soft calfskin at its head and foot. 'I can just hold on to the top of it,' she said fearfully, hating the thought of being bound in position. 'You don't have to tie me down.'

'We'll see about that!' said the officer. He grinned and took a rattan from the wall. 'Maybe you'll be braver than the other girls who've tasted this cane on their soft little bottoms.' He looked at her more keenly. 'So are you going to approach the bench yourself or do I have to frogmarch you into place?'

'I'll walk!' Fern said with conviction. She tried to remind herself of how much worse a jail sentence would have been. At least here they treated you wonderfully despite the rigorous punishments.

'Get all the way over,' the man said as she neared the piece of furniture. 'And stick that naked little bum right out!'

Bastard! Fern knelt against one plane of the surprisingly cool leather then shuffled closer to the centre of it on her bare knees, keeping her dress tucked under her armpits. Now that she was closer she could see that it was a large inverted V, just like a double-sided children's slide. When she lay flat her head and arms were supported on the downward slope of one side, whilst her hips and legs sloped down the other way. The way that was closest to her tormentor and his rattan!

As Fern's naked tummy wriggled nervously against the smooth surface, she wished he'd just use the long slender stick on her arse and get it over with.

'Let's see how this bottom's shaping up,' the security guard said.

Fern winced as she felt his large palms running over her helpless buttocks. He pushed the pinafore dress even further up her back, then renewed his taunting fondling of her bum.

'It's an ideal bum for thrashing, isn't it, my dear? Wonderfully small and creamy – just as the wise judge said.'

At least only the officer and the vaguely sympathetic Lydia would be around to see her being thrashed. Oh, and that grinning trolley boy with the carnations when he appeared! As Fern lay over the whipping stool and thought about her small but enthusiastic audience, she heard the door behind her opening. She tensed at the clamour of sound.

'Met those six on their way back from the swimming pool,' the breathless voice of the flower boy said.

Fern looked over her shoulder to see three damp-haired couples in their mid-thirties entering the punishment chamber. She herself seemed to be one of the younger inmates here. Not that her youthfulness was going to do her bottom any good!

'Now that you've arrived we can get started,' said the officer firmly. He walked in front of Fern then hunkered down so that his face was close to hers. 'You've said you'll try to take the cane without being tied down. If you fail I'll bind you in place before delivering the remainder of the strokes to your tethered bottom. As its your first taste of the rattan I won't repeat any strokes on account of your failure to lie still.'

Fern felt absurdly grateful that he seemed to care.

'Thank you, sir,' she murmured as quietly as possible, then gripped more tightly at the leather edge. She wanted him to like her and be gentle with her, but she didn't want the watchers to overhear. After all, she wanted to make friends with the other inmates and joke with them about the stupid regime. She couldn't do that if she proved to be a wimp or a teacher's pet!

'Stroke one of the rattan coming up,' the official said.

Shouldn't that be coming *down*, Fern thought. Then all coherence went from her brain as the implement connected with her naked buttocks. 'Aaaah!' she yelled, and her backside seemed to take on a life of its own and half leaped off the leather slope. Christ, that had stung like a thousand bees! Fern reached back and rubbed frantically at the hot red stripe, as if hoping to massage the pain away.

'Don't rub your bottom without permission. Grip the edge,' Arramerci said.

He hadn't been named well, Fern thought dazedly: he seemed totally without compassion. But she'd agreed to this punishment – to every punishment they might inflict here. Reluctantly she took hold of the sides of the trestle again.

The second stroke was equally severe, but at least she was expecting it. It stained a line across the curvy centre of her naked cheeks.

'Two,' said the officer with obvious satisfaction. 'We sometimes make the more disobedient girls and boys count the strokes out loud, and then thank the officer. Sometimes they lose the place and we have to start again.' He smiled as he walked in front of Fern and ran the cane through his fingers. 'Their bad bums end up very sore indeed.'

'I'll count if that's what you want, sir,' Fern whispered, no longer caring about the watching inmates.

'No need, Miss Terris. We're letting you off lightly today,' he said then disappeared behind her.

Fern tensed her bottom. After an agonisingly long wait she heard and felt the third swish of the rod. She yelled, as it connected sharply with the curving-in part of her buttocks. Then she impotently drummed her feet. Was this really them letting her off lightly? To avoid such shame she'd be discreet when she seduced her next man!

Officer Arramerci laid on the fourth behaviour-modifier at the tops of her thighs and, because the punishment was beyond endurance, Fern pushed herself back and scrambled from the trestle. 'Too much,' she whispered, standing up and frantically rubbing at her punished parts.

'You've two to go yet,' said the man.

She looked at him miserably. His features were impassive. As she watched, he ran his fingers along the cane from curved handle to thin tip.

'Go back over like a good girl,' he entreated her gently, 'and take the other two strokes.'

'And if I don't?' Fern asked, cupping her sore cheeks.

'We'll tie you down and deliver them anyway. You'll hate us for it, which isn't what we want. You'll also feel ashamed of yourself later. After all, you *agreed* to this, Miss Terris. Agreed to a short sharp shock rather than a dingy cell for life.'

'I know but I didn't think it would hurt this much!' Fern sniffed, stalling for time.

'Of course you didn't – you were ignorant about such things. You've been ignorant about a lot of things. Here at *Compulsion* we're dedicating each day to putting you right.'

'And in a few months I'll be free to go?' she prompted.

The guard nodded. 'If we could see that you'd truly repented of your crimes and learned a new way of interacting with the world we'd let you walk out of here tomorrow.'

'Two more, then,' Fern muttered resignedly, and walked the few steps towards the punishment slope.

Going over it again was supremely difficult. She fought for self-control and courage. God, to again expose her bare bottom to that searing punisher!

'After this thrashing the rest of the night is yours,' the officer said. She heard the encouragement in his voice. 'You can order a special meal, go for a swim, choose a video from our extensive library. We've a music room, a sauna, a spa ...'

His words swum round Fern's brain but she couldn't quite turn them into pictures. All she could think about was her raised and waiting bare bum. 'The last two now, I beg. Get it over with,' she whispered, scared that at any moment she would try to escape and undergo the further humiliation of being led back and tied firmly in place.

'The lady gets what the lady asks for,' her tormentor murmured, sounding amused and exultant.

Fern heard the swish of the rattan then felt its unique burning impact on the middle part of both cheeks' full swell. She moaned and twitched both buttocks, then waited in an agony of suspense for the sixth.

'Are you thinking about the crimes that brought you here?' the man added.

'Yes, sir.' She couldn't remember her crimes. She'd been reduced to the status of a trembling red-and-white bottom.

'Think of each thrashing as bringing you closer to new awareness,' the officer said.

She was aware of her arse. She was aware of his right hand. She was aware of the horrible swishy cane in it. As she mused, her corrector applied the cane for a sixth and final time to the backs of her thighs.

'Six of the best,' he said with obvious satisfaction.

Fern wriggled her striped sore hindquarters, trying to find a movement that would relieve them. Six of the worst, more like!

'You can stand up now.'

Her knees felt stiff, and she got carefully to her feet. She put her hands at her sides in a desperate attempt to keep them from cupping her punished bottom.

'You can hold your arse if you want,' the man continued. He looked somehow smaller and more approachable now.

'Thank you, sir. Can I pull down my pinafore dress as well, sir?' Fern whispered, trying not to look at the other grinning inmates.

The officer nodded: 'You can do anything you like!'

Gratefully, Fern put her relatively cool palms over her hot sore orbs. She could feel the bands glowing against her fingers. She had a sudden urge to go find a mirror and look at her well-warmed bum. *I took my thrashing well*, she thought, and felt a rush of pride, a surge of achievement. *And I'll make damn sure I don't get caught when I have sex next time!*

Aloud she said: 'Can someone show me back to my room?'

'I will. And you can walk back without keeping your knickers round your ankles!' Arramerci answered.

Blushing, Fern stooped to remove the offending pants. Then, more haltingly, she started to free her pinafore from her waist, edging it carefully over each centimetre of punished bottom. 'I'm ready to go back now, sir,' she murmured, turning towards the door. The officer hurried to open it. He kept pace with her as she walked slowly along the corridor – for now not her superior but her equal.

'Phone down for the meal of your choice,' he said, 'then join us later for a movie in *Compulsion*'s cinema if you wish.'

'I haven't been to the cinema for years,' she said. There were lots of things she hadn't done in years, she realised.

'Gives you insight into different lives, different motivations,' the officer said.

'It's not one of these educational things?'

'No, it's a thriller,' he replied. 'We're showing a psychological drama tomorrow night, and a comedy the next if that's what you prefer.'

She didn't know what she preferred, Fern realised with a pang. Throughout her life she'd mainly shopped and partied. She didn't even know if she liked doing either – they were just what people of her social class did to pass the time. 'I'll go to them all, if I may,' she said thoughtfully.

'You may,' said the officer. He smiled as he imitated her precise queen's English.

Fern felt surprised at his mimicry: this was just the way she had been brought up to speak. She wouldn't put on airs and graces with the man, she mused. There was no point, given that he'd made her bare her bum and submit

71

to a thorough caning. She wouldn't get away with playing the lady of the manor here!

She ate, then bathed and changed. Yet another guide, a bearded man in his forties, took her to *Compulsion*'s auditorium where she watched a recent movie with rows of other equally relaxed inmates, twenty women and ten men.

'Are there more women prisoners here, then?' she asked the guide as the film ended.

'No, more men – but the women are more open to different options,' the officer told her. 'If the man's always gone down the pub of an evening he'll try to do something like that here, like making illicit home brew.'

'You can't drink here?' asked Fern, as the film ended and they walked slowly from the large darkened room. She'd been craving a vodka for hours now, especially before approaching the bench for them to pronounce sentence on her poor backside.

'Not legitimately if you're here for drink-related offences like you are,' the man replied.

He knew of her crime, then. Did he know of the punishments she'd had?

'If I reshape my life for the better will I be allowed some alcohol?' she asked hopefully.

He smiled back at her: 'You'll be allowed anything – you'll be free to go! Obviously by then your priorities will have changed so you'll no longer drink to excess.'

They walked up two flights of stairs then reached a crossroads of four corridors. 'Isn't my room this way?' Fern asked, pointing to the left as the officer turned to the right.

'It is love, but I have to take you to Dr Marshall first for your inaugural review,' her bearded companion said.

'Yeah?' Fern's heightened sense of wellbeing wavered. She could still remember the spanking she'd received from the man, and the way he'd let Rob bare her bottom.

'Dont' worry. It's just a quick pep talk,' the officer said, and smiled.

They reached a glossy teak door, and the man knocked. Fern heard Dr Marshall calling for her to come in. The officer made a gesture with his hands that indicated she should enter.

'You'll be fine, dear,' he said, turning to go.

Taking the smallest steps possible, Fern opened the door and walked through. The psychiatrist was seated behind his desk. He was writing quickly.

'Fern! Take a seat. Help yourself to tea from the urn,' he instructed, adding another word to the page.

'Oh. Right,' Fern stammered.

He raised his head. 'Only if that's what you want, Fern.'

She no longer knew what she wanted – except that she didn't want to be chastened or humiliated again tonight.

The psychiatrist smiled at her as she carefully poured herself some of the scented Earl Grey.

'Settling in all right?'

She nodded. 'I like my room – and the cinema.'

'Good, good.'

Fern felt something in her body lift again – somehow she wanted to please the man, to earn his respect.

'I know of your misbehaviour here so far,' the man continued, 'but you've been soundly thrashed for that, so we won't dwell on it further. It took time for you to build up your current misguided beliefs so it'll take time for them to change.'

'If you could just tell me what counts as doing wrong . . .' Fern started.

The psychiatrist shook his head. 'I could give you a list, and you'd learn it off by heart, but that wouldn't change your basic psychological make-up. We want to show you what works in practice and what doesn't. That takes longer to achieve.'

'I'll achieve it!' Fern said. She felt too alert to drink her tea. Felt . . . *sexual*.

'Most of the inmates say that, but they all earn a few sore bums along the way,' Dr Marshall replied.

'I'm a fast learner – you'll never have to punish me again,' Fern declared. She wanted hugs not humiliation. She wanted the subject to change.

The psychiatrist raised one eyebrow. 'You obviously

have the motivation to pretend to change – at least your tender little rump does!' He gazed into her eyes for an uncomfortably long moment. 'Whether that change is deep and lasting remains to be seen.' He looked down at his notes. 'Over the ensuing months we hope you'll discover an acceptable value system. We trust you'll put together a valid philosophy that will last for the rest of your life.'

'I will, sir.'

'Then go, sleep, dream. Your gardening work begins tomorrow,' he said softly.

'I . . .' Fern searched for words that would keep her in his room a little longer. 'Thank you, sir.'

She wanted him inside her. Wanted to be held and helped. She loved the idea of him thrusting into her gently as she lay on her back and he cupped her punished cheeks. She opened her mouth to murmur a few seductive words, then closed her lips again. No – he wanted her to think before she acted. To forge a better future. To change the life she'd led so far. Gathering all her willpower, Fern walked from the room without touching or propositioning Dr Marshall. At least she'd made a start. She smiled as the officer returned to take her to her warm safe room. For the first time in years she went to bed feeling loved and clean.

Five

The next morning after breakfast Fern dressed in her favourite knee-length denim shorts, a plain white T-shirt and her matching denim waistcoat. After a moments consideration, she left off her bra and left the waistcoat buttons undone. After all, she might be working with men in *Compulsion*'s vegetable plots and gardens, so wanted to look her sexual best. She might not rush clit-long into another thrusting encounter, but she still wanted to be dressed to thrill.

As she finished outlining her pout with a scarlet lip pen, she heard two short knocks on her door. 'Coming!' Fern called. She wondered when she really would come next in the sexual sense. She hoped it would be soon. She'd been too tired to play with herself last night, but her dreams had been of probing thick phalluses. 'Ready for anything!' she said brightly, waltzing out of the room.

Bill Stark stood there in the corridor. His mouth was set in an even more displeased line than that of the day before. His hands were pushed deep inside his pockets. 'I plan to get a good eight hours work out of you today,' he said sternly. 'I had to do your job when you went and got yourself caned.'

As if she'd actively chosen to feel the rod on her bum!

'I'm a good worker, Mr Stark,' Fern said. Then shivered, because she knew it wasn't true. She'd never done anything more strenuous than drying a dish before. God knows how she'd get on in *Compulsion*'s gardens, or how she'd fare with this squat unsmiling man. Rough-hewn people like him often hated her fine bone structure, her well-modulated voice, her opulent upbringing. He might well decide to tell the officers that she deserved a further taste of the paddle or swishy cane.

'I'll try my hardest to please with my work performance, sir,' she continued, using her most obsequious voice as she followed him along the building's corridors.

They reached what seemed to be the back door, and walked out into the gentle morning sunshine. She breathed the ozone-fresh breeze, then walked towards the stretching fields of feathery-topped produce – presumably carrots. Bill motioned into the distance with his walking stick:

'Those strips of earth contain turnips, potatoes, peas.'

'You'd think they'd be cheaper to buy,' Fern said thinking out loud.

'Not when we get our labour virtually free!' he muttered, looking at her legs in the cut-off denims.

'But one of the officers told me I'll get a wage here,' Fern exclaimed.

'Aye – a couple of quid to keep you in hair ribbons,' the man answered. 'You'll not be in the top tax bracket here, my silly lass!'

He was a patronising bastard, but he was also her boss, albeit temporarily. Fern took a seat on the nearest fence and surveyed the sprawling vegetable plots. She'd hold her tongue whilst she was in his employ rather than risk holding her chastened arse cheeks. 'I'll work hard for my two pounds,' she said.

'Then get off your lazy backside before I decide to tan it for the next hour,' Bill Stark replied.

He tapped his walking stick against the bare backs of her legs as he marched her over to the patch of earth she was to work on. 'We're going to grow heather and export it. We want a well-nourished soil so you've to dig all this peat into the ground.'

Briskly, Fern opened one of the four-foot sacks of peat and scooped handfuls of the rich brown sphagnum onto the ground. She used the spade Bill Stark handed her to turn the old earth over, digging in the new peat. She did it again. And again. And again. Her armpits ached as if they were bruised by the time the man said she could stop for a rest.

'There's decaffeinated coffee in my flask, and wholemeal tuna baps in the picnic box in the shed,' he said.

Fern flopped down on the ground: 'I could murder a glass of beer and a sausage roll or two!'

'Dr Marshall says a healthy mind needs a healthy body,' Bill Stark continued. 'Says too much junk food can lead to a brain that thinks garbage.'

Pretend to be part of the system. Comply! 'Makes sense to me,' Fern murmured, smiling at the man, hoping he'd look on her as if she was a favoured granddaughter. 'I'll go and get that healthy snack from the shed.' She walked away across the field. Climbing over a fence, she started to thread her way through the ten glasshouses that would take her to her destination. Then she froze as a male voice called her name.

'Miss Terris?' He stepped out of the nearest see-through door. He wore dungarees and a blue and white checked shirt. He had glossy brown hair and a knowing secret smile, both scary and seductive.

Fern stared at him warily. 'How come you know who I am when I don't know you?'

The youth grinned some more. 'I've been introduced to your arse. I saw it squirming under the paddle the other day.'

So he'd been in the assembly hall. Fern coloured and tried to step past.

'No – wait,' said the boy. 'We've all been through it. I've felt a stiffened birch on my behind more often than I can count.'

'What's your point?' Fern muttered. She was thirsty, worn, sore, and badly wanted that decaffeinated coffee.

'Point is, I've a drink that'll take your mind off things.' He looked quickly round the complex. 'Bill Stark gone for a piss behind the fir trees? Then come inside!'

Warily the twenty-four year old followed him into the square glass house. Large tomato plants bearing red and reddening fruit covered every surface except the floor.

'Great, isn't it?' said the boy, gesticulating. 'Means no one can peer in whilst we imbibe.'

Imbibe, huh? He was educated like her. He looked sure of himself. She might just find a soulmate here.

'Welcome to my Happy Hour,' the youth added, staring hungrily at her T-shirt moulded breasts.

The attraction was mutual! Fern was glad that she'd unfastened the buttons of her denim waistcoat. She'd need this boy on her side if she was to help herself to any of his booze.

'*Voilà!*' he continued, and, reaching behind three of the largest plants, brought out a litre-sized green glass bottle. 'It's full of sloe gin,' he said.

'You have a still?' Nothing would surprise her about this place.

'We wish! No, the gin is smuggled in by newcomers and by inmates on weekend passes. We just pick the sloe berries here and add them – you can taste the result.'

He opened the bottle and poured a half inch of purple liquid into the cap: 'Enjoy it!'

Fern reach for the tiny container and tipped the contents into her parched mouth. It was strong and sweet with a soothing yet heightening afterglow.

'More?' she asked hopefully, moving closer to the sun-kissed man.

The boy grinned and dipped his middle fingers in the liquor, then held them out for her to suck. Blushing, Fern licked the purple alcohol from his fingertips.

'Take it all the way in this time,' murmured the boy, placing his finger in the bottle neck again before holding the dripping digit out to her. Brain and belly craving the forget-me-not liquid, Fern took his middle finger deep into her mouth.

When the last droplet of gin had disappeared inside her lips, she backed away.

'Get down on your hands and knees,' commanded the boy, 'next course is the main course.' He lay down and unbuttoned his dungarees then pulled his shirt up, before dribbling a capful of the strong spirit over his flat warm belly and the dark hairs just above his groin.

'Couldn't I just have a cup?' Fern mumbled, feeling

78

ashamed yet excited. Part of her wanted to arouse and satisfy this strong sure youth. Another part of her just wanted
to drink her way into near-oblivion, into sleep.

'If you're nice to the publican you may find the pub gives
generous measures,' the gin-holder said. He smiled up at
her from his relaxed waiting stance on the ground, his shaft
standing to attention. 'I heard you never went a day without a liquid lunch, even had piña colada's for breakfast,
Miss Terris.'

'Oh, I usually just have brunch,' Fern said.

For a second she felt triumphant – she could still ver-
bally give as good as she got! Then she looked down at the
bottle the boy was still clutching and knew that she wanted
an alcoholic drink more than anything else in the known
universe. She wasn't an alcoholic, but she had used spirits
almost every day for the past six years, in the same way
that some people eat biscuits with their coffee. Giving up
liquor or sugar or cigarettes could take time.

And the time didn't have to be now! Each cell calling out
for the potent liquid comfort, she got down on her hands
and knees and centred her mouth above the youth's belly.
Then she put her open lips to the top of his pubic hair and
licked the liquid away.

'Let's have that licking further down, sweetheart,' murmured the boy.

He sloshed more of the sloe gin around the root of his
shaft. Fern hoped he'd get some in his rod's sensitive eye,
but he was obviously wary of that and held a protective
palm cupped over his prick head. Fern pushed her bum
back and lowered her head down and prayed that no one
would come in. But why should they? Bill Stark thought
she was having her wholemeal lunch in the shade of the
shed. Only she and the youth knew what was happening.
She and the youth and his thickening, lengthening shaft.

'Tongue it for me, baby,' he whispered.

Fern did as she was bid, licking sweet sloe gin from the
matt shaft and mouthing salty pre-come from the shiny
glans which immediately produced more liquid excitement.

'Deeper,' begged the youth.

79

Fern started to use her curled palm like a close-fitting vagina, strongly finger-frigging his hardness whilst giving a gentler tongue bath to the more sensitive penile head.

'God, yes!' He lifted his well-muscled hips and cast down his eyes.

Fern watched through her lashes as his lips stretched wide in increasing ecstasy. She moved the foreskin up and down, finding a medium rhythm that took his cock's tip in and out of her mouth. She put her left hand between his firm thighs and cupped the thin-skinned giant marbles, using the middle finger of that same hand to stroke the crease of his arse.

'Got to ...' muttered the boy, as she tongued his smoothness over and round. 'That's so ...'

But she never got to know what that was, for at that second he pushed up and spritzed the salty contents of his scrotum between her rounded lips.

Tired from the strain of staying on her hands and knees, Fern swallowed the sap then lowered herself over him. They lay there for a few minutes.

'You've got a tongue like velvet!' the youth said dazedly.

'Earned me a drink, has it?' Fern replied.

'My love, it's earned you the bottle!' he said, gratefully handing her the container.

Fern sat up and lifted it to her lips. She drank deeply. Choked slightly, then recovered. Then she drank some more. Jesus, it went down as smooth as single cream!

'Maybe I could come here every lunchtime?' she said, glad to have access to a mood-altering substance.

'No promises about the liquid lunch, sweetheart,' the youth said. 'Don't know if my cock could produce as much juice as it did today!'

Fern stiffened. Why did he have to go and spoil things by being crude again? She'd been starting to relax, feeling that they were equal. Now he was reminding her that she'd prostituted herself on her hands and knees for a couple of drinks. 'Want to see how much liquid *I* produce?' she asked, lying flat on her back and spreading her legs. 'See how much you can excite me with your hot tongue?'

A spur to his male ego should do the trick! She'd get him to lick her to orgasm. He'd be assuming he could then fuck her hard, but she'd coolly turn him away. It would serve him right for being such a pig about the alcohol. She'd leave him with a cock like iron, begging for a second release.

'Oh, I can excite you, sweetheart,' the boy said. 'Believe me, I know just how to excite you.'

Fern slid her right palm under her T-shirt and over her right breast: 'Touch my tits, then, lover.'

'Uh, uh. A good hard spanking over my knee will have you creaming yourself.'

'You presumptuous little . . .!' Fern tried to sit up but he took her arms and held them above her head. 'That's what the officers think, but they're wrong,' she said, blushing.

'No, dearest, they're never wrong.'

She couldn't bear the way he was looking at her: so assured, so gloating.

'Then that means you're also turned on by being punished,' she said.

The boy kept staring at her: 'Looks like it. At least, I've hardened under the whip a few times. But like a lot of the people here I can swing both ways.'

'You mean you like to discipline people too?' Fern said, her eyes searching futilely for a means of escape.

'Babe, I just love it!' he smiled.

She played for time: 'But I haven't done anything to *deserve* a spanking.'

The boy's eyes widened. 'Yes you have – you've turned into a taunter and a tease.' He held her wrists more firmly and stared down at her, his lips tightening.

Fern was glad that she was still lying on her shorts-covered bum. 'I'll tell one of the officers,' she warned.

'Tell them that you've been drinking when it's against the rules? They'll smell it on your breath. We've a nurse here and a medical laboratory. He may choose to do a blood alcohol test.'

He probably would, Fern thought, staring up at his triumphant face.

'If you go before the court for being drunk, the judge will give more than a spanking!' the youth said. He sat up and put the bottle safely away on the upper workbench. He leant his back against the table legs and took hold of Fern by the waist. 'You can struggle, in which case I'll bare your bum for longer and thrash it harder,' he said quietly, 'or you can lie over my knee and take your spanking like a good little girl.'

She couldn't acquiesce to his demands – she just couldn't! At least Dr Marshall and the officers had had a certain authority. This boy was probably a couple of years younger than her. He was a fellow inmate. Someone whose only claim to eminence was that he'd added freshly picked sloes to smuggled gin!

'Go shove it up your arse!' Fern muttered, trying to dig her back and backside closer into the ground.

'That's not nice,' the boy said. 'That really isn't friendly.'

'You want friendly?' Fern continued, 'Join a singles club.'

'You were pleased to see me a moment ago, my love. Sucked awfully good and rubbed firmly but not too hard at my prick, like you'd had lots of practice. Reckon you've often had more than a piña colada for lunch.'

Fern closed her eyes. She wouldn't listen to him any more. She'd think about something pleasant, think about anything. She retensed her muscles and dug down again too late as he took hold of her by the waist and flipped her over, before pulling her with obvious enjoyment across his lap.

He held her there with one hand whilst he refastened his dungaree straps with the other. 'I just want one of us naked, darling – the one of us that has titties,'

'Please don't strip me. I've got to get back to work!' Fern said.

'Fine by me if Bill comes looking for you. Vital discipline always takes priority over other tasks. He'd love to see me turning your pale bum to scarlet.'

He would too, Fern realised, squirming. Hadn't Ms Lenn mentioned that he liked to watch?

'I could slide down on your shaft now, instead,' she whispered enticingly.

'He's just come, baby. He can wait.' The youth seemed immovable.

'You could do the phoenix position,' Fern pleaded. 'You know, you hold my ankles high in the air and thrust forward. Means you go in so deep! And I can't move, and . . .'

'I'd rather watch you wriggle as I heat your bottom, angel,' the youth said.

Somewhere to the left of them a door opened and closed. 'Is Mr Stark on his way?' Fern gasped.

'Could be any of the gardeners,' said the boy. 'Some of my colleagues are tending the orchids that we export.'

'I thought orchids were always imported,' Fern said, trying to take his attention away from her backside.

'Good try, but now it's time to talk about your bad bum,' said the boy, putting his fingers to the single button of her shorts and neatly undoing it.

Fern tried to shove her tummy more firmly into his in an effort to stop him pushing the front zipper down.

'Naughty,' said the boy. 'Such obstinacy has been noted and will be dealt with.'

Christ, he sounded like some middle manager giving the office junior a strict talking to!

What could she say to stop him baring her bottom and subjecting it to the weight of his palm? She'd already sucked him till he squirted his seed. She'd offered the silky hollow between her thighs. That only left her bumhole up for grabs, and she had no intention of giving his cock access to her virgin anus.

'Please don't spank me,' she whispered, deciding to grovel. 'I've been punished so much already. Oh, please!'

'Tell me what's been done to these cute little cheeks so far,' grinned the boy, pushing down her shorts and stroking her through her white cotton briefs.

'I . . . Dr Marshall spanked me for being seductive in the van.' *God, this was so humiliating!*

The youth sniggered: 'I hear Rab got in on the action too?'

'Yes. He bent me over a fence and tore off my knickers.'

The bastard obviously knew most of the details so it was pointless trying to save face. Save bum, more like! At least whilst she was talking about the chastisements she'd received the youth wasn't thrashing her. 'Then I got paddled for getting up late or having sex for ulterior motives, or something.' She tried desperately to keep the conversation going. She could remember each correction and each message, but not which pain went with which explanatory words.

'I remember you taking the paddle,' the boy murmured, squeezing her taut full globes through her pants. 'You didn't half wriggle!'

'Well, it hurt,' Fern whispered, 'and everyone was watching and ...'

'We were all watching your pussy juices glistening on your legs.'

Damn him! Fern tensed her bottom, her calves and her toes.

'What's made your bum most sensitive so far?' continued the youth gloatingly.

'The ... the rattan.' She'd been shocked beyond words at the severity of each stroke; the fact that the thin rod could cause such radiating bands of anguish. And the officer hadn't been meting out the lash with anything like full force. 'He just raised his arm halfway and flicked his wrist and ... Jesus!' she continued.

'Wish I'd seen you moving your arse for that one!' her castigator said.

Fern trembled as he fondled her helpless little bum.

'Time I pulled down your pants,' he added, reaching for her elasticated waistband. 'I prefer to spank naughty girls on the bare.'

Remember that the alternative is a whipping ordered by the judge, Fern told herself as she felt her bottom being exposed. She screwed up her eyes and clenched her small fists and waited. She soon felt the youth's surprisingly soft hands sliding over her newly denuded cheeks. She sensed that he'd raised his arm dauntingly far back, and was holding it there. Then it made noisy contact with her left buttock and she squealed.

She drew in her breath, then let it out fast and wailed again as he spanked the other naked orb. She flinched her legs as he slapped with equal zeal over her bottom's sensitive crease.

'How many am I getting?' she gasped.

'As many as you deserve.'

'None, then,' Fern muttered.

'You said I had to turn you on,' the boy said, a knowing smile in his voice. 'And I am.'

'Are not!' She sounded petulant, then winced as he started berating both helpless nether cheeks again.

After another twelve or fourteen spanks, he stopped.

'Let's see how aroused this little pussy is,' he said.

Fern inhaled hard as he shifted her upon his knee so that he had greater access to her labia. She let her breath out in a shamed gasp as she felt one thick digit probe her entrance and slide into the hot oiliness within.

'You're soaking, sweetheart. Your cunt gets off on this.'

'So does your cock!'

'It's not wise to be rude to the man who's blackmailing you when your bare bum is over his lap,' her tormentor said.

He was right, damn him to hell. He could do what he liked to her poor arse in this Godforsaken greenhouse.

'Sorry I was rude,' Fern mumbled, trying to restore the status quo. '*Please* don't spank me again!'

'I'm not going to spank you. I'm going to give your arse a taste of the cane!' the youth murmured.

In an instant Fern had levered herself up off of his lap and had scrabbled backwards until she was sitting against the greenhouse's side wall. Vehemently she shook her head from side to side: 'No way!'

'You just want my tongue on you, huh?' said the boy.

Fern nodded warily.

'Okay,' he continued, 'I'll lick your clit before I take my cane to your arse.'

'You will?' Fern spread her bare thighs far apart, grateful that he was going to let her orgasm. By the time he'd lipped her to climax he'd hopefully be too tired to punish

85

her poor bottom again. Forget the cane, she told herself, then shivered in anticipation as he crawled quickly over and dipped his head between her legs.

Aaaah, that felt good! His tongue was light yet firm as it made contact with her clitoris, tracing its thrilled wet walls from tiny foot to tip. His mouth lapped gently round the fleshy nub, bringing renewed pleasure to the area. Bringing ecstasy close, then closer still.

Fern lifted her spanked sore cheeks from the ground and pushed her clitoris closer to his tongue in an unseeing gesture. She felt the thirty second warning go off in her head. Felt . . . nothing suddenly. She opened her eyes to see the boy sitting back on his haunches. He grinned.

'I'll finish bringing you off if you agree to take the cane.'

'Fuck you!'

Fern started to plunge her own right hand towards her mons. She was so close, so hot, so desperate.

'Uh, uh.' The boy grabbed her hand. 'Ask nicely for your orgasm. You'll come under my tongue or you won't come at all.'

Still pinning her wrists in one hand, he bent his head and gave her begging bud an experimental licking. Fern moaned and moved her hips towards his face. 'Easy, sweetheart. You haven't yet asked for that caning,' he taunted.

Fern swallowed hard. 'Isn't there another way?'

'Not when I want to soundly stripe that pretty bum!' said the youth.

God, he was a louse – but he was an exquisitely licking louse. And her clit was so needy.

'Right, I'll take a thrashing, but for God's sake finish me off first,' Fern begged.

'I'll think about it.'

The boy licked across the tip of the nub. Fern moaned low yet loud.

'Quite liked that, didn't we?' He repeated the gesture. He then licked slowly round the widest part of the clit in a way which kept her panting with desire but not quite able to go over the carnal cliff.

'Keep the same rhythm,' she whispered brokenly.

'Say *pretty please*,' the youth jibed.

'Pretty please,' Fern moaned, beyond caring. What did it matter that she was stripped to the waist in a greenhouse in broad daylight with a stranger who'd just soundly spanked her bare bottom? All that mattered was that ever-nearing rapturous come.

'Maybe I'll lick to the right. Maybe I'll lick to the left,' the boy teased. He did both. Fern whimpered in amalgamated lust and frustration. 'I'll take the cane as often as you want to give it to me,' she begged.

'Ten strokes?' he queried.

Fern hesitated and the boy stilled his tongue.

'Twelve!' she gasped, and was rewarded by thirty seconds of rhythmic licking.

'And will you ask for most of them on the lower swell where it hurts more?'

'Yes, sir. Take them all there!' She was cresting now. The boy stayed true to his tonguing tempo. 'Take them with Bill Stark watching,' Fern added gutturally, then cried out and came and came.

The orgasm seemed to start deep inside her mound and spread swiftly out to pleasure her dusky folds; her belly, her anal furrow. Her buttocks felt particularly alive – the skin prickling, tingling. The boy kept licking, helping out each last wave of rapture, till she gently pushed his silky head away.

'Worth waiting for?' he said arrogantly.

Fern nodded with heavy-lidded relief. 'Please – just hold me for a while,' she murmured sleepily.

The boy gazed at her for a few seconds, then abruptly nodded. He put his arms around her shoulders and she leaned against him, her insides still pulsing with recent delight.

When she woke, she had no idea how much time had elapsed. Two minutes? Two hours? Bill Stark had warned her not to wear good jewellery in the gardens, so she'd left her gold watch in her room. The youth who'd tongued her was sleeping on his watch wrist, so she couldn't see.

Standing up slowly, Fern parted some of the thickly growing tomato plants, and peered through the gap. She could see a man of around Bill Stark's height hoeing away far in the distance. If Bill was angry at her for being late back she'd simply pretend that she'd fallen and hurt her ankle. They were too civilised to add pain to pain!

She'd foolishly agreed to a caning – but the caner was asleep! Feeling she was winning at last, Fern started to tip-toe out of the greenhouse, and reached one anticipatory hand towards the door. Immediately she touched the handle a loud buzzer went off. The boy sat up and stared at her. Fern froze into a startled statue.

'As you can see, I've had to set up an alarm system to stop naughty girls escaping,' the boy said. 'I've fallen asleep during prolonged chastisements before.'

So she was in for a prolonged chastisement, was she? Fern's spirits fell. She damned her needy clit, damned her easy words, damned the fact that she'd originally gone into that London store and lain down behind the lingerie. But she didn't want to think about why she was here.

'You probably got the rattan last time,' said the boy. 'Long whippy cane with a curved handle?'

Fern nodded and backed away.

'Don't be shy,' the youth continued. 'You wanted a dozen bare bottomed strokes, remember?'

'I just said that because . . .' *Because I needed to come more than anything else.*

'And now you must accept what you asked for,' the youth cut in.

Fern reached for the door but found it shut fast.

'Locks automatically when it's closed,' the boy explained. 'I rigged it up myself.'

She swallowed: 'To take women prisoners?'

'No, to make sure that girls who've agreed to a caning get the thrashing they deserve!'

Fern reached the furthest wall. There was nowhere to go. She could throw a tomato plant at him but the heavy pot would break the glass and that might attract a vengeful officer and ultimate judiciary. God knows, the last thing that she wanted was to spend another half hour standing with her nervously bared bottom before the bench.

'Grip hold of the far end of the work surface,' the boy instructed.

'And if I don't?' Fern asked.

'I'll cuff your hands high up your back and leave them there till I've finished striping your little buttocks!'

Reaching into a drawer of the work station he dangled the metal handcuffs in the air.

'All right, all right – I'm bending,' Fern muttered. She looked covetously at her pants and shorts which lay discarded on the floor, taken off for her spanking. She wished that the T-shirt and waistcoat she was wearing covered even an inch of her pink rear.

'Ready in a mo,' she continued under her breath. It was awful, having to lean forward and expose her naked rump like this at his bidding. She dipped forward and felt the rough wood rubbing at her belly. She curled her fingers round the furthest edge. Trembling, she laid her face, shoulders, breasts and waist along the surface of the wood, and felt the vibrations as her pitiless lover walked up behind her. She heard something scrape against the ground as he lifted it from the floor.

'Look at it, sweetheart,' he said.

Fern turned her face in the direction of the latest sound and stared at the thick rod lying on the work station.

'It's a bamboo cane,' the boy said. 'Much less flexible than a rattan.' He gave her a slow lazy smile. 'Kiss it and I may not use it so hard.'

Shrivelling up inside, Fern put her lips to the smooth yellowish staff.

'It stings less than its thinner friend,' continued the boy, 'or would do if you hadn't pleaded for so many.'

Fern cleared her throat. 'But you had me by the clit!'

'You have to think through action and reaction, honey. Dr Marshall will tell you that,' said the youth, running the bamboo through his hands.

Fern stiffened: 'You won't tell him about us, will you?'

'Who knows?' The boy's eyes flickered.

'You can't,' Fern said, realisation dawning, 'because

that would mean admitting that you climaxed without permission. You came in my mouth when you were supposed to be at work.'

She stood up, and turned to reach for her shorts. She felt the youth's firm arms encircle her waist.

'You still agreed to this thrashing love, and the good psychiatrist says we mustn't break our promises.' He stroked her bum teasingly and laughed low in his throat when she flinched at the contact. 'And you also orgasmed knowing that it's against the rules. You'll feel Dr Marshall's birch or whip for that. He won't spare you.' He edged her reluctant body back over to the work surface. 'Now let's give that naughty bottom a strong taste of the cane.'

Fern bent, gripped then tensed. She jerked her buttocks from one side to the other after the first lash striped both cheeks. It seemed to fall exactly across the centre.

'Bull's-eye,' the youth chuckled. 'Now let's warm the flesh slightly further down.'

Fern held her breath: hadn't he said it hurt more there on the lower swell? She yelled as he swished the cane. It certainly did!

She stiffened as the youth stepped closer and ran an exploratory thumb along the backs of her legs.

'How about a nice stingy one there, angel? Just to delineate where bottom meets thigh?'

Fern moaned and shook her head then tensed her bum. She jumped up after he doled out the reverberating stroke. 'I can't bear it!' she wailed, palms cupping her poor inflamed bottom.

'You said you'd bare it for twelve, sweetheart.'

'But sir, it really hurts!'

Maybe if she called him sir, if she kissed his feet, if she was really, really nice he'd show some mercy. Would he really make her take a dozen hard strokes? 'If I could even wear my shorts,' she whispered.

The youth shook his head unequivocally: 'Seeing the stripes appear is half the fun.'

'You could see them later, sir.'

'Darling, don't make this more difficult.' The boy whisked the bamboo rod through the air as if getting his wrist muscles ready. 'I want to see your sore little bottom wriggling *now*!' He took hold of her right arm and started to turn her back towards her fate.

Wincing in anticipation, Fern lowered her body reluctantly and gripped the wood.

'Four!' said the boy, and applied the cane further up.

Fern trembled, but stayed in place. The fifth stroke cut slightly more diagonal, brought tears to her eyes. Automatically, she put her palms back to protect her punished bottom. She jumped up again. 'Dr Marshall says punishment must be just and fitting!' she cried.

'Your arse is here, and His Highness isn't!' sneered the boy.

Fern heard a click, then heard the youth gasp.

'No, but I'm here,' a vaguely familiar voice said heavily.

She turned to see the bearded officer who'd escorted her to the cinema some time before. He'd been a kind officer, a helpful officer. He was looking at her with concern now.

'Who said you could cane this girl?' he asked the boy.

'She was . . . leading me on, sir,' the younger man muttered.

'I was not – I was just on my way to the shed to get a sandwich!' Fern said.

The officer looked from one frantic face to another. 'Why did you come in here, Miss Terris?' he asked.

'I . . .' Fern looked round at the tomato plants as she searched for inspiration. 'I wanted a tomato to add to my snack, sir,' she said.

'That's what we grow them for,' the older man answered, looking at the younger one. 'You should just have given her it.' He put a fatherly hand on Fern's back. 'Put on your pants and shorts, miss. I'll escort you back to your room for a meal and a rest. This callow youth had no right to thrash you.'

'Thank you, sir. I'd appreciate that,' Fern said.

For once her words were true. She felt sticky with sexual joy, and sore with the cane's cruel excesses. She wanted to bathe then doze then drink coffee and eat pizza. Each cell of her body craved quiet and rest.

She bathed, phoned down her lunch menu then slept. She woke to a gentle knock on her door and let in a smiling waitress. She ate the wholemeal pizza and sipped the hot coffee. Afterwards, Fern sat by the open window reading a magazine.

'Enter,' she called, as she heard a second knock at the door.

The friendly officer stood there again, only this time he didn't look so friendly.

'You've been accused of drinking alcoholic substances on the premises,' he said dispassionately. 'You're to appear immediately before the bench.'

'Has that boy said something? You saw how he bullied me!' Fern made her eyes pleadingly big as she drank in his paternal features.

'An independent witness saw you engaged in oral copulation,' the man continued evenly. 'Seems there was something more than bullying going on.'

'He made me!' Fern said.

The officer raised one eyebrow: 'He says you traded your body for a few sips of his sloe gin.'

Fern swallowed: 'Can he prove it?'

The officer looked at her indifferently. 'That's for the judge to decide.'

That hellish courtroom. Those smirking faces in the long wooden rows, just waiting to hear of her punishment. She'd been so sure that she wouldn't get caught out again! Feet dragging, Fern followed the man along the corridors until they came to the sombre judgement seat. Slowly she approached the bench.

She looked up at the magistrate. It was a woman this time. An unsmiling and remote-looking middle-aged woman.

'Fern Terris, you are charged with using mind-altering substances,' she said. She paused as Fern looked at the ground, then forced herself to make eye contact. 'How do you plead, my girl?'

They could do tests, Fern reminded herself. 'Guilty,' she whispered. Maybe if she came clean they'd let her off with it this time.

A deep groan came from outside. Fern raised her head. 'Your greenhouse friend has been tied facing the wall outside. We're thrashing him with his own belt to teach him not to be so keen to take his trousers off,' said the judge, looking pleased with herself.

'I see, M'Lord,' Fern replied. She wished she could see. Wished she could watch the bastard flinch from each stroke. But she daren't suggest it. She could only try to look repentant and pray that they wouldn't warm her own bum for her various crimes.

'Do we have her inaugural report?' the judge asked, her eyes sweeping the room.

'I'm putting a dossier together now,' said Dr Marshall's strong sure voice. 'If it would be easier, I could deal with her myself in my chambers.'

'No,' Fern whispered, looking back up at the woman. 'Please – no!' She wanted Dr Marshall to see her as an intelligent and thoughtful woman. She couldn't bear to be demeaned in front of him. And what if he brought in the sadistic gloating Rab?

'Very well, Dr Marshall – she's all yours,' the judge confirmed.

Fern hung her head. She didn't look up even when the psychiatrist touched her elbow.

'Take your shorts and panties off, put your hands on top of your head and walk in front of me to my office,' he said.

'Oh please no! I ...' She couldn't bear the thought of him staring at her jiggling little bum, at the spanked sore flesh and overriding cane marks.

'Do it voluntarily or I'll cuff your wrists to a collar behind your neck and lock your feet apart with a spreader,' the doctor said coldly. He slapped lightly at her denim-clad rump. 'Come on, Fern – you know you did wrong. You broke the rules and now you must pay the consequences. Get those lower garments off now!'

To be stripped forcibly would be even worse than doing

93

it herself. Eyes downcast, Fern shucked off her shorts. She hesitated, then pulled down her pants and kicked the clothing away.

'Palms flat on your head,' the psychiatrist reminded. 'It's a long slow walk to my office. I wonder how many strangers we'll meet along the way?' he smirked.

Fern stared fixedly ahead and tried not to think of her poor denuded rump as they walked up the stairs of the courtroom.

'Turn left, my dear,' Dr Marshall instructed, but his tone indicated that she was anything other than dear. Fern knew that she'd let him down, that she'd put alcohol before the work ethic. That she'd used her body for non-sexual motives once again.

Another corridor. Another place to be seen and smiled at. Two women in their late twenties came walking along carrying armfuls of CDs.

'Have you visited our music library yet, Miss Terris?' the psychiatrist enquired.

'No, I . . .' Fern cringed as the strangers grew closer. 'I haven't had the time.'

'If you decide to *make time* you'll find it relaxing and musically eclectic,' the psychiatrist added.

Fern nodded miserably: the man really did see every aspect of her life as being under her own control. Well, under *his* control for now. God knows what he was going to do to her! He'd already bared her bum – the situation didn't look good.

'Mandy, Jess – meet Fern. She's been a naughty girl. Been drinking,' he said in a jovial tone.

'Been caned as well,' said Mandy, walking round behind Fern.

Hugely embarrassed, Fern turned the opposite way to hide her bare bum. *Please don't make me do this, Dr Marshall*, her eyes pleaded.

'Come, come, Fern, show the ladies your nice red bottom,' he said convivially. His own eyes were determined and calm.

'What if I don't?' Fern muttered under her breath.

'You'll receive extra punishment for insubordination, my sweet.' He slid a hand over her chastened rump. 'Turn round now and grasp your ankles to really show the girls your sore posterior.'

Tensing her tummy muscles and thighs in shame, Fern reluctantly obeyed.

'Can I touch her?' one of the girls asked.

'Intimately, if you like!' Dr Marshall confirmed. 'This is a punishment walk. She deserves to be humiliated.'

Fern forced herself to stay bent over in place as a female finger slid between her labial lips.

'How come she's been thrashed yet isn't wet?'

'Got time out to bathe away her juices before we discovered her latest set of crimes,' Dr Marshall replied. 'I'm assured she enjoyed a spectacular orgasm. She was in one of the greenhouses at the time, and people several yards away heard her climax. Said she sounded like a donkey that's just been kicked.'

They were making her bend like this and listen to this just to shame her. *Ignore them*, Fern told herself, and tightened her grip on her ankles as she stared at the floor. She must concentrate on getting through the next corrective session then slip quietly back to her room for a cool shower. Maybe if she was extra good from now on they'd give her one of those weekend release passes and she could drink all the spirits her slender body could take.

For now she was taking a strange woman's touch on board! The unasked-for exploring finger moved up to trace the cane stripes and she shivered with desire and humiliation at Mandy's caress. The touch was indifferent, yet somehow pleasing.

'Bet you begged real pretty when you got those,' the voice belonging to the fingers said.

Fern wriggled. She'd said all sorts of things under the boy's hands, tongue and cane as she'd bared her bum and pubes in the greenhouse. But she didn't want to be reminded of them now in the corridor with the punitive Dr Marshall looking on.

'Time we delivered those CDs,' the other woman announced.

Fern held her breath, then let it out as the digits on her derrière withdrew. She started to straighten.

'Did I tell you to let go of your ankles?' Dr Marshall said.

'No, sir.' Calf muscles stretched tautly, Fern bent fully over again. She heard the girls' heels clicking away along the corridor, then stiffened as she heard them greeting a man who was obviously walking Fern's way.

'Ah, Nurse Bryson – meet our newest recruit, Fern Terris,' Dr Marshall said.

Fern lifted her head up and to one side and squinted at a small wiry man in his forties. He was wearing a white tunic and trousers and looked more like a surgeon. A male nurse, no less!

'Should I shake her hand or her bum?' laughed the man.

'Her bum, I think – she does seem to be offering!' the psychiatrist snorted.

Fern screwed her face up in consternation and let her head hang closer to the ground. She winced as the nurse squeezed one hot buttock, then the other.

'If she hadn't admitted her guilt,' the doctor said, 'we would have been sending her to you for a blood alcohol test.'

'Been administering a lot of those lately,' the man admitted, 'there's sloe gin and cherry brandy and some kind of home brewed beer going the rounds.' He fondled the cane stripes on Fern's thighs. 'We've been busy birching the secret drinkers. I had to send two guilty young men for a leathering just the other day.' He gave Fern's bottom another sly nip. 'Well, got to be getting on. One of the boys who wants to start work on building an outhouse needs a tetanus injection.'

'And I've got to lecture this bad bottom,' the psychiatrist said.

The nurse walked briskly away. Fern felt an admonishing hand on her rump.

'Miss Terris – continue the punishment walk to my office,' Dr Marshall said.

Gratefully she straightened, flexed her calves and stumbled on.

When they reached Dr Marshall's quarters, he preceded her in. 'Now bring that chair into the centre of the room, my dear.' Trembling, Fern obeyed him. The psychiatrist sat down and patted his lap: 'I want that bad bum under my hands as we chat.'

'Couldn't I just ... well, stand in the corner?' Anything but being bent over his knee – that was so humiliating.

'No, I want you to think of your helpless bottom as we talk about your many wrongs.' He smiled grimly, then continued, 'I want you to be aware of how vulnerable those nether cheeks are. You'll get the message much more strongly if I spell it out whilst I fondle your hot sore bum.'

Swallowing hard, Fern walked over and stood sideways to his knees. Tipping forward she let her weight carry her down, down, down, till her fingers touched the carpet. The psychiatrist shifted his hips till her legs stretched out more tautly and her flanks were directly under his wandering hands.

'Your bottom hurts, doesn't it, Miss Terris?' he whispered.

Fern writhed in embarrassment: 'You know it does!' *God, he was hateful!*

'And you're wishing that you hadn't disobeyed my orders, because you don't want me to punish your poor cheeks any more?'

'I don't! I'll be so good! I'll never touch illicit alcohol again, I swear it,' Fern gasped out, writhing. She felt him palm both her buttocks.

'Never touch alcohol, or just make sure you don't get caught?'

The latter was true – but she had to convince him otherwise. She had to make him spare the rod on her already chastened bum. 'I'll try to control my cravings, sir. If there was a recovery programme that could help?' she asked obsequiously.

'Such programmes are for weaklings. You merely have to overcome the craving for sugar,' the implacable doctor said. He sighed, as if he'd been forced to give this talk many times before. 'Getting rid of the yearning should take about six weeks. Thousands of others have done it before.'

'Yes, Dr Marshall.' In his own way he seemed to believe in her – if only she could believe in herself. If only he would regard her as an equal. It was hell having her bare bum displayed over his knee! 'I'll be a good girl,' she added humbly, hoping to find favour.

'You still have to be punished,' the psychiatrist said.

'Yes, Dr Marshall,' Fern whispered. Her groin was throbbing with an odd mix of arousal and shame. His belt was rubbing against her side. She wondered if he was going to use it.

'Getting drunk with a stranger and having sex was irresponsible,' the man continued. 'Do you know how many unwanted children are born that way?'

'I . . . we didn't have intercourse, sir.' Only because she'd sucked the boy off first, she realised. She'd forgotten to put in her contraceptive cap that day.

'If you behave like a cheap tart you have to dress like a cheap tart,' the man said, 'so your punishment is to be dressed in our prison uniform.' He patted her naked bottom. 'Go to the lowest shelf in the cupboard by the window and bring your outfit to me now.'

Slowly Fern approached the shelved recess, then squatted down and reached for the small pile of garments. Wincing inwardly, she brought out a cut-off style blouse, skirt and shoes all in a glittery silver effect.

'Bring them to my desk. Stand before it. Strip.'

Fern swallowed hard at the psychiatrist's words, and considered making a run for it. But where would she go? Much as she hated the demeaning regime, spending a few months here was still her best bet. As they'd said, she'd be ill-fed and under-entertained in a conventional prison. Here she had access to cinematic films, fresh air, good food.

'Nice body, shame about the uniform,' she quipped as she edged off her T-shirt and denim waistcoat. Naked, she stared at the silvery scraps of clothing she was expected to put on.

'Approach me. Hold your arms up high,' the watchful doctor continued.

Fern couldn't quite meet his gaze as she did. Her nipples hardened and the pink hillocks around them tingled and swelled as they neared him. She wanted so much for those same breasts to be kissed and held! She wanted this to be a trip towards pleasure rather than punishment. She'd even be willing to accept both.

'You said I was to be honest. I'd like you to hold me,' she mumbled, starting to toy with one of the many leather-bound notebooks on his desk top.

'All right then,' said the psychiatrist, 'just a hug.'

Before he could change his mind, Fern stepped between his seated legs and pressed her nude warm body against his, her pubis pressing into his lower torso. She lowered herself into a sitting position on his lap, her arms around his neck.

She felt his manly arms round her waist and back, holding her tightly. For a moment she felt loved and safe. She grazed her teeth against his nearest earlobe and started to flick the very tip of her tongue against it. She felt the space between her breasts go hollow as he abruptly let go.

'A hug is not the same as foreplay, Fern. You'd do well to remember that.' He pushed her gently from his knees and stood up, handing her the silvery cut-off blouse. 'Now put this on.'

The top was like rough glitter on the outside but was reassuringly smooth and cottony on the inside. Still she looked like a parody of the cheapest street walker as she put it on. The material was toughened and shaped at the chest area to form two oversized silvery conical breasts. The blouse stopped six inches above her belly button. It was cut away at the back to show her shoulder blades.

'Turn round. Let me see how it looks so far,' Dr Marshall said.

Fern licked her lips. This was so cruel after their earlier closeness.

'No, hands up in the air like a ballet dancer,' he continued. 'Pirouette.'

'And if I don't?' she stalled.

'If you don't I'll throw the skirt away and you'll spend

the next two days in the gardens showing off your pubis and your arse.'

Fern glowered and tensed her hands into fists, but she still pirouetted. She was pink-facedly aware of her denuded lower half.

'Good girl. Now put on the skirt.'

Fern picked up the silvery scrap. It was a ra-ra skirt that stuck out in a tiny circle. She slipped it up over her tummy and fastened it at the back. Only by bending precariously forward could she make the minuscule garment cover her genital triangle. She straightened quickly as she realised that tilting forward left her bottom completely revealed at the back. Trying to ignore the doctor's knowing smile, she leaned backwards to conceal part of her bum with the hateful skirt. This then revealed her mound of Venus. Damn it! Whilst wearing this she'd have no hiding place for her most vulnerable charms.

'Don't I get to wear panties?' she muttered, feeling very sorry for her poor bare bottom.

'No, you've behaved like a tart and tarts show their pussies to strangers,' said the man.

'For how long?' she whispered, trying to picture wearing this outfit outside.

'For the next two days, then we'll review the situation. We can have a nice long chat with you over my knee.'

He pushed the silver stilettos towards her. 'Don't forget the shoes, sweetheart. They're a must for the lady gardener.'

Fern looked at the tapering heels and her heart sank further: 'I'm to wear those whilst working in the grounds?'

'Of course. After all, this is your uniform until Wednesday.' He smiled, 'I'm sure it'll gladden Bill Stark's soul to see you stumbling about in it.'

Fern slid her feet inside the towering strapless shoes: it wasn't Bill's *soul* that she was worried about! She wouldn't be able to walk and dig nearly as quickly in this get-up, which meant . . . . 'What if he has me punished for shoddy work?' she whispered nervously.

'What of it, angel?'

Fern thought fast: 'Well, I'm already being chastened by

being made to wear this hooker's get-up. Further correction wouldn't be fair!'

Smiling, the psychiatrist picked up his rolled gold pen and made a note on her file. 'You're wrong, Miss Terris. We're dealing with cause and effect, remember? You fucked a stranger for alcohol. In the real world that could lead on to any number of unpleasant things.' He closed the leather bound book. 'We're reproducing such a set-up here, only we're being thoughtful enough to limit the consequences. Means you won't be found murdered in a ditch.'

No, only thrashed in a soundproofed room! Fern held back the words. She still had to get the good doctor on her side, make him like or even love her. She had to find a way to earn an early reprieve from here. 'I understand, sir – I'll do better,' she murmured obsequiously.

The doctor's stare hardened: 'You'd do better if you didn't lie to me by putting on that submissive voice.'

Defeated for now, Fern toed the carpet with her calf-tautening shoes.

'It's too late to go back to work today. Wear your uniform tomorrow and the next day from morning till night, though,' the man continued, waving his hand towards the doorway.

Fern hesitated: 'I'm free to go?'

'Go anywhere in the building, at any rate!' the man sighed. 'Let's face it, you're nowhere near earning yourself a weekend pass to the outside world yet.'

Still, Fern reassured herself, at least she hadn't earned another well-spanked bum. Carefully she started the long walk out of his surgery and towards her own room. The weather so far had been blissfully warm and there seemed to be few insects around the gardens. Maybe wearing this outfit wouldn't be so bad.

'Been bad, I hear!'

Bill Stark greeted her with those words the next day. He sounded pleased that she'd been caught doing wrong, he sounded gloating.

'I've already paid for it,' Fern said quickly.

'And if I don't get a full day's work out of you, you'll pay for it again.' He looked Fern up and down as she closed the door to her room. 'On you go,' he said, waving his hand for her to precede him. Fern was all too aware that he was enjoying the view of her jiggling naked bum.

Everyone else at *Compulsion* did too! As she walked past the reformatory's many rooms, women winked and men whistled. Head dipped in shame, Fern concentrated on not tripping whilst wearing her ridiculously high shoes. If she fell they'd see even more of her nether cheeks than they were seeing already, and God knows which part of her anatomy Bill would grasp to bring her to her feet.

Eighty steps. A hundred steps. A hundred and sixty. At last they reached the heather garden she'd dug over in a previous session.

'Keep going, love,' Bill said grinning widely. 'You're to make a rockery for the rarer plants this time.'

Her calves aching, Fern walked on and on and on until they came to a field full of boulders and slate and the type of flat stones which can skim across water.

'Take thirty or forty of them over to that bare flower bed in the next field,' Bill Stark said.

Fern looked wearily at the rocks: 'Have you got a wheelbarrow?'

Grinning, the man shook his head: 'Sorry, love, the gardening budget wouldn't run to another one. You'll have to carry them singly by hand.'

Bastard! Fern opened her mouth to protest, then thought better of it. He was a formidable man, a man she sensed would be merciless. And she was some distance from the reformatory now and had a completely bare bum.

'As you wish, sir,' she murmured, and saw the head gardener's mouth tighten in frustration. He obviously itched for an excuse to punish her. Damn it, she wouldn't give him one!

Tensing her thighs and pushing her shoulders back, Fern teetered over to the rocks and picked up a head-sized boulder. Straightening she turned towards the next field and walked till she reached the fence, hugely aware of Bill Stark close behind her. She tried not to think of her bottom twitching as she moved on the precarious heels.

Reaching the gate, she rattled it – it was securely locked. 'I can't open it, sir,' she muttered.

Bill's voice came mockingly from behind her: 'Nor can I.'

'Then how . . .?' She turned to him, her skirt riding up to show her close-trimmed pubic patch. She put the boulder in front of her and squeezed her legs together as he leered at her triangle.

'You'll just have to bend over it each time and set the boulder on the other side, won't you, sweetheart?' her staring boss said.

Fern closed her eyes for a second. If she did what she was told her bum would be completely open to him. If she didn't he might arrange to have her soundly thrashed or teased almost to orgasm.

'Not gone shy, have you, love?' the gardener continued. 'Let's face it, half of the reformatory has already seen or felt that pretty bum!'

Deciding to choose humiliation over a raw, whipped bottom, Fern approached the fence with the boulder she was holding. Wincing, she pressed her belly to the wood top and let her arms and head go over, over, over until she was close enough to the bare flower bed to put the rock down.

'Not often we see the moon on a sunny day!' the man sneered as Fern bent over the fence and the ra-ra skirt showed each bare centimetre of her creamy rotundities. Blushing, Fern straightened up and teetered towards the pile of rocks again. When she was bent fully over the fence she sensed his palms only millimetres away from the flesh of her raised buttocks.

'Your bum's just a bit too plump,' he murmured, obviously aching to spank her sun-warmed extremities again and again. She heard a note of satisfaction enter his voice.

'When we fill the vacancy for a gym teacher she'll sort that lazy soft bottom out.'

Six

'You want me to pretend to be a gym teacher?' Sonia Shendon said. She stared across the desk at Robert Greene her boss and wished once more he was her lover.

'Well yes, they've apparently got such a vacancy,' Robert replied. He stood up and began to pace the room, something he always did when he was agitated or excited. 'If you were willing to infiltrate them and find out exactly what's going on?'

'What do you *think* is going on?' Sonia said. As Robert walked past her she stretched out her dark-stockinged legs and let one of her black patent shoes dangle.

'Something . . .' Robert Greene cleared his throat, 'well, either over-punitive or sadomasochistic. On her first day at the reformatory one of the inmates smuggled a note into a shipment of vegetables. It said she'd heard two other inmates being spanked and caned.'

Sonia watched her boss pace and pace: 'So why don't we just interview her?'

'We did, but she withdrew her complaint.'

Sonia nodded and ran her tongue over her full lower lip. God, it was great to have an excuse to talk about punishment and pleasure with forty-year-old Robert. One candid look from his aloof grey eyes had her labia turning to throbbing liquid heat. Each time she walked past his chair she wanted to stroke his black hair, tinged with grey. She wanted to bury her face in one of his big sure shoulders and slide down his suited chest and belly, and . . .

She forced her thoughts back to the present. 'Okay, so let's assume I become their gym teacher and report back to you. Then what?'

Robert sighed wearily: 'If the regime they're following is too controversial we'll have it quietly closed down.'

Sonia thought further ahead: 'Why not close it down publicly? Might be worth a promotion if you were seen to put another part of the penal system to rights.'

Robert grimaced and walked to the window then walked back to the centre of the room. 'Problem is, as Head of Penal Liaisons, I'm supposed to have my finger on the pulse all the time. But this set-up hasn't been approved through the usual channels. I mean, all the paperwork's been filed with the official stamps, but those of us who're usually involved in a new initiative haven't been asked to sit on any committees or draw up a charter of rights.' He opened his hands in a half shrug. 'Yet we can't go in with all guns blazing, because there's serious money coming from the top.

'Cue Sonia Shendon, spanking spy!' Sonia said.

She noticed her boss's jawline stiffen as she said the spanking word and wondered if that was all that was stiffening. God knows she'd tried to tempt him by wearing lycra tops that clung to her 38C specials. When that hadn't worked she'd left her bra off so that her breasts hung conical and free. He'd seemed to notice each flaunting act – leastways his pupils had widened. But he hadn't reached for her willing waist or hungering hips.

Now she realised that he might want to cane or whip these selfsame hips. Was that the offer he'd been waiting for? Sonia stood up and stretched her body across the desk as if reaching for the far drawer. She felt her thin summer skirt tautening against her curvy bottom. 'I've read about girls that enjoy a good thrashing,' she said. She hesitated, then opened the drawer and blindly pulled out a pen. She looked round to see Robert staring out of the window, his ears reddening. He'd noticed her position, then, but wasn't going to react.

Damn the man! Was his wife really so marvellous that he had no need for a mistress? The few times she'd met the distinctly horsey-looking Mrs Greene she hadn't been impressed with her. And Robert worked such long hours that

106

he couldn't exactly spend much time doing the happy families bit. Couldn't he see that he'd make her, Sonia, happy by pleasuring her quim?

He obviously didn't want to spank her, she thought, straightening up from the desk and tugging down her skirt a little. But he was still going on about this punitive reformatory. Could that mean *he* wanted to be spanked? 'You've got a nerve sending me so far away from home!' she said, slapping lightly at his trousered buttocks. She flexed her palm back, ready to repeat the hard flat blow.

'Whether you take up the challenge or not is up to you,' Robert said cooly, moving swiftly away.

Sonia stared but could see no hint of a bulge in his groin area. Maybe he just didn't fancy her? Yet he always stared before looking away.

'What do I do?' she asked resignedly, retaking her seat.

'Just go along for an informal chat. We'll have had you recommended by someone high up, so my guess is they'll ask you to start the job immediately. Hint that you're a firm disciplinarian. I'll provide you with fake references and a CV.'

Sonia nodded: 'And when I'm doing the job?'

'Try to see and hear various spankings and canings,' Robert said worriedly. 'Take details of who is punishing who.'

The personal assistant nodded and picked up her pen. She heard her boss take a deep breath.

'You may have to ... mete out chastisements of your own in order to keep up the act,' he added.

'Consider it done,' Sonia said after a moment's hesitation. She figured there could be few worse punishments than the sexual denial he was currently subjecting her to. And a tiny part of her Venusian mound tautened and tingled at the thought of punishing grown up naughty girls.

Seven

That bitch deserved to be punished! Fern cried out as Melissa deliberately bounced the ball against her right shoulder during their netball game. She felt relieved as the new gym teacher, Sonia, blew the whistle and jabbed her middle finger at the culprit.

'Melissa Brown – see me tomorrow morning for chastisement!' She glared at the reluctant teams, her mouth downturned, her eyes watchful. 'This is supposed to be a *friendly* game to work off excess energy. Not an excuse for a foul.'

Everything was foul here, Fern thought. Ms Lenn had started tying her hands in front of her at night to make sure that they didn't stray towards her own clitoris. The *Compulsion* guards still wanted to use orgasm as the carrot, and were equally eager to apply the stick to her buttocks. In the few weeks she'd been here she'd enjoyed a few rapturous climaxes and plenty of spanked-bottom pain.

'You're to attend the correction centre,' the guard said the following morning, popping his head around her door.

Fern blinked up at him from her chair: she'd been expecting Bill Stark to collect her as usual and take her to work in the gardens.

'Whose bottom's being corrected?' she asked, shifting her own weight more firmly upon her shorts-clad bum.

'You'll find out soon enough,' said the man evenly.

Deciding just to watch and learn, Fern tidied up her breakfast tray then obediently left her room. They walked together to the third floor punishment hall. The man knocked, then walked away quickly.

'Enter,' a woman called.

Fern's stomach flipped over at the new teacher's voice – Sonia's voice. She was still an unknown quantity when it came to chastising a bare bum. Some said she used the rod on your arse for the most minor infraction. Others swore that in the time she'd been here she hadn't as much as raised her sweetly reasonable tone. *Don't let the bitch get to you*, Fern told herself, breathing deeply. She kept her head high and mouth firm as she walked slowly into the large well-lit room.

The room contained a piece of furniture shaped like a padded king-sized bed. It held a whimpering naked female. Two rectangular boards were fastened to the fixture's foot. Each board was shaped like a stockade so that it held one of the girl's ankles, forcing her legs apart like a pair of scissors so that whoever wished had total access to her shaven quim.

Fern stepped closer, squinting. Now she could see that the naked girl was the previously aggressive Melissa, the netball player whom Sonia had promised would soon see the error of her ways. Melissa's arms were bound firmly to the couch's two other corners. Only her bare breasts and tummy moved up and down as she breathed.

'You hit Fern, didn't you, Melissa,' Sonia stated matter-of-factly.

The bound girl nodded: 'She's taller than me; she had an unfair advantage at the netball game!'

'An admission of guilt in the form of "Yes, I hit her, Miss", was all I was looking for, dear,' the sports teacher said.

Melissa kept her full lips open, her eyes downcast. Her nipples stiffened. 'Sorry, Miss Shendon,' she muttered.

'How long should she be fucked without total fulfilment for hurting you?' Sonia asked lightly, turning to Fern.

Fern felt the guilty heat rush to her face. How had the older woman known she wanted Melissa to be punished? Was this a trick? She moved her hands into a half shrug. 'That's . . . up to you, miss.'

Two dark blue eyes studied her, then the teacher smiled conspiratorially. 'Normally it would be, but I understand

110

that you've been here a few weeks longer than I have, so I'd appreciate your advice.'

Was the sports teacher trying to find out how far she, Fern, would go? Or did the woman herself not want to order or administer the sexual punishment?

'As you're commanding me to set her sentence, I think she should be pleasured without orgasm for half an hour, ma'am,' she replied. She figured she was sounding fair and reasonable. She really wanted the bitch squirming on some thick cock for several days!

Smiling, the sports teacher nodded to a muscular dark-haired youth in the corner whose erection was already moving vertically up his belly.

'Half an hour's shafting, with long breaks between to pleasure her tits,' Fern added, beginning to enjoy her new power.

Melissa shivered and stared at the pulsing maleness before her.

'So be it,' Sonia said casually, looking from one girl to another, 'though I wonder if you'll want a half hour's shafting plus extra breast fondling, Fern, if your own turn ever comes?'

She'd make damn sure that it didn't, Fern thought rebelliously. She stared at her naked counterpart and felt her pubis start to pulse a little.

'Ask nicely for your fucking, Melissa, you bad girl,' Sonia said.

'Please take me to the limit then keep me there, sir,' the girl whimpered ashamedly, looking from the teacher to the erect youth then turning her gaze away from Fern.

'Watch how we teach people obedience on the pleasure platform,' Sonia said, staring at Fern.

The sports teacher then nodded to the boy, who approached Melissa and knelt between her tied-apart legs, his manhood jerking. The girl's tummy quivered as he looked her up and down. The youth slowly stroked her underbelly, then the shaved honey blonde triangle. Next he ran a teasing finger down each immobilised tender thigh.

Fern watched, fascinated, as the girl's perfect white face

111

turned perfectly pink. The netball bully had become such a shy and nervous girl since having her legs spread in the correction centre. How she trembled at each knowing touch and tried to pull her helpless tummy away.

Being fondled whilst in a fixed position was obviously hard to take. The victim's separate squeals soon merged into a low wail of frustration.

'I haven't started yet,' whispered the boy lustfully, teasing the tip of his cock against her eager canal.

'Does watching that excite you, Fern?' Sonia asked.

'Yes, ma'am,' Fern said uncertainly. She was aware that her breathing had quickened, that she felt tremulous, but didn't know if it was sexual excitement or just general pleasure at seeing her enemy squirm. Until now she'd only been attracted to men. She pushed away the thoughts which threatened to follow. She must concentrate on not getting her bottom spanked throughout this session, concentrate on getting out of here for good.

'Tell the foolish little Melissa that she must please you,' murmured Sonia, pushing Fern forward.

'No! Really! I haven't ever . . .'

Hardly conscious of her own actions, Fern swatted at the sports coach's arm then started to back away. She stopped as she reached the wall. She looked around the room in search of diversion, and, finding none, reluctantly looked at the gym teacher again.

'The door is locked and you can't run from your fears when they're inside you,' Sonia said.

Christ, the woman had only been here a few days and already she sounded like Dr Marshall.

'I just – I'm not into women,' Fern said with an apologetic grin.

'But Melissa would be into you. I mean, it would be *her* tongue up *your* sex. You'd just receive the pleasure. You could close your eyes and pretend it was a man.'

'But . . .' Fern looked at the naked staked-out girl. The youth had just withdrawn from her mound, leaving her whimperingly pre-orgasmic. Why not squat on her face and further shame the little bitch?

'Sports teacher's orders!' Sonia continued, smiling coolly.

Despite her uncertainty, Fern found her own mouth twitching into an answering smile.

Could she really make this *Compulsion* inmate lick her to orgasm? Warily Fern walked round till she was above Melissa's face. She stared down at it. Tendrils of hair lay damply against the smaller girl's hot cheeks. Droplets of sweat testified to her struggle for a climax, the pleasure-led wetness beading her fringe, and trickling down her throat to her flush-tipped breasts.

Yes, she could conquer the girl! Triumph expanded in Fern's chest as she took hold of Melissa's blonde hair and pulled it back till their eyes met. 'Apologise profusely,' she murmured.

The girl sniffed and swallowed: 'Please . . . I'm sorry I hit you, Fern.'

'*How* sorry?' Fern pressed on.

The girl hesitated then lifted her unsatisfied loins up and whispered: 'Make them let me come and I'll do anything you say.'

Fern felt a sensation widening her lower belly, and enjoyed the growing stirrings of potential. 'Please me with your mouth, and I'll think about ordering an end to your lack of satisfaction,' she said. She took her time in getting the position right, squatting over the girl's face, her lower lips to the girl's soft upper lips. 'Tongue me thoroughly,' she warned.

Blushing hotly, the girl put her uncertain mouth to Fern's mons.

This was different – wonderful! Those helpless lips sucking and licking away whilst she looked down at these vulnerably spread young thighs. 'Lick harder, bitch,' murmured Fern, enjoying the girl's shame as much as the increasing sexual excitement. 'Concentrate, or we'll have to fuck you for another hour without coming, or more.'

The girl licked on. Fern closed her eyes and concentrated on the growing gratification. If she wanted, she could make this sexually-frustrated girl lick her all day! At the thought more heat rushed to her loins, spreading through her labia. She looked at the bondaged contours and felt her arousal increase. An unquenched clit, a subservient tongue, a girl tied in position whose only task was to pleasure her ... Ecstasy rushed through her soaked pubes and Fern came and came.

But it would be a long time till Melissa was allowed to come. Once again the rampant guide approached her. He was obviously keen to tease her velvet canal with his iron rod.

'Fifteen minutes left of your half hour to go,' he taunted, 'so don't get *too* excited, my sweet.'

'No, sir,' Melissa said gutturally. Her wettening petals and gaping sex belied her words.

The boy slid in slowly with consummate self-control. Fern could see his cock entering the prisoner's crevice inch by exquisite inch, a slow-won pleasure. The girl couldn't see this – but she could obviously *feel* it. She gave a long ragged sigh of relief. Which soon turned to a whimper of frustration as he kept her close to the edge, but wouldn't let her go over it.

'Such ·impatience,' he whispered, flirting with her help-less female parts. 'Such a long ordeal left.'

'I'm sorry I threw the ball at Fern,' the girl moaned. 'Oh God, please – I'm so sorry!'

The youth circled his hips round and round, tormenting her hot slick innards: 'Twelve long minutes of near-rapture left to endure!'

Despite her bonds the girl managed to raise her Venusian mound a tiny fraction but the boy pulled back, edging a little way out of her. Sinking down she submitted to his blissful baiting again.

'Good girl,' he said. He continued to pleasure her till she was whimpering and wriggling, her limbs mutely begging.

'Make her come now,' said Sonia Shendon, watching closely, and the thrusting guard did.

And how! Fern watched enviously as he moved his mus-cled bum almost lazily back and forward, big self-assured thrusts going right up the tethered pussy, taking it further and further.

'Thank you,' Melissa moaned. 'Thank you for letting me co . . .'

Her climax started mid-word, causing her head to tip back and her nipples to harden and her mouth to open.

'She won't throw any more netballs at anyone for a while,' Sonia Shendon said to Fern and the guard with a wink.

Fern stared dazedly at the implacable sports teacher then at Melissa. She pushed her hair from her eyes only to find her wet palm sticking to the equally damp chestnut locks. Each bead of perspiration told of her initiation into lesbian sex. Until now, only a couple of boyfriends had kissed their way to her core like that, though she'd wondered if . . .

'Fern, you seem confused,' Sonia said gently, walking over to her. 'I can arrange an impromptu therapy session with Dr Marshall if there's something you want to confess or talk about.'

'No! Nothing! Can I go work in the gardens now?' She didn't want to think any more about her latest orgasm or the way it had been achieved.

'You can, but go by the gate at the left. The fields you've been working on have been given over to some of the senior officers for a prolonged disciplinary session. You'll be cutting the lawns on the south side today.' She smiled lopsidedly at Fern: 'You can go back to your room to shower first if you like.'

To shower off the sex juice created by Melissa's mouth moving over her mound of Venus! Blushing, her inner thighs slicked with sexual satisfaction, Fern walked squelchily from the room.

She bathed in tangerine bubbles and drank mandarin juice. Then she changed into a pair of black cord shorts and a scoop-necked white T-shirt. She was glad that the days spent wearing that ra-ra prison uniform had passed. Now life was back to normal – if life could ever be normal once you'd had your clitoris licked by a woman. Not that that meant she was necessarily bisexual or a lesbian. After all, Sonia had *ordered* Fern to push her pubis against the girl's lips, and if she hadn't obeyed she might have had her bare bottom spanked very badly.

Talking of spanked bare bottoms, hadn't the woman said there was going to be a punishment taking place in the part of the gardens Fern usually worked on? She could sneak over and see it if she dared to go via her usual door. Not that she actually *wanted* to see other inmates being thrashed or kept on sexual tenterhooks, Fern told herself guiltily. It was simply in her best interests to know what was going on here so that she could avoid such chastisements for herself.

She heard the sound thrashing long before she saw it. She heard the cane's savage swish, followed by a gasp of breath and a sharp high cry. Fern hesitated: now she was getting close to the corrective scene she wasn't sure whether or not she dared go ahead with her spying plan. One part of her was hugely curious and a little excited. Another part of her said that this wasn't politically correct and that she should have no part in it; should walk away.

Curiosity and excitement won. Holding her breath and keeping her arms in close by her sides as if to take up less room on the planet, Fern walked silently over to the bushes. Hunkering down behind them, she parted the foliage and peered through the newly created gap. Then she exhaled hard and bit her lip as she saw that she was a mere eight feet away from ten bare bottoms that were held firmly in place.

What on earth was happening? Being careful not to make a sound, Fern shifted towards her right leg so that she could peer diagonally at the scene before her. She saw that the miscreants' necks and arms were locked in a device that resembled the latter day stocks. Only the stocks before her were long enough to hold up to a dozen wicked necks and sets of arms in place leaving the related bums completely unable to protect their tender selves.

Raising her eyes, she saw a guard she vaguely recognised from her weeks at *Compulsion*. The man strode towards the long desk which was just inches away from the helpless inmates' heads.

'What shall it be this time?' he said, looking at the rods, whips and martinets before him. Fern watched every waiting bottom twitch. 'On reflection, I think the two-fingered tawse will warm up an arse or two,' the guard continued, picking up the long leather punisher. He ran the implement through his hands then took his time strolling behind the restrained young bums.

They were very varied bums, Fern realised, scrutinising the row of vulnerable bare bottoms. Eight of them were well-rounded and female, whilst the two more oval-shaped hirsute ones were male. The posterior immediately in front of her was slightly plump, and curved into a pair of equally curvy thighs. Each inch of flesh was lightly suntanned. Each inch of flesh was also anticipating a somewhat more painful tan.

As she stared, the guard stopped behind a slightly darker girlish derrière. The unfortunate bottom flinched as did the bottoms on either side of it.

'Putting weedkiller on the mange touts, failing to water the saplings – so many misdemeanours,' the guard said mockingly. Again the waiting buttocks puckered up then untensed.

The man pulled back the leather tawse then brought it smartly down over one of the helpless cheeks, creating a pink spreading punishment mark. As the girl squealed and moved her bum from side to side he laid on the implement again. 'Save your whimpers till that bottom's been out in the sun for an hour, Theresa, giving me a nice warm canvas,' he said mockingly. 'I like to take my time turning a hot pink bum a pretty red.'

Fern squinted at the furthest female backside. The soft flesh was already glowing all over, as if it had tasted the bat-shaped paddle. It writhed as the guard's footsteps moved its way.

'You needn't wriggle that scarlet arse at me and hope you'll escape further whipping, Rose,' the man said emotionlessly. 'I haven't finished correcting that wicked little posterior yet.'

He hadn't *started* correcting some of the others! Fern sat

down silently on her own bum and parted a lower portion of the bushes. She felt safer squatting on her most tender charms, carefully protecting them. God knows what this bastard would do if he found her lurking here. Her crime would be eavesdropping, and she could easily envisage her punishment. There was room for two more naughty bottoms in those hateful stocks.

'Well, young Keith, what have you to say for yourself after planting the bulbs too shallowly?' the guard asked, walking up to yet another bared posterior.

'I'm sorry, sir. I was tired, sir,' muttered the youth.

'And now I have to *make* you sorry,' the guard continued, beginning to unbuckle his belt.

Keith's bottom was still relaxed, his eyes presumably trained on the punishment table before him which held all the admonishing implements. He obviously had no idea, Fern realised, that the guard was about to thrash him with the strap from his waist. As she stared the uniformed man flipped back the belt then walloped the youth's helpless buttocks six times.

'Oh! Ah! Aaaah!' The boy's yells increased as each of the lashes were laid on.

Still, Fern knew that at some stage his manhood would pulse and lengthen as desire and pleasure replaced the stimulus he initially felt as pain. Her point of view prevented her from seeing the boy's erection, but she could see the girls' sexual excitement glistening on their legs. The inmates before her were all subconsciously into being erotically tormented. Dr Marshall believed that she, Fern, was subconsciously into this too! Fern wasn't quite convinced. Still, she had to admit that watching a bum being corrected was somehow enlivening. She could feel her heart's increased tempo; her armpits fast dampening despite her recent shower. There was a particularly cheeky upturned girlish bum in the centre of the stockades, and Fern found herself wanting the guard to cane it hard.

At last the guard turned his merciless attention towards that particular waiting rear. 'Oh dear, Sylvie, we seem to have neglected your posterior so far, don't we, sweetheart?'

The bottom in question quivered, but Sylvie didn't answer. 'I'll have to pay it particular attention now,' the man said, his voice containing a smile. He walked over to the table and let his right hand hover over the cat-o'-nine-tails, the variously shaped martinets and the wooden-handled razor strop. 'I wonder, should we warm your arse uniformly with a nice wide paddle or stripe it with a Victorian rod?' He handled the leather, rubber and bamboo implements, swishing them through the air then slapping them lightly against his palm as he stared over at the trembling Sylvie. 'Which punisher would make a naughty bottom good?'

The rod won. Smiling, he picked up a reformatory cane and ran it through his fingers. Fern could see the tension in the girl's naked shoulders increase. The main muscles in her bottom tightened up as the guard strolled round towards those selfsame buttocks. After a moment or two Sylvie couldn't hold the position and had to let her muscles relax.

It was then that Sylvie's tormentor applied the punitive stick to her bare hindquarters, causing a thin red stripe to appear across the centre of the previously creamy flesh. The blonde girl cried out and moved her poor bottom from side to side the little she could given her body's position in the stockades.

'Such a loud noise for such a little girl,' mocked the guard, lining the rod up again.

'Sorry to interrupt!'

The voice seemed to come from directly behind her. Fern squeezed her knees together and closed her eyes and waited for an authoritative hand to fall on her shoulder. She opened them again as she heard the guard's voice reply.

'What can I do for you, Ms Lenn?' he asked.

'An altercation over in greenhouse three. If you could deal with it directly?' the admissions officer said briskly.

The man nodded: 'I'm on my way.'

He set the reformatory rod down on the ground, then turned back to Sylvie's bum with its single scarlet stripe enlivening the middle. He fondled both cheeks, and ran his palm over the backs of her tautly expectant thighs. 'I'll be

119

back soon, love. Just think about what's in store for that disobedient little bottom. Just enjoy the sun on that wicked arse whilst you can.'

Sylvie shuddered, and a new string of liquid appeared from her sexual sanctum and trickled its shameful way from her inner to her outer thigh.

Fern cautiously employed her peripheral vision. It showed that Ms Lenn was a mere ten feet from her hiding place. Luckily she had stopped just in front of Fern's level rather than behind it – for now the admissions officer couldn't see. But the older woman would only have to take a few steps back and turn to her right to espy the crouching observer. *I won't be bad again if I get off with this*, she told herself fervently. *I'll be so good.*

But goodness was a relative term to Fern, and as soon as the two guards disappeared from sight she felt the urge to approach the hapless victims. Why, they wouldn't know who was walking up behind them, so their bottoms would be wonderfully quivery and apprehensive. In fact, they'd assume it was the guard! And if she didn't speak they'd *continue* to assume it was the guard. Which meant that . . .

Awareness sank through Fern like a leaden bomb. She couldn't thrash them hard, she told herself. Well, she could – but she *shouldn't*. There again, she'd had her own arse warmed whilst she was here – why not dish it out rather than accept it for a change?

Fern stood up and flexed her arms and legs to their fullest potential. Then, her limbs re-energised, she walked slowly towards the helpless row of bums. She'd just have a peak and see which of them were the most excited. Look but not touch. There again, caressing the pleasure-led pouches between either youths' tense legs couldn't hurt. Part of her wanted to hear them catch their breath, see their testes tremble. Fern stopped, all other thought departing, as she reached Sylvie's exquisite rear.

The girl had the kind of bottom that grown men cried for. Each creamy cheek was perfectly rounded. The skin looked like the purest flesh-toned velvet: Fern could tell that it would feel equally silky smooth. The cleft between

120

the adorable orbs was deep and dark yet slender. The girl's thighs were equally well-exercised and trim.

Only one thing broke up the creamy poised surface – and that was the vertical cane mark. Its initial painful redness had already faded to a ragged pink. Drawn by a force that seemed not of her making, Fern reached the middle finger of her right hand towards the sore reminder of Sylvie's wrongdoing, and ran her curious digit lightly along the ridge.

Sylvie gasped in either arousal or fear. Fern took a step back, then remembered that the girl couldn't see her. Sylvie would merely be assuming that the controlling guard had returned. The guard who said, 'bad girl's need sore bums', and, 'time I taught your arse a lesson' – then did so. Did what she, Fern, could do now!

Heat rushing to her pubis, Fern picked up the reformatory cane. It was a long cane. A thick cane. A cane to be reckoned with. The type of cane that wasn't easily forgotten by an insubordinate bum. Wishing that she could taunt the girl, she ran the cool rod warningly over the helpless bottom.

'Please,' Sylvie whispered. 'Show mercy, please!'

They hadn't been merciful to Fern, when she was being paddled in the assembly hall or clit-teased in the dining room. Driven by a sudden desire to get her own back, she arched the surprisingly bendable cane. Sized it up with the underswell of the rump before her then flicked it sharply into place.

'Aaah!' Sylvie's entire bottom flinched, and the muscles in her thighs puckered up and smoothed out then re-puckered.

Fern waited till her victim's buttocks stopped moving, then lined up the rod again. She'd teach this beautiful brat not to get complacent. She'd show this pretty young bum who was in charge!

She made the helpless backside taste the cane further up this time, so that it left its glowing mark a third of the way down the girl's writhing posterior.

'I'm sorry I was bad,' Sylvie whispered, flexing her thigh

backs lasciviously and trying to push her pubis towards her harsh caner. 'I could make it up to you.'

Aware that to answer the girl would reveal her true identity, Fern reluctantly kept silent.

Sylvie continued to plead for clemency: 'I could take you deep in my throat, suck you so good.'

Shameless little bitch! A strange anger sweeping through her belly and chest, Fern swung the cane and watched the scarlet proof of her rage appear across Sylvie's disarmed buttocks. All the strength in her body seemed to surge into her mobile right arm. The girl was a shameless tease and wanton temptress. She was a goddess whom she'd reduce to the status of a waiting naked arse.

She pulled back the rod again. Sylvie's hot cheeks quivered. Fern saw a flash of grey and white from the corner of her eye and froze into place. She could see two tiny figures in the far distance – presumably Ms Lenn and the punishing guard had completed their mission. They were slowly approaching, returning by a different route.

No matter. They were obviously wrapped up in their own conversation or lacked long-distance vision. Least-ways, they didn't appear to have seen her. Reluctantly dropping the punitive rod she'd been using on Sylvie, the twenty-four-year-old backed away. Hurrying to her original hiding place, she ducked down behind the bushes and parted two of the leafy lower branches to create a new observation place.

Slowly the stick figures drew closer, closer, closer, gaining feature and form till they were in line with the stocks, a mere ten feet from Fern. She let out her breath and leaned forward, confident that she was fully concealed. They had no reason to suspect anything.

'Back to work!' the guard said in a lilting tone. He winked at Ms Lenn. 'Which of the inmates are you planning to take away with you?' he asked the admissions officer.

'The boys – they're needed in the command station,' smiled Ms Lenn.

'They need their bare bums commanding!' growled the guard.

The admissions officer shrugged: 'They've been allocated a task that's more genitally based, but every bit as exacting.'

'Just lift the top wooden section above each youth, then. That releases them,' the man said.

As Fern stared, the older woman freed both youths. They shrugged themselves gratefully out of the stockades, then rubbed their necks and upper arms before putting their hands shyly over their half-hard manhoods.

'You'll be keeping those at full mast for the next hour or so,' explained Ms Lenn. She turned to go and the boys obediently got into place behind her.

'Don't do anything I wouldn't do,' the guard murmured to the woman, before picking up the rod. He walked towards Sylvie's waiting bum. 'Now, where were we sweetheart?' He stopped and stared at her reddened arse.

God, what an idiot she'd been, Fern realised, seeing what the man was seeing. She'd added several cane marks to Sylvie's previously singly striped cheeks!

'Ms Lenn – can you fetch the dogs? We appear to have an interloper,' the guard shouted. 'A somewhat *sadistic* interloper.'

'They'll be with you in a few moments,' the woman yelled.

Fern hugged her bare knees and wished she was wearing a more substantial garment than these lightweight shorts. They could be pulled down or birched over so easily. She should come out of her hiding place, she told herself. She should own up to her caning crime before she was caught.

She peered through the bushes at the remaining girlish bums. God, some of them were glowingly crimson! She looked at the thin riding whips and thick straps they might use on her own arse, and felt her courage contract. Maybe they were just bluffing about the dogs – she'd never seen any. Even if they did have a mastiff or two, the creatures weren't already familiar with her scent.

The scent of arousal. The scent of fear. The scent of uncertainty. Fern tried to concentrate on the guard's latest actions to take her mind off the smell of her own vaginal juice. Damn, he was freeing the beautifully bottomed Sylvie!

'Lie under the table on your tummy, love. It's cooler,' he told her. 'And help yourself to the mango juice in my flask.'

'I thought I was scheduled to stay in the bottom garden all day?' Sylvie muttered, looking up at the man with obvious confusion.

'You were,' he confirmed, 'but ... well, seems someone else gave you a sore bum whilst I was dealing with that trouble in the greenhouses.'

'That explains it!' Sylvie said, her eyes widening. 'I wondered why you'd suddenly started to cane me really hard.'

'Nah – being naked in front of me is almost shameful enough for you!' grinned the guard. He reached out and stroked her waist-length honey blonde hair. 'Though a couple of cane strokes livens that pretty bum a treat and makes you behave even better.'

Blushing, Sylvie toed the ground with one naked foot, then walked stiffly towards the table and crawled obediently under it.

Like a dog would, Fern thought. She bit her lip as she remembered the canines were due, and looked nervously over her shoulder. She swallowed as she saw beige and brown shapes rushing over the flower beds, vegetable plots and fields.

Don't let them see me, she silently pleaded. She bit her lip as four of the dogs raced her way. *Don't let them smell me* she thought wildly. She gave a little squeal as they neared her, they were a mere fifteen feet away. Their tongues were lolling, they were wagging their tails, they were ... upon her. Fern squealed and fell over as four tri-coloured King Charles spaniels leaped on her chest and started to lick her arms, neck and face.

'Get off!' she gasped, laughing with relief at the realisation they were friendly. She looked up at the guard and felt her sense of humour die. Their gazes locked. Fern didn't want to be the first to speak, for words would reveal her wrongdoing. She felt her chest lighten as Ms Lenn hurried up. Maybe the older woman would step in and refuse to let her be punished. Or maybe they'd let her off with a spanking.

'Fern – you weren't supposed to work this section today,' the admissions officer said.

'I know, Miss. I . . . got confused.' She tried to make her voice small and sweet.

'You mean you got *curious*,' Ms Lenn corrected.

Curiosity wasn't such a bad crime. Fern cleared her throat: 'I suppose so. Yes.'

'What else did you get? Hot pussied?' asked the guard.

'Don't answer that yet, Fern. Wait and tell Dr Marshall,' Ms Lenn said quickly.

'Dr Marshall's on his way?' Fern felt her mouth and tongue go dry.

'Uh huh. Here he is now,' the guard murmured gloatingly.

All three of them looked towards the reformatory to see the psychiatrist strolling a steady path from its open doors.

He was wearing a single-breasted cream suit. It would have made a lesser man look lightweight, but it made Dr Marshall look unruffled by the heat, at ease in his environment. Fern tugged down the legs of her shorts to protect her thigh tops from whatever discipline he might have in store for them.

The wait was a long one which Fern found psychologically daunting, but at last the doctor reached them, and nodded to all three parties.

'What's been going on, Fern?' he asked, turning to her and raising his eyebrows.

'I . . . was curious about the bottom garden, Dr Marshall, and I sneaked a look.'

'That's not all she sneaked,' said the guard. 'She picked up this reformatory cane and used it on one of the girl's bare bottoms.'

'Which one?' Dr Marshall squinted at the remaining girlish buttocks in the stocks.

'Sylvie. I'll call her for you.'

The man did, and Sylvie crawled out from under the table and slowly approached them.

'Turn your back to us. Bend over and touch your toes,' said the guard, 'Dr Marshall wants to inspect your chastened bum.'

'I . . . as you wish, sir.' Her facial cheeks immediately turning the colour of her lower ones, the girl did as she was told.

'See what I mean?' queried the guard.

Fern gazed, like the others, at Sylvie's multicoloured bottom.

'I only laid on this one,' the man continued, tracing the lightest of the stripes. 'She marks real easy and is basically a good girl.'

Dr Marshall stroked his beard with the fingers of his right hand and nodded: 'So some unauthorised person laid on the rest?'

The guard nodded with increasing certainty: 'And how! She certainly did.'

'You said *she* rather than *he* when talking of the culprit,' the implacable doctor continued.

'Yeah, the dogs sniffed *her* out of the bushes.' The guard pointed an accusatory finger at Fern. All four of them stared at her, frowning.

'Prove it!' Fern said.

Dr Marshall turned his searching eyes on hers till she looked mutinously at the ground. 'Oh Fern, our studies show that you are more than capable of applying such a thrashing,' he murmured. Ms Lenn nodded sadly in agreement.

'That doesn't mean I did it!' Fern said.

'True,' the doctor looked from punished girl to punishing girl. 'Sylvie, why were you having your bottom caned in the first instance?' he asked.

'For not paying full attention during gardening duty. That's why we're all here sir. I failed to mend the boundary fence, which means an inmate could have escaped or an unwanted outsider could have crept in,' the blonde girl explained nervously.

Dr Marshall's eyes swept over each inch of her nude body: 'What were you doing when you should have been fixing the fences, my dear?'

Sylvie started to braid her hair into plaits, her movements fast and jerky. 'I . . . have to confess that I was in one of the glasshouses, sir, drinking sloe gin.'

Join the club, Fern thought. She looked more closely at the girl's upright breasts and slender waist, yet felt no sense of solidarity. The girl looked too straight to be a genuine inmate. She was probably an *agent provocateur*. God, if she'd been left alone for a few more minutes with that thick rod in her hand and that bare arse just waiting for each stroke, she'd have . . .

'So you hadn't finished thrashing her when the interloper took over?' Dr Marshall continued, addressing the guard who was now looking towards the stockade's remaining bottoms.

'No, but I hadn't planned to lay on so many as *she* did.' He looked sourly at Fern.

'Really? When a boundary fence and the very safety of *Compulsion* is at stake? I'd have thought that warranted the most rigorous correction,' the psychiatrist continued.

'When you put it like that, sir,' the guard said, his right hand flexing.

Sylvie's own palms had crept round to cover her poor bare bum.

'Sylvie, it seems like we have a little unfinished business with your naughty young *derrière*. Get back into the stocks,' Dr Marshall said.

'Oh please don't warm my bottom again!' Sylvie whispered, holding onto her orbs with even more conviction.

'We have no option in the circumstances,' the psychiatrist said.

The girl turned towards the stocks and looked at the powerless rumps imprisoned there. She looked back at the others, then took a step towards Dr Marshall and put her palms flat on his shirt over his nipples. 'Sir, you could punish me by withholding my ultimate pleasure for an hour.'

Fern felt her own jaw and tummy muscles tighten as if of their own volition at the girl's provocative words. How could Sylvie prostitute herself like this before an audience? Had the girl no dignity? She wanted Dr Marshall to thrash

127

that perfect round bottom until the girl squirmed and begged for release.

'Sorry, your chastisement isn't negotiable,' the psychiatrist said evenly. 'So get that bottom in the stocks now before I double the thrashing you're about to get.'

Sylvie ran her tongue over presumably dry lips as she turned towards the waiting wooden restrainer. She exhaled then walked slowly towards its cruel confines. She hesitated, then lifted the top half of the section that would hold her neck and arms in place. She stopped and Fern thought that she was going to turn round again and plead for mercy, but instead she positioned her head and shoulders correctly and let the hinged portion slide smoothly down in place. The girl then moved her buttocks the little she could, as if reminding herself of the limits of their freedom.

'Good girl,' the guard said lasciviously, picking up the cane.

'No – Fern's to do the thrashing,' Dr Marshall said quickly.

Fern stared at the psychiatrist: 'Me? I can't!'

Well she could – would love to, in fact. But she sensed a trick. The man was just trying to psyche her out, find out how willing she was to dole out a caning. 'I mean, she hasn't done me any harm,' she added cunningly.

'Hasn't she? Aren't you working in the gardens this term?'

Fern nodded. 'Uh huh.'

'Well, your hours there are long because Sylvie and the others in the stocks here didn't pull their weight last season.'

'I see,' Fern felt her pubic pulse quicken. 'If you put it like that . . .'

She contemplated Sylvie's naked cheeks, seeing the creamy untouched patches of skin between the punished sections. If she could just line up the rod and strike these paler bits. But she mustn't look or sound too whip-happy. She must appear unsure of her tormenting role.

'Don't you think Sylvie deserves to have her bum

128

heated?' Dr Marshall asked in a low voice that seemed the height of reason.

Fern shrugged: 'I guess so, but . . .'

'Don't you have good reason to chastise her, Fern?' He put the reformatory cane in her nerveless right hand.

'If it's what you want, sir.'

'Isn't it what you want, Fern? Isn't that bum just too pert, too perfect? Don't you want to redden it and make it squeal?'

God yes, she did. She wanted to mark and pain that pretty posterior. Wanted to . . . Fern drew back her right hand and raised the reformatory cane. She drew in her breath as she started to bring it down on the girl's bare bottom. She exhaled and muttered a half-formed, 'What the . . .?' as someone grabbed and held her wrist.

'Just checking,' Dr Marshall said, taking the rod from her before it could reach Sylvie's tensing bum.

'Checking what?' Fern queried, going pink.

'Checking that you really were willing to cane a bum that's been overdisciplined already.'

Fern scuffed with her sandals at the dust underfoot: 'But you said . . .'

'If I asked you to jump in the lake would you do it?' the psychiatrist queried.

'No, but . . .' She opened her hands in a half-shrug, hating the way he had of twisting things. 'You told me to cane her and I feared you'd thrash me if I didn't,' she fibbed.

'Don't lie, Fern. You'd thrashed her already, did so as soon as the guard left,' he murmured.

'Prove it!' she said vehemently for the second time.

'I can, now. That's why I had you brandish the rod,' Dr Marshall explained. He took her hand and pulled her closer to Sylvie's nervously twitching bum. 'See these marks?' He used his index finger to trace the red horizontal blotches.

Fern squinted at them: 'Yes. So?'

'These are caused by the tip of the cane. In other words, the end of it has been the main part making contact with Sylvie's backside.' He pursed his lips together as he studied the different shades of pink and scarlet. 'That's because you're not used to laying on the rod and have caused it to fall in a diagonal line.'

The doctor turned his attention to one of the unmarked bums further down the stocks. 'Watch closely, Fern, and see how a caning should be applied,' he said. He lined up the reformatory rod and applied it smartly so that it landed parallel across the creamy expanse. The girl grunted low. A uniform line appeared all the way across her wicked bottom. 'See?' the man continued. 'A good mark, a sore stripe and no bruising – the ideal chastisement for a lazy gardener.' He smiled mirthlessly at Fern, 'Don't worry, my dear, I won't bruise you either though I'll give you the hottest bum.'

'No – don't!' Fern took three steps back and bumped into Ms Lenn.

'Take your punishment, my dear,' the older woman said. 'You know you deserve it.'

Fern swallowed convulsively: 'But I . . .'

'Sneaked out of the wrong door. Neglected your gardening duties,' the doctor cut in.

'And thrashed poor Sylvie's backside,' the guard said looking covetously at the various canes.

'I know, but . . .' Fern tried to think up an excuse. 'I thought this was a public humiliation,' she said quickly, her brain working overtime, 'you know, like the latter day stocks, when anyone could throw rotten fruit. I thought I was *supposed* to discipline these bottoms! I mean, there was this set of whips and birches and these bottoms held and bare . . .'

'Fern, you lie so badly,' Dr Marshall replied.

'Prove it!' she muttered childishly.

'Oh, don't start that again.' He turned to the guard. 'Can you let the others go? I'll need all my concentration to teach Fern's fibbing arse some truthfulness.'

The guard nodded then walked to the wooden restrainer and freed the naked girls.

They left with him. Fern, Ms Lenn and Dr Marshall stayed.

'Fern – take off your shorts,' the psychiatrist said.

'Can't I just . . .?'

'Procrastination will earn you further punishment and that arse is already due a severe thrashing,' the man continued.

Trying not to think of the sore bum that awaited her, Fern unbuttoned and pulled down her summer shorts. She kicked them off.

'And your sandals,' the man instructed.

She obeyed him and stood on the warm dust in her newly bared feet.

'Now, Fern, you can't expect to get to keep your panties on,' the doctor said.

'I . . . No, sir.' Deciding that to mimic obedience might lessen her correction, Fern pulled down her white pants with pink rosebuds.

When she was naked below the waist, the man pointed to the recently de-peopled stocks. 'Get in the middle one, my dear. That'll give me ample room to swing the birch from any angle.'

The birch! Fern quivered and felt hugely aware of her bare little bum. Hadn't the birch latterly been used on only the most intractable British criminals? Hadn't it eventually been banned?

But normal rules didn't apply here – and she'd agreed to follow *Compulsion*'s unorthodox regime; had signed official documents to that effect. It was better than a lengthy jail sentence, Fern reminded herself as she walked towards the wooden stocks. She put her fingers to the upper section and pushed, surprised at how well oiled it was. She stretched her neck and arms into the requisite grooves.

Seconds after she got into position the hinged wood slid down, holding her *in situ*. How ingenious, Fern thought, moving her fingers and toes. She felt fully restrained, yet almost comfortable within the stocks' confines. Not that her bare bottom was going to be comfortable for long – not with Dr Marshall about to birch it soundly. It was about to become hot and red and sore. She winced as he walked before her and went up to the table and selected the twig-stiffened punisher. One lash would bring heat to almost half of her captive posterior, the birch was so wide. And she had no idea how many lashes she was about to get on her exposed cool orbs.

Fern tightened her lower cheeks so that she scrunched up her bum and made it as small and tight a target as possible. She held and held and held it like that until at last her strength gave out and she let her buttocks relax. Then she flinched and squealed as a smarting pain covered the top half of her arse. Damn him, he'd been patiently waiting his moment!

'Count each stroke for me, Fern, then thank me for it and ask me for the next one,' the psychiatrist said.

'And if I don't?' Fern muttered.

'If you don't I'll add a birching to the backs of your thighs to match each one planned for your recalcitrant little bottom. Your hips will be begging for mercy by the time I'm through.'

She felt his smooth fingertips trace the crease at the bottom of her nether cheeks, and shivered with mixed shame and delight.

'Thank you for using the birch on my bad bottom, sir. Please give me another taste,' she whispered with obvious reluctance.

'Your wish is my command. Just think about *why* you're getting this,' the doctor said. He used the birch a second time. Each individual twig left its hot trail, a trail which seemed to fuse with the others till her entire backside felt fiery and tight.

'Thank you for . . .' Again Fern acknowledged the horrid stroke, though she couldn't quite bring herself to ask for its successor. Her bottom already felt like an oven-baked apple. Would the thorough and all-knowing doctor turn it into a roasted chestnut before he was through?

'Tell me why you caned Sylvie,' the psychiatrist said.

'Because . . .' *Because I could.* She searched for a reason that would make sense to the academic who was birching her. 'She was rude to me! She sensed I was hiding in the bushes. She said she would tell the guard when he came back and that I'd receive a thrashing on the bare.'

'You're lying to me again,' Dr Marshall murmured, and Fern knew by the change in the air currents around her that he'd raised the birch high in the air. 'Sylvie has a pretty bum, doesn't she?' he continued, his voice low.

Fern tensed at the sudden change of subject. 'If you like that sort of thing,' she said warily, wriggling her own small bottom.

'You mean you don't?'

'I . . . well, I'm heterosexual,' she explained.

'So you keep emphasising,' he said. She tensed as she heard the birch swishing warningly in the background. 'I think you've told me this before.'

Well, I'm telling you again! Fern spat out. She clenched her teeth together and balled her fists. Christ, the man was an irritant!

'Are you so cynical about life that you can't even acknowledge beauty, Fern?'

She tried to shrug but found she couldn't within the confines of the stocks: 'I like beautiful men, paintings, flowers,' she murmured.

'Yet you can't appreciate a smooth pert female bum?'

'I . . . just not my thing.' Her words sounded flat.

'I suspect it's very much your thing,' the psychiatrist pressed.

Fern heard the grating edge in her own reply: 'Then you know fuck all about it!'

She could hear the smile in Dr Marshall's voice: 'Oh Fern, why such rage?'

'It's you – you make me mad!' she spat out.

'My words make you mad.'

'Same thing, isn't it?' she returned, tired of his pedantic musing.

'Not at all. We still have to teach you about such important distinctions.' Dr Marshall said.

'Right, teach me with that bloody birch. Just quit all the analytical bullshit,' Fern muttered. A sore bum would be preferable to listening to this!

As if in answer, Dr Marshall ran the birch twigs over her bum, a caress with potential cruelty. 'That's nice, isn't it, Fern? Quite stimulating?'

133

She shivered as the blood rushed to her pubis. She might as well be truthful, given that he seemed to read her mind with unerring precision. 'I . . . guess so. Yes.'

'You could have just done this to Sylvie – teased her with the stiffened twigs and made her defenceless bottom slither about within its confines. Instead you picked up the rod and used it full force on her helpless arse.'

Fern moaned quietly as he continued to stroke her twice-birched bum with the multi-fingered implement. Amazing that the sticks which had brought such pain could now give such pleasure to her exposed silky flesh! She could feel the gelatinous liquid starting to leave her aching centre. She could sense her areolae expanding, the nipples craving contact, growing stiff.

'Did Sylvie cry out when you caned her, Fern?' the man murmured.

'She . . . um . . . groaned a bit.' It was hard to remember the girl's pathetic noises: she'd just wanted to concentrate on making the flesh flinch and quiver; on generally enlivening that complacent arse.

'Did you make her bum pink, Fern?'

Her own bum was awash with lust now: 'I guess so.' She'd wanted to make both cheeks the deepest sorest scarlet. Had wanted the poised young beauty to submit totally, to beg.

'It was a beautiful bum, wasn't it, Fern?'

She was nearing climax now, each caress with the birch sending more wanton weight to her mound of Venus. Desperate to reach orgasm, she pushed her hips back against the traitorous touch.

'It was a beautiful bum, wasn't it, Fern?' the psychiatrist repeated, stopping the sensuous strokes with the birch and obviously waiting for her answer.

'God, yes!' Fern muttered, beyond covering up her motive now. 'It was all golden and smooth and pert.'

'And you wanted to touch it, didn't you Fern?' he prompted.

Lust made further lies impossible: 'I suppose . . . just curious. Yes!'

'But you couldn't admit that to yourself, so you picked up the rod,' Dr Marshall confirmed. 'You wanted to beat the beauty out of that bum, make it less sensuous. You wanted to tame it before Sylvie's beauty tamed you.' As he spoke he ran his thumb over her clitoris and kept repeating the light sure pressure.

'Ah ... aaaaah ... aaaaaaaaaaaaaaaah!' Fern's body went into rapturous spasm after spasm as her pussy pleasured into release.

Climax here at *Compulsion* was unlike any climax ever known before. It intensified when the guards and the psychiatrist talked and touched her. Increased when they lewdly tormented and teased each genital inch.

'Caning Sylvie must have been like foreplay for you, dear,' Dr Marshall said, patting her still-wriggling lower cheeks as if they were the smooth head of a puppy. 'You were so hot and wet.'

Fern kept her eyes and mouth tight closed, still slave to the incredible pulsing thrill between her legs and above them. Dr Marshall was exquisitely skilled in the art of making a woman orgasm. Dr Marshall was ... about to birch her again.

Eight

Fern tried to push her belly inwards against the stocks as she sensed the psychiatrist reach for the merciless implement of chastisement. 'Sir,' she muttered, 'Do you really have to take the birch to me again?'

She quivered as the man rubbed the stiffened twigs across her bare flanks and the backs of her thighs, as if readying the defenceless curves for the lash to follow.

'It's my solemn duty to re-educate you, Fern,' Dr Marshall said.

'Then does it have to be here, in the bottom garden, with people walking past?' Though she could only see the occasional figure in the outlying fields, every so often she could hear laughter and voices behind her.

'A thrashing here should shame you into being fairer to others,' the man said. He paused, presumably to let his words penetrate her brain, then added, 'Anyway, you're getting off lightly – there's a more punitive setting than this.'

'Yeah? Where?' Fern shot back. When he was talking to the back of her head he wasn't birching her bare bottom, so she was motivated to keep the conversation going.

'It's a hidden part of the building we keep for our most intractable miscreants,' the psychiatrist said.

The girl cleared her throat: 'What happens there?'

'Buttocks are taught the most prolonged painful lessons.' He seemed to savour each word.

Fern searched for ways to save her own bum from such a tutorial: 'I'm sorry I caned Sylvie, okay?'

'Tell her, not me. And *be* sorry, don't just *say* it, my girl.'

She drew in her breath as he ran the birch over her

137

naked rump again. She sensed him pull the implement back, and waited for the smarting to emblazon its trail across her captive bum cheeks. Instead she felt a trickle of liquid make its slow way from her labial lips to her inner right thigh. Damn, she must be leaking arousal again!

'Lucky you, this thrashing's been put on hold for a while as you've just started menstruating, Fern,' the doctor murmured.

So the wetness she'd just felt had been *blood*! She'd thought her stomach felt slightly stretched and weighted, but her menses weren't due for another two days.

'Let's get you to the nurse for a couple of painkillers,' Dr Marshall continued briskly.

Fern flexed her limbs as he pulled open the top half of the stocks, freeing her. She walked carefully over to her pants and flexed her toes, ready to slide the garment on.

'Don't bother covering your pubes – wait till the nurse has had a look at you,' the psychiatrist added.

Wincing at the thought of strangers seeing her birched bare bottom, Fern clutched tightly at her briefs, shorts and shoes. Still, she told herself, feeling her pink buttocks tingling as she hurried after Dr Marshall, she should count her good fortune in having her punishment brought to an early end. Each limb still languid after her recent all-encompassing orgasm, she followed the man mutely to the medical bay.

When they walked into the antiseptic white room, she immediately recognised the man dressed in a white tunic, who had taunted her many days before in the corridor. She'd been forced to walk ahead of Dr Marshall showing off her sore extremities. The man had come along and mocked her unclothed state. This time she wouldn't take any cruel comments, Fern decided. She was obviously excused from punishment due to menstruation. She might as well make the most of it!

'Nurse Bryson – Fern's period has started early,' Dr Marshall said, guiding her to the surgical couch and pushing her gently onto it.

Fern sat rather than lay on its padded length and wondered how the psychiatrist had known when her menses were actually due. Aware of the male nurse's eyes raking every inch of her body, she put both hands shyly over her pubic mound.

'Right, love, let's take a look at you,' the small slightly balding man said.

'No thanks,' Fern muttered. She looked up as Dr Marshall started to leave the room, and added, 'Hey, don't leave me!'

'I'm busy, Fern,' the psychiatrist countered. 'I was studying the new inmate's background reports when I heard you'd been causing trouble in the grounds.' He recommenced his long sure stride across the room. 'Now that I've dealt with your bad bottom, I have to return to my work.'

Fern blushed slightly at his shaming words, then called out: 'That's all I need, being left with this mincing medical creep!'

Dr Marshall turned, his hand curved round the handle of the door. He stared thoughtfully at Fern till she dropped her gaze, pretending to turn her attention to the rolls of bandages and first-aid tape on the shelving.

'Nurse Bryson, you have my permission to teach Fern manners,' he said smoothly, 'though you can't thrash her for the next couple of days until she's recovered from her menstrual tiredness and any period pains.' He smiled coolly at the pouting twenty-four-year old. 'After all, we want a bum that's fully concentrating on the sensation of being severely whipped, rather than one that's registering menstrual cramps!'

He left. Fern made to follow him, but Nurse Bryson swiftly strode to the door, turned the key then pocketed it.

'Now, Miss Terris,' he murmured, 'it's my duty to teach you politeness as the good doctor said.'

'Oh, and don't you just love it!' Fern replied tensely. She was already wishing that she'd been civil to the man or even fawning. It had been foolhardy to call him a creep.

'Put your feet in those loops,' the male nurse ordered.

Scowling, Fern did as she was asked, anxious to avoid

further argument. Then she gasped as the man pulled a lever which caused the straps to tighten round her feet and pulled them high in the air. Damn, they were the kind of stirrups formerly used on pregnant women! Now, with her legs held high and captive, he had total access to her naked bottom and quim.

'Let's wipe all this warm pussy juice away,' the man continued.

Fern shuddered with shame as he used a tepid cloth to dab away the proof of her earlier climax and the trickle of menstrual blood.

'I can see every inch of your bum,' the man continued. 'I can tell that it's recently had a mild taste of the birch.' Fern clenched her teeth to hold back the sarcastic comments. 'I'd love to warm that arse properly,' Nurse Bryson added, 'but I'll just content myself with putting a tampon in.'

He brought over the paper-wrapped cotton rod and unwrapped it, then slowly parted Fern's labia. To her surprise a prickle of excitement spread through each pinkened leaf at the contact. 'Oh, I think young Fern quite likes having her pussy lips fondled,' said the man, repeating the touch. He ran his middle right finger over her tender tissues again and again and again and again and again.

'Ah! Uh!' Fern could hear half-formed guttural noises coming from the base of her throat. Her bare thighs trembled.

'Now don't be too noisy, my pretty patient,' the nurse murmured, putting the tampon to one side of the medical couch, 'or I'll have to take you more fully in hand.'

He could do what he wanted when he wanted – as long as he kept caressing her! The girl gave herself up to the sensations of bliss. Who'd have believed that she'd be ready to come again so soon after being brought to climax in the stocks? So soon after being birched?

She felt so wanton having her legs stretched up and apart like this; felt helplessly open. She moaned longer and louder as the man found her clitoris and slid his thumb round its swollen circumference.

'Can I enter you?' the man whispered, taking his hand away from her clit but continuing to stroke her mound of Venus.

'I ... guess so,' Fern muttered, not wanting to appear too eager. Then when he made no move to probe her she added, 'Do what you like – just let me come!'

She opened her eyes as the man's shadow fell across her, then shut them again as she felt his shaft at the entrance to her womanhood. For such a small man his phallus had a very inflated tip. Fern strained to hold her stirruped legs even more apart and tried to lift her hips up, desperate to encourage him in.

She exhaled long and hard with relief as his cock impaled her inch by exquisite inch. God, she loved the moment of penetration! His hardness stimulated her outer and inner labia, her sugar walls. He pulled out a little way and indirectly excited her distended clitoris. He pushed back in and thrilled her interiors again. If this was what being shafted in the stirrups was like she'd have a pair added to her box of sex aids, Fern thought, squirming with shameful pleasure. This equalled the joys of a vibrator any day!

The man put his palms flat on her breasts and palpated them through her thin T-shirt. 'D'you like that?' he murmured gloatingly.

'I guess so!' Fern gasped, then amended herself. 'Yes, I love it. Please, sir – I need it!' she said, as he started to move his hands away.

In. Out. In. Out. Her birched bum rubbed against the surgical couch. Her traitorous tits rubbed against his hands. Her quim enjoyed his shaft's sensual stimulus.

'I could keep your legs imprisoned like this for hours, just tease you with my prick,' Nurse Bryson said.

Fern breathed hard and fast as new arousal spread through her helpless loins: 'Let me come, sir!' she begged.

'Come on the shaft of a mincing medical man?' he taunted, circling his cock round and round.

Fern wished she could move her helplessly suspended thighs. 'I didn't mean to call you names ... I shouldn't have!' she gasped, getting close to a climax.

141

'No, you shouldn't,' her tormentor added. 'Such a wicked girl doesn't deserve relief.'

He pulled almost out of her and held himself on his firm arms so that only an inch of his cock remained to pleasure her. 'Ask nicely for another inch,' he ordered coolly.

'I . . . I'm asking nicely,' Fern stammered. Dazed with lust, she tried to push her belly nearer to his thick long rod.

'Say pretty please,' smiled the man.

Fern shook her head and tried again to thrust her hips upwards. In answer the man put his hands on her tummy and held it down.

'Say it,' he prompted.

'Pretty please,' Fern half-sobbed, writhing and moaning. Her sex was a desperate sheath of desire.

'Pretty please what?' the man continued, keeping her waiting.

Fern took a deep breath: 'Pretty please shove your cock right up me and let me come!'

'Pretty please with sugar on it,' taunted the man, sliding half of his sexual stimulus into her.

'Pretty please with sugar on it!' Fern begged.

She gasped with relief and gratitude as he pushed fully in to her pulsing depths and began to move with a rhythm she could rely on. 'Thank you, thank you, thank you!' she all but wept. She moved her hot bum against the couch and remembered tasting the birch and being held in the stockades. She remembered and convulsed with pleasure and promptly came. As her crevice contracted on Nurse Bryson's cock, his own mouth opened in obvious silent rapture, and he squeezed her breasts and made a series of half-strangled little groans then flopped satiatedly over her heaving chest.

They slept. When Fern awoke her ankles were free of the stirrups and the man had made her peppermint tea in a Wedgewood teapot.

'It soothes upset tummies,' he explained, handing her a half-filled cup.

'Mine feels fine,' Fern murmured, sipping the hot beverage. Her two intense orgasms had rid her belly of any cramps, leaving her mons blood-scented and sweat-slicked.

142

'You can shower here and put on one of my spare medical uniforms,' the nurse added, as if reading her thoughts. They were all seers or magicians here, Fern thought dazedly. They could both bring pain and make it go away.

She felt good now – inwardly cleansed. After she'd showered and dressed she felt even better. She sat chatting to Nurse Bryson for half an hour whilst she ate wholemeal sultana scones spread with *Compulsion*'s own-produced honey to give her blood sugar a lift.

At last she left the medical bay and started the walk back to her room.

'You the new doctor?' asked a girl in her twenties. 'The inmate in Room 105 has been asking for an enema.'

Fern looked down at the borrowed white tunic and trousers she was wearing. They obviously made her look the medical part! For a moment she contemplated making some female squirm at the end of a colonic tube.

Then she shook her head. 'No, Nurse Bryson's still in charge. Best see him about it.' She wondered if the other inmates saw him when they wanted sexual pleasuring too. No matter – the main thing was that the girl would have her purging done by a trained professional rather than an opportunistic hack. Fern went to bed feeling very pleased with herself, knowing that she'd had the opportunity to be bad but had chosen to do some good.

Four days later she felt less pleased, for it was then that she had to complete her birching for caning the hapless Sylvie. She quivered as yet another grinning guard led her to Dr Marshall's office. She breathed in, out, in, trying to find a calming rhythm as she approached his desk.

Damn him – he might at least acknowledge her presence! She stared at the psychiatrist's pursed lips as he finished the document he was writing, then coolly studied her from feathery fringe to peephole shoe tip.

'You acted impulsively when you spied both the rod and young Sylvie's bare bottom, didn't you, Miss Terris?' he murmured.

'I . . . suppose so.' She hated it when he was this formal. Hated it when the safety of her poor bum was at stake.

'In other words you showed a lack of control?' he continued.

Fern gulped. 'Yes, but I've been controlled since then, sir. I could have pretended to be part of the medical team, I could have administered an enema, but I didn't. I was good – I told the truth!'

'You told the truth because you'd just enjoyed an orgasm in the stirrups,' the psychiatrist continued.

Fuck it! The male nurse had obviously been telling tales out of school. 'Maybe that's true, but . . .' She couldn't think of further words which would redeem her.

'It's true that when the masochistic part of your personality is satisfied you behave much more fairly,' the man said. He smiled, eyes raking her cream ribbed top and emerald dirndl skirt. She'd been told not to wear trousers for this punishment session. 'Right, let's see if you're willing to bow to an intelligent authority, obey a few stringent commands!'

Fern cleared her throat: 'Am I to go back to the bottom garden, sir?'

She trembled as she remembered the firm stocks and the table of long whips and canes which stood in front of it.

'No, as you've behaved like a silly schoolgirl you're to be taught discipline in the school room,' Dr Marshall said.

Slowly Fern walked beside him to the specially equipped suite that had been turned into a very large classroom. Four other girls and one boy, all in their twenties, already had their bums bent over their desks. Their heads didn't face the bearded teacher at the front – instead, their poor bottoms did. Three of the bums were vulnerably bare, with the pupils' knickers at their feet.

'I see some of your adult pupils need to learn a workable philosophy,' the psychiatrist murmured.

'Not to worry! I'll soon thrash their misguidedness out of them,' promised the man.

Fern looked dully at his black teaching cloak, black shoes and black trousers. Then she noticed the tan leather four-tailed tawse in his large right hand.

It was about a foot and a half long and half an inch thick. Its width covered three wicked inches. The four fingers of the punisher looked slightly worn at the ends. How many luckless bottoms had been thrashed by this pitiless implement? How many inmates had howled and begged?

'I'll behave,' Fern whispered.

'Angela said she'd behave, then we found out she'd been stealing from the girl in the next room because – how did you put it, Angela? – "It was only a few jumpers".' He shook his head and walked over to the culprit's naked buttocks, caressing them softly again and again. 'As if people aren't shocked and sickened to find their rooms ransacked. As if clothes can't have sentimental value or just be essential for practical use.'

Fern looked at the thieving girl's bare bum. It already bore three or four overlapping tawse marks.

'I'll put the jumpers back, schoolmaster. I'll buy her extra ones!' Angela whimpered, tensing her bum.

'Not good enough! You'll also give her victim support by listening to her feelings and anxieties,' the schoolmaster instructed, pulling back the tawse then laying on another lash.

Angela cried out and wildly swung her bottom from side to side as if trying to shake off the horrid stinging sensation. Fern noticed, though, that the girl didn't jump up from the desk.

'She's here to learn control, so she knows better than to refuse her punishment,' the man said, looking at Fern closely.

Fern nodded, too wary to form a reply.

'This is Fern Terris,' Dr Marshall cut in, pushing Fern forward slightly. 'She did a bit of impromptu caning of her own so we're trying to teach her forethought and restraint.'

'I'll do my best to make her tender parts better,' the teacher promised, running the four-tailed tawse through his hands.

He smiled emotionlessly at Fern. 'Right, girl, bend over that desk by the window, your bottom towards the blackboard. You can keep your skirt and pants on until you do or say something bad.'

'I'll be the perfect pupil, sir,' Fern murmured, hoping she sounded suitably obsequious. If it spared her pale nether cheeks, she was willing to say the right words, to pretend that she had fully reformed. She genuinely thought she was becoming a better person – more thoughtful and inward looking. She'd just lapsed for a few moments when confronted by Sylvie's captive pert arse.

Now she had to present her own arse for possible punishment. Wincing at the ignominy of the situation, Fern settled her tummy upon the hard wooden desk and let her head and arms hang down heavily. She hoped that if she was good she would get to keep her skirt on for the full tutorial hour. She prayed she could be so ingratiating and deferential that the teacher wouldn't have to pull down her pants.

'Right, Miss Terris – tell myself and the other pupils what brings you here,' the schoolmaster said.

'Today, you mean?' She looked at the wooden floor close to her nose and tried to keep the words light and factual. 'Well, I was spying in the bottom garden when . . .'

'No,' said the man, 'I mean what crime brought you to *Compulsion*?'

Fern stiffened. She'd have to be careful here, have to avoid implicating . . . She cleared her throat: 'I got drunk alone in the lingerie department of a megastore after hours. I set the place on fire by mistake and injured a security guard.'

There! The life and crimes of Fern Terris revealed in a few well-chosen remarks. Fern relaxed over the desk, secure in the knowledge that she'd simply repeated the version of events she'd told the police and Dr Marshall.

'You felt it necessary to mention the fact that you were *alone*,' said the teacher silkily. Fern stiffened as she heard his footsteps growing closer to her bent-over bottom and taut backs of thighs. 'That suggests to me that you're lying, that you really had an accomplice in your crime.'

They were just trying to psyche her out, Fern told herself as she remained bent vulnerably over the desk: they couldn't prove it. Surely they couldn't punish her for an unproven lie?

'Lift your pretty skirt right up your back, Fern,' continued the schoolmaster.

'And if I don't?' Fern muttered, stalling for time. She didn't know which was worse – being treated like a child or being chastised like a grown-up.

'Then I'll have to get Sylvie, the girl you caned, to undress you and administer the thrashing,' the black-cloaked educator said.

'Right, I'm pulling my skirt up!' Fern confirmed quickly, cringing at this new threat. She couldn't bear for the more spoilt blonde girl to disrobe and wallop her. She would rather take her chastisement from a man. A man who was doing this to help her in the long term, rather than a woman who was out for revenge on Fern's poor bottom. Nevertheless, Fern gritted her teeth with shame as she removed the emerald material from her pantied bum and edged the hem up her back to reveal her cream cotton panties.

'I'll give you two hard tastes of the tawse over your knickers,' the schoolmaster told her, 'then we'll have another little talk.'

Fern gripped the legs of the desk with both hands and waited for the leather to warm her bum cheeks. She was suddenly aware of the schoolroom clock ticking, tocking. One of the adult male pupils coughed nervously and a girl sneezed. *Take the lash bravely then thank him for it*, Fern told herself, *be suitably fawning*. Be . . .

A wide band of pain exploded across her pantied orbs. She yelled and kicked her feet, flexing her ankles.

'You're here to learn control, remember, Fern,' the schoolmaster said sternly. 'A lack of restraint will be severely curbed.'

'Sorry, sir. The tawse hurt more than I realised, sir,' Fern muttered, getting reluctantly back into position. She waited silently for the second stroke to fall.

This one bit further down, at the lower curve of her cheeks which were more sensitive than the upper. Fern wailed more loudly and jumped up from the desk. Breathing hard, she rubbed her pantie-covered bum, helping to diffuse the soreness. She stopped mid-rub as she saw the teacher's unsympathetic face.

'I'd hoped that you'd behave like a big girl, Fern, but as you aren't you're going to have to lie across my lap like a baby.' He looked her up and down, his gaze distant. 'Not that we at *Compulsion* would ever physically chastise children. That's out and out cruelty and bullying. That's wrong.' He took hold of her wrists and began to lead her across the room. 'But a young woman who's masochistic like yourself ultimately benefits hugely from each whipping.' He settled himself in his armless big wooden chair, still holding her before him. 'Trust me, my dear. This spanking is a form of therapy!'

Fern wished that he'd let go of her so that her hands could therapeutically soothe her own bum.

'We're trying to teach you control today,' the schoolmaster reiterated, 'so I'd like you to bend over my lap of your own volition.'

'And if I choose not to?' Fern said softly, suspecting that she didn't want to hear the shameful answer.

'Then Sylvie will hold you over my knee whilst I tan your arse.'

Fern pictured the scene and shuddered. 'Right! I'll do what I'm told,' she forced out, wondering why it never got less degrading to say such acquiescent words. She'd thought that after a few weeks here she'd know the drill, be able to give the staff flip answers. Instead they genuinely humiliated her – and then excited her – every time.

'I'm waiting,' prompted the man. He let go of her wrists and patted his trousered knees. 'Get this bottom under my hands so that I can redden it.'

Fern sucked in her breath and pulled up her shoulders and bent, almost in slow motion, from the waist. She found purchase with her hands and stretched her legs back until the soles of her feet were on the classroom floor.

'Push your legs back further till you're on tiptoe. A whacking stings more with the pupil's legs held tautly,' the schoolmaster said.

Fern cringed inwardly but obeyed. How she wished

148

she'd stayed bent over the desk tasting the leather tawse on her cotton-pantied bottom! Now she felt even more disarmed and humbled as she was held over his knees.

'First I'm going to smack you over your pants. Then I'm going to pull them down to admire the heat and colour the spanking has provided. Finally I may display you to the other pupils as a warning of what happens when a naughty girl jumps up to protect her bum,' the educator said.

He stroked her trembling hemispheres through the smooth material which clung to them. 'I'm going to enjoy punishing this bottom, Fern. It's well-rounded yet nicely pert, and your thighs are smooth and taut and coltlike. I'm looking forward to making them kick and beg.'

She wouldn't beg, Fern told herself – not with the other pupils listening and probably laughing. She was only willing to plead for mercy when there weren't too many others around.

'Yes, sir,' she mumbled reluctantly. She really wanted to call him names and kick his ankles. She didn't want to enrage him, she thought, gasping as the first slap ricocheted down. The softness of her panties muffled the actual sound of the slap, but the heat still radiated across one helpless orb.

The schoolmaster treated the other hemisphere to an equally focused spank. Soon he got into a sure hard rhythm. He spanked first one buttock then the other, and seemed impervious to her gasps, flinches and grunts.

'I'll do whatever you want!' Fern yelped at last. The man stopped spanking her. She exhaled slowly, and used every last ounce of effort to keep her palms flat on the floor. She so wanted to reach them back to protect her flaming posterior, to massage just a little of the shameful sting away.

'Do what's best for everyone, including yourself,' the schoolmaster said.

Damn it, he'd obviously been to the Dr Marshall School of Instant Wisdom! 'I . . . I'll do what's best for everyone,' Fern repeated obsequiously. She winced as the teacher started to fondle her buttocks, bringing new heat to her flanks and to her loins.

'We're trying to turn you into a useful citizen, Fern, not a mindless parrot,' the man corrected.

'Yes, sir. I'm sorry, sir!'

'You're sorry you got found out – not sorry that you've caused chaos throughout your short lifetime,' the bearded master said.

Fern opened her eyes and stared at the floorboards, as if they somehow held the answers. The answers which would protect her defenceless raised backside! The man might keep spanking her for not telling the truth about what had happened in the store that night, yet she couldn't admit to her real drunken plan.

'Reach back and pull down your pants,' the schoolmaster instructed.

Fern swallowed, but obediently reached back with her left hand, steadying herself with her right hand. Awkwardly she groped for the elasticated waistband, hooked her thumb under it and pulled. She felt the cotton start to drag its slow way down her feverish small buttocks, bringing fresh heat to each well-spanked inch.

When her panties were at the tops of her thighs she stopped pushing, unable to reach further without moving from her bent-over position.

'Good girl, now walk over to the mirror and have a look at your sore bum,' the teacher said.

'The mirror?' Fern muttered dazedly. Her thighs and pubis felt strangely weak. She wasn't sure if she was capable of standing.

'It's next to the door. Get over there now or I'll repeat that spanking,' the man said.

Finding a new strength, Fern squirmed backward till she was able to drop from his lap, landing on her feet in a squatting position. She felt the liquid arousal on her sex lips and inner thighs and winced. She wouldn't let him see that she was wet! She wouldn't show him that she was daunted! She'd . . .

Unsure of what else she'd do, Fern turned towards the door and immediately saw the mirror. It was a narrow full-length one with a bamboo frame. Probably made from canes they'd worn out through thrashing girlish bottoms, she thought sarcastically, and felt another long line of moisture thread from her womb.

Pants at her feet, she shuffled towards the reflective surface. She reached it, and stared at her confused flushed face. Her eyes were glassily bright, the pupils hugely dilated. She looked down at her breasts to see the nipples straining through her creamy top. Another sexual signal started to leak from her pouting lower lips. Desperate to stop it, Fern pushed her bare legs together. She wished she was alone and could touch her craving clit.

'You're supposed to be contemplating your red bum – not admiring your face,' came the teacher's voice.

Fern flinched and looked over at him. 'Sorry, sir! I'd started to daydream.'

'Daydreaming's a reward at the end of a working day, not an alternative to it!' said the man.

'I see, sir. I'll pay more attention, sir.' Fern took her time turning her back to the mirror. The longer she could spend over here by the door the less time he'd have left to warm her arse!

When her bottom was facing the reflective glass, she looked over her shoulder at it.

'Describe your bum vis-à-vis your personality,' the teacher murmured, with a smile in his voice.

Fern turned to look at him: 'Sir, I don't understand.'

The man continued to gaze at her. 'Well, is it the bum of a liar? Of a cheat? A bum that's attached to a shallow person or a deep and meaningful one?'

Damn him – she hated the self analysis bit! Fern looked reluctantly again at the reddened contours of her bottom. She saw how the teacher's fingers had strayed over her thighs and the edges of her hips so that the colour splayed over a wide area of tenderised flesh.

'It's been a thoughtless silly bum in the past, but now it's learning its lesson,' she said, licking her lips and wishing that she could stop blushing. She halted, feeling secretly pleased with herself. That should impress him: she'd admitted past liability yet shown that she'd changed for the better.

'And is it a bum that's learnt control?' the man continued.

'Oh yes, sir. Yes!'

The teacher flicked the tawse against his desk top. 'So much control that you impulsively grabbed a rod and caned Sylvie the other day?'

Drat! She'd forgotten that was why she was here. She should have incorporated the scene into her apologetic repertoire. Fern looked dully at the reflection of her sore bum and realised the man wasn't through with it yet.

'Right girl, come back over my lap and take a spanking on the bare,' the schoolmaster continued.

Taking uncertain small steps, which were partly due to her shame at going over his knee again and partly due to the restrictiveness of her ankle-based panties, Fern approached the man.

She knew from the weeks spent at *Compulsion* that the second spanking was even more daunting than the first one. It was hard to lower yourself over a man's knee for the second time, knowing that he was going to increase the sore stingy redness of an already squirming hot bum.

At last she reached his chair and stood waiting, the fronts of her legs touching the side of one of his. She wished he wouldn't scrutinise her naked pubes and thighs quite so closely. Wished that he hadn't suddenly shifted his focus to her pink-cheeked face.

'A naughty girl's bottom should be across the teacher's knee,' said the man, flexing his fingers.

Quivering with uncertainty, Fern bent at the waist.

Lying obediently over a male lap never got any easier, she realised as she got awkwardly into the correct position. She knew that from the first echoing spank she'd want to put her palms back to protect her naked rear end. That earlier spanking over her pants had been hard and demeaning. But she knew that she'd feel more helpless and ashamed now that she was to be spanked on the bare.

'Mm, that rump's started to pink nicely,' the schoolmaster murmured, fondling her taut globes and equally tense nude thigh backs.

Fern closed her eyes and wished that she could similarly close her ears to his belittling words.

'I'm just wondering how many spanks you deserve for lying to me and for caning poor Sylvie,' the man continued.

Fern knew better than to suggest a lenient session. 'As many as you think fit, sir,' she said.

'As few as you can get away with, you mean,' the schoolmaster retorted.

Fern could sense him staring down at her wriggling contours. She breathed quickly and shallowly as she waited for his large palm to fall.

Silence. Stillness. The wooden boards under her hands felt reassuringly smooth. She inhaled lavender floor polish and wondered who cleaned the many rooms in *Compulsion*. She forgot all about such trivia as the first spank radiated sharply across her waiting bum. God, that smack had hurt! The man had toasted his hand over the crease in her backside, which was hugely sensitive. Fern reared up for an unthinking moment, then abjectly got back into place.

'That hurt, didn't it, Miss Terris?' the man mocked. He fingered the newly heated flesh so that she squirmed further. 'But it didn't hurt as much as Sylvie's bum did when you took the rod to it, my dear.'

'No, sir. I've apologised for caning Sylvie, sir.'

'And now your own cheeks must say sorry.' He fondled her helpless hindquarters again.

He doled out a second spank on her right buttock and a third one on her left. The noises were loud and reverberating. He warmed her wriggling thighs with spanks five and six. He obviously wasn't going to stop at six of the best, Fern realised, as her quivering orbs registered spanks seven, eight, nine, ten and eleven. 'Now where shall I place the twelfth spank?' the schoolmaster said.

Fern prayed that it wouldn't be across her buttock crease, for the sharpness of that particular smack seemed to spread right through her.

'Shall I do it here? Or here?' the bearded man continued, laying his palm on her upper buttocks, then on her lower curves, then on her legs.

'On one of my upper cheeks, please, sir,' she whispered raggedly, her bum a pleading hot swathe.

Somewhat to her surprise, her tormentor did as she asked, dishing out a mild slap to her nearest rotundity.

'You think your poor bottom has had enough,' he said, 'but I know a way to make you take a little more.'

'I beg – no more sir,' Fern muttered, her buttocks already red and glowing. She groaned low in her throat as the man slid his index finger between her labial lips.

She continued to make little guttural sounds as he penetrated her digitally inch by delectable inch. God, she was wet and close to climax! Until he started to finger-fuck her she hadn't realised how aroused and in need she was. 'God, yes, like that!' she gasped, as he pushed even more firmly inside her. Then she cried out in confusion and loss as he withdrew.

'Put it back!' she whimpered.

'Only after you've had your remaining twenty spanks,' the schoolmaster replied evenly.

Fern licked her lips: 'But you said I was nearing my limit, so . . .'

'Now that you're more aroused you'll feel each spank less keenly, my pretty miss.'

'Isn't the whole point to make me feel each spank as much as possible?' Fern asked, trying to push her hungry clitoris against his hand.

'Oh, you'll feel the heat fully after you've come, sweetheart. And your bottom will be a bright red reminder for the rest of the day.'

A spanked bum didn't really stay red all day, he was doubtless just trying to shame her.

'Right – lay on the last twenty spanks,' Fern mumbled, willing to endure the pain for the ensuing pleasure. 'Then please put your fingers up me again.'

'I'll think about it,' said the man, and she sensed that he'd raised his palm over her poor raised *derrière*. She shut her eyes and waited for the additional spanks.

The first one went low across her thighs and she automatically tried to flinch away. But its successor landed further up and felt surprisingly pleasant. As the man got into his rhythm, Fern found herself pushing up her bum to meet each stinging spank. My God, she was actually welcoming this, enjoying it! Willing each heat-bringing slap to fall.

After the twentieth spank had landed her bottom felt bereft, craving further chastisement.

'Let's see if we can make that little clit of yours as hot as your arse is,' said the man. He laid the pad of his thumb above her sensitive bud. 'Come on, sweetheart, I want your pussy to do all the work. Rub against my fingers.'

Her pubis a weighted curve of desire, Fern did as she was told. She moved her bare hips in tiny insistent thrusts, wriggling against the stimulus. She used his finger the way she would use her own. It was physically demanding moving her loins round and round, but she was almost at the apex of arousal, the rapture in her clitoris equal to the unusually gratifying pain of her bum.

'Don't expect each thrashing to afford you as much joy as this one did,' the teacher warned, and she moaned with shame at his awareness. 'For every time a girl arches back to enjoy each spank, there's five times that she tries to protect her bottom from further punishment,' the man said.

'Yes, sir. Won't expect . . .'

She was fast going beyond words, beyond logic. She could focus only on the incredible near-nirvana of her clit. She whimpered as she felt his thumb trace the outline of her little nub.

'Wonder what Dr Marshall will say when I tell him you thrust your bum up for that spanking?' he taunted.

'Please, sir, you don't have to tell him!'

'Tell him that you demonstrated your sub side? Oh yes, I do.' He slid his thumb over her flesh again. 'In fact I may have to put it on the noticeboard: *Fern's Bum Begs Nicely for an Additional Spanking.* What do you think?'

Fern orgasmed, her voice a strained high series of yelps, her palms moving convulsively on the floorboards. She thrust her hips more strongly against the man's hand as the elation coursed through.

'That's it, sweetheart, let it out,' he murmured, sounding pleased with himself or with her or with the universe.

Fern obliged mightily, then slumped, spent, across his knee.

When she finally opened her eyes the room seemed brighter, as if the sun had become trapped in the south-facing classroom. She shifted slightly, and found her labia stuck wetly to the folds of the teacher's cloak. She heard a girlish sigh somewhere to her left and remembered the other adult pupils who must have heard if not seen her sati-ation and shame.

'Permission to go back to my desk, sir,' she whispered, wondering how much there remained of the tutorial.

'Permission denied, girl,' said the man. She stiffened, then heard the genuine approval in his voice. 'You endured your ordeal well, so you don't have to remain for the rest of the lesson.' He helped her from his lap then looked at the other bums before him. 'These other arses have yet to learn the same measure of respect.'

Fern looked at the bare bottoms in question and, for the first time, felt no desire or anger. She was too overwhelmed by the force of her recent orgasm to react to another's thrashed bum.

'Go back to your room and rest, Fern,' the schoolmaster continued, as if understanding that she needed concise clear orders. 'You'll need your strength three hours from now – Coach Sonia Shendon's organising baseball on the south pitch.'

Smoothing down her dirndl skirt and holding her crum-pled pants in her right hand, Fern said goodbye to the man and cast a last confused glance at the bent-over pupils. She wondered if she'd ever again enjoy such a spectacular or-gasm and wondered how she'd summon up the energy to take part in Sonia's game.

156

Nine

Sonia stared at the small black punisher which the guard had just handed her.

'It's a ferula. Just flick it against the backs of their thighs during the hockey match if they seem to be slacking,' the man suggested with an encouraging smile.

'Right. No problem.' Sonia ran her right forefinger and thumb over the eleven inches of thick rubber which ended in a paddle shape. Would she really be able to go through with this? She'd never physically chastised a human being before.

She'd even managed to avoid correcting Melissa for that netball foul the other week! Instead, she'd arranged for one of the youths to withhold the girl's pleasure. And she'd got one of the other inmates, Fern Terris, to lower her sex lips upon the bondaged girl's face. The frustration and humiliation the troublemaker had suffered before being allowed to orgasm had been punishment enough.

But now she'd been handed a ferula – and was expected to use it. She'd given the impression at the interview that she'd often disciplined one of her erstwhile lovers; that she believed in corporal punishment for very serious crimes. Robert, her boss, had told her what to say and the way in which to say it. She'd managed to sound just like the other staff at the reformatory – or at *Compulsion* as she now knew it was internally called.

'Okay, girls and boys, let's bully off!' she exclaimed, glad to be breathing the fresh sea air as she walked round the sunlit hockey pitch.

She smiled at the reluctant adult players as they awkwardly toed the grass. The girls were dressed in tiny pleated

157

grey skirts which hardly covered their small bare bottoms. The boys wore equally skimpy shorts, with large cut-out sections which revealed their naked bum cheeks and manly cracks. This was a *punishment* game – a demeaning game. A game designed to show them how their victims had felt.

For both hockey teams were made up entirely of men and women who'd committed fraud. Sonia had read their case files, which showed every crime from printing their own ten-pound notes to writing cheques which bounced to the ceiling. These inmates had cheated, faked, embezzled, swindled and lied. And now they'd pay with sore bums and equally stingy thigh backs. 'Make an effort, Arlene,' Sonia shouted, running up behind one motionless female and flicking the thick hard ferula against her pale white thigh.

'Ouch!' Arlene muttered, taking three hasty steps forward. She turned round and spat on the ground before Sonia, obviously daring her to use the ferula again.

It was a challenge to the sports teacher's authority. An unequivocal challenge. Sonia looked over at the others. They were all watching her. The guard on the outskirts of the field gave an encouraging nod. Could she fully flog this girl? Lost in thought, Sonia flicked the rubber chastiser against her own outer thigh. She winced and looked down at the flesh there. A long pink mark had appeared below her shorts hem. It stung.

More importantly, it had interrupted her negative thought chain. It had made her concentrate on the matter in hand. *It could do the same for Arlene!* Sonia tried to keep the uncertainty and excitement from her voice as she turned to the nearest youth.

'Les – fetch one of the big armless wooden chairs from the changing rooms and bring it here to the side of the pitch,' she ordered. Then she looked at the others. 'Okay, go back to the game, and put your backs into it! I'm going to give Arlene the thrashing she so richly deserves before I oversee the rest of the match.'

'Yeah? You and whose army?' Arlene muttered, but she made no effort to run away. Inmates at *Compulsion* rarely did, Sonia realised. Oh, they muttered and protested about their canings before they took place, and cried and begged during them, but something deep in their psyche made them secretly crave that same discipline and stay for more.

Just as Arlene now stood in place, anticipating the flogging she was about to get. Sonia could sense that the girl's eyes were trained on the rubber implement. It was smaller yet thicker than a paddle, well suited to an over-the-knee chastisement that was meant to last for some considerable time. Arlene had already tasted it on her thigh backs and must still be feeling it smarting through her tender flesh.

'I'm not used to playing this game,' she muttered now, kicking at the clumps of grass with her pristine hockey boots.

Sonia looked sideways at her: 'I was looking for enthusiasm, not expertise, my dear.'

'And it's hot out here for running,' the girl complained.

Sonia shook her head in exasperation. 'Just keep a perspective! You're wearing lightweight summer clothing and there are sports drinks on the table over there!' She looked the girl up and down. 'Arlene, don't start making excuses now. You've been lazy and rude and you're going to get your bottom tanned. There's an end to it.'

The raven-haired inmate put her hands back and fruitlessly tried to pull her pleated skirt further over her cheeks. 'You'll thrash me with everyone watching?' she whispered nervously.

'I'll thrash you whilst they continue their game,' the sports coach confirmed. 'They won't have time to watch your arse reddening but they'll hear your screams.'

Sonia swished the little implement through the air. She felt well pleased with her words, which sounded controlled and suitably ominous. She had a feeling that Arlene and the others would be much more ingratiating after this. A hot bum could, in time, produce a cooler logic. Scarlet flesh could help a blue mood to dissipate.

Pleasure usually followed punishment here, making the lash and spank more bearable. Sonia wondered if she could bring herself to touch Arlene in an intimate and climax-bringing way. She'd only fantasised about Robert during the past two years, though she'd had a couple of drunken one-night stands when he was on holiday with Mrs Greene or being particularly distant. They'd been young disco-dancing men, though. Satisfying a hockey-hating woman was something else!

We have countdown. She winked at Les as he finished puffing his way across the field with the oversized chair. Most of the chairs here with armfree like this one, designed for the victim's lap-based chastisement.

'Just put it there,' she told the youth, pointing at an area of grass near the perimeter fence.

Arlene looked at the chair, then glanced with peripheral vision at Sonia.

'Now to teach a bad bottom some goodness,' the sports coach murmured, taking a seat and settling back. She stared at the girl: 'Get your arse over here now. You'll get double if I have to come and get it.' Again she felt pleased with herself. This was the sort of thing Dr Marshall said.

She thrilled inside as the luckless female approached. Even if she was only able to give the girl a few cautionary taps it would act as a warning to the others. From their stance in the middle of the field they wouldn't be able to see if she was turning Arlene's bottom red or just pink. Maybe it took time to learn how to warm another's but-tocks. Maybe it took a coldness she didn't have inside her. Maybe you had to feel really enraged.

'Hurry up!' she said as Arlene dragged her steps. The in-mate took six slightly bigger moves until she reached the side of the chair. 'I'm waiting!' Sonia continued, and tightened her tummy muscles and thighs a little to more easily hold the girl's weight. All elbows and knees, the black-haired complainer lowered herself onto her teacher's lap and let her head flop down.

Sonia looked at the girl's glossy dark hair, and felt a rush of affection yet when she looked at her small pert bum she felt a flood of rage. This girl had money, breeding, in-tellect – yet had chosen a deceitful way to making a living. She'd sold reconditioned car wrecks to unsuspecting owners, although she'd had the opportunity to study medicine or law.

'You always take the quick fix, don't you Arlene?' Sonia said, starting to lift the scrap of skirt from the girl's bottom. 'On the hockey field you do as little as possible just as you've always done in life.'

'Don't like hockey!' the girl muttered.

'Then you should have asked to play an alternative sport,' Sonia countered.

'Don't like exercise.'

'But you need it to improve your mental and physical wellbeing. It'll help sort you out.' Just as the ferula would help sort her out now.

Sonia ran a warning hand over the girl's alabaster cheeks. 'I'm going to make your little rump sting until you plead to be allowed to work out on the hockey pitch,' she threatened.

'You'll have a long wait then!' Arlene said, snorting. She'd obviously decided that being humble wasn't doing her any good. Or maybe on some level she wanted her correction to begin. If so, she wouldn't be disappointed.

Aiming to mark across the centre of the girl's buttocks, Sonia lifted the rubber punisher and brought it smartly down.

'Ah! That hurt!' Arlene gasped, jerking her bum and tensing her upper legs.

'It was meant to hurt,' Sonia murmured, realising that she was genuinely ready to make the girl beg.

'I thought . . .' the raven-haired girl spluttered, 'well, people said you wouldn't whip an inmate.'

'Then after today you can tell them that I do – and hard.'

She lifted the ferula again, looked at the pink mark that the little punisher had made and struck immediately beneath it. She doled out a third and fourth stroke further down before the girl had time to complain or plead. But complaining seemed more Arlene's way.

'If you give me too many I'll tell the doc!' she muttered, wriggling and kicking.

'I'll tell him that you failed to take your thrashing with dignity and obviously need a repeat performance,' Sonia said.

Arlene slumped further over the older woman's lap, then jerked her head and shoulders up as Sonia struck her smooth young thigh tops. 'Thinking of going someplace?' Sonia asked as the girl reared out of place.

'I . . . no, miss,' the girl muttered, letting her silky head flop down again.

Sonia fondled her fast-reddening bum. It was now a nervous bum, a sorry bum. A bum which flinched and tensed and quivered. The sports coach gave it another two sharp tastes of the ferula on its lower curves, and it trembled and writhed some more. 'Wish you were on the hockey field now?' Sonia taunted, rubbing the rubber against Arlene's hot sore orbs.

'I'm neutral!' Arlene muttered.

'Oh dear, a proud girl who won't admit defeat earns herself a much more scarlet bum,' the teacher said. She looked at that bum – the bum of a liar and a charlatan. It was a bum that deserved to cringe.

By welding the front of one damaged car to the back of another equally traumatised vehicle, Arlene could have killed the unwary new driver, or at least maimed him horribly. She'd put cash before compassion. Put self-interest before common sense.

The girl's actions could easily have resulted in the death of a wonderful man like Robert Greene, the Head of Penal Liaisons! At the thought of losing the man she'd spent the last two years in love with, Sonia raised the daunting little ferula again. And brought it down on Arlene's right buttock, then on Arlene's left buttock, then on Arlene's crevice. She warmed Arlene's upper bum, lower bum, and the quivering backs of her thighs. She was going to teach this small bare bottom to be fair to others, to show respect, to start thinking before acting. She was going to make its bitter young owner sweetly beg.

By the time she'd finished making the ferula rise and fall, Arlene was pleading really prettily. Sonia looked down at the girl's reddened haunches. She told herself that she was glad she didn't have to pleasure the younger woman – Arlene had already come by rubbing against Sonia's leg.

'Right, girl,' she said, pushing the squirming inmate from her lap. 'Let's get you standing by the sports drinks table, with your naked bum facing the other players.'

Sniffing loudly, Arlene momentarily squatted in place. Liquid desire could be seen smeared across her inner thighs and pubis. Satisfaction shone from her newly relaxed hot face.

The girl looked strangely compelling, Sonia thought, as Arlene stumbled off to take up her humiliating position by the table. Though she didn't look as alluring as that Fern Terris had the other day. No matter! Sonia forced her mind back to safer channels. Surely she didn't really want a girl she could pleasure and punish? After all, she'd set her heart and her loins on Robert and conventional sex.

Ten

That baseball game last night had been a demanding one! Fern stood under the hot shower for moment after moment and let the water jets revive her well-exercised arms and legs. Sonia had proved to be a fair but exacting sports coach and the other team members had been worthy adversaries.

Now however, she had to lose her competitive edge and replace it with the work ethic. She had to be ready for another day spent digging in the gardens. Fern yawned at the prospect and soaped her tanned taut thighs. She was glad that she wasn't in the older woman's hockey, rounders or football teams. There was a limit to how much exercise a former party-girl could take!

At last Fern left the reviving spray, breakfasted in her bathrobe, then changed into a military-style cream shirt dress with metal buttons. It was cute but not conniving: she didn't feel like flirting today. Felt a bit remote, a bit languid. She left her room and suddenly felt scared.

'Time for your first parole hearing,' said the guard who had been waiting in the corridor.

'You mean I've to face a panel?' Fern stuttered, her mind flooding with half-formed questions. 'But I haven't prepared!'

The guard grinned. 'That's the whole idea, pet. They're looking for authentic progress not verbal dexterity.'

At least she was dressed conservatively, Fern told herself as she followed him to the long narrow interview room.

It held an equally long narrow desk. Three men and three women sat behind it. Each of them smiled at her, their looks frankly assessing.

'Fern, just tell us about the crime which brought you here,' the oldest woman, who was in her late forties or early fifties, said.

Stopping to search for the right word or phrase, Fern told them the half-truths she'd told everyone else. She used terms like 'past mistake' and 'now reformed' and 'useful citizen'. Two of the panel scribbled on their blotters – the others just stared. Was she winning them over with her rehabilitation speech? Was she a candidate for swift parole? Would she be out of here by this time next week?

'Call Dr Marshall as a character witness,' the man at the top of the table said.

The guard left and returned with the bearded psychiatrist. Fern smiled at him brightly. He looked at her, his mouth set, and coldly shook his head.

'I'd hoped to be able to talk of Miss Terris's improved behaviour,' he told the watchful board. 'Unfortunately we found out three hours ago that she's still lying to herself and to others.'

'Am not!' Fern muttered, toeing the ground. She wondered what they'd heard, seen, discovered. She hoped she could find a plausible story that would make any wrongdoing right.

'Fern, this is your last chance to tell the truth about why you were loitering in that department store,' the psychiatrist said evenly.

'I've told you the truth already!' Fern lied.

'If you continue to lie like this you'll receive your most stringent ever punishment,' prompted the eldest of the female board members.

'I've nothing to hide,' Fern muttered, convinced that they couldn't prove otherwise.

'Very well, we have no option but to bring you before the bench again for an internal court hearing,' Dr Marshall concluded. He nodded to the guard. 'Take the prisoner to Courtroom One. We'll try her immediately. And use the handcuffs. If she receives the penalty she deserves for this continual self-delusion she'll probably try to escape to save her bum.'

A few moments later Fern found herself stumbling towards the seat of judgement, dreading the prospect of standing before yet another magistrate. The ones she'd already encountered had made her keep her skirts raised whilst they thrashed and fondled her bare backside.

News of her latest trial had spread quickly round *Compulsion*. As Fern sat in the dock awaiting the judicial hearing, inmates filled seat after seat in the public gallery, and began murmuring amongst themselves. Again and again Fern smoothed the plain shirt dress over her knees as if to remind herself of her own increasingly unprovocative nature and wholesome desires. They couldn't find her guilty of anything – could they? Nurse Bryson had teased Fern in the stirrups then penetrated her, but she hadn't actually *seduced* a man for weeks!

'The court will rise,' said the clerk as the magistrate entered. Or was he a judge or a justice of the peace?'

Fern stared at the man as he took his seat. Jurisprudence had never been her strong point. Not that it mattered, *Compulsion* doubtlessly had its own legal framework, its own punitive regime.

When the judge sat, the inmates in the public gallery did likewise. 'The prisoner will stand,' he said, frowning at her. Fern hastened to do as she was bid.

When did you go to the store. Why? Why? Why? Forcing back a yawn she answered their questions by reiterating her recent criminal history. 'I'd like to offer the security guard I injured some victim support when I leave,' she finished, remembering how the schoolteacher at *Compulsion* had suggested this act of reparation to Angela the petty thief.

'How magnanimous of you to give up your precious time, Miss Terris,' the judge said.

Fern wanted to stick out her tongue at the man, but she knew better. She kept it firmly against the floor of her mouth. It was a mouth that was no longer nervous and dry, for she knew she'd fooled them. She knew that they couldn't produce evidence that would show there was more to the truth.

'Bring on the witness for the prosecution, Wanda Miles,' ordered the clerk of the court.

Wanda! Fern felt the cold shock ice its way through her. No, it couldn't be! She'd been so careful to protect the slightly older girl, had never once mentioned her name to the police or the other prisoners. She still wouldn't implicate Wanda in the arson incident, no matter how often they warmed her backside.

As she watched, Wanda walked slowly in and was guided towards the witness box. She was dressed in the backless silver blouse and tiny ra-ra shirt that comprised *Compulsion*'s punishment uniform. As she teetered forward on the silver high-heeled shoes the stiffened skirt lifted further at the back to reveal a well-thrashed red bum.

How could they hurt her like that? They'd pay for this! They'd ... Fern tugged impotently at the handcuffs.

'State your name, age and occupation,' the opposition lawyer said to the costumed brunette.

'I'm Wanda Miles. I'm twenty-eight. I've recently been working as a stablehand,' Wanda said.

'And before that?' the lawyer prompted.

'I was ... supported by my parents, sir.'

Too right she was, Fern thought. She wondered if Wanda was really working with horses. Maybe she'd been told to say that by her attorney as a means of sounding gainfully employed. Wanda had been like her – a party animal. Someone who shopped by day and danced by night.

She sighed. Mind you, Wanda had fled the city after the fire that night. Fern had fruitlessly tried to contact her whilst out on bail awaiting trial. But Wanda had obviously feared she'd be implicated in the security guard's injuries, and who could blame her? She wasn't to know that Fern was willing to cover up Wanda's part in the crime.

'Tell us what happened on the day of the fire,' the opposition ordered.

Wanda nodded gently: 'Fern and I had been drinking in a wine bar. We were ... flirting with each other.'

Christ, Wanda was going to tell the truth! Fern closed her eyes. How could her friend say such damning words within earshot of strangers? She, Fern, had been so careful with each lie.

'You mean you were building up to a lesbian dalliance?' the prosecution asked.

'I think so, sir. Fern was putting her hand on my upper arm, ruffling my hair at any opportunity.'

'And you welcomed this, Miss Miles?'

'I . . . wasn't sure.'

You seemed reasonably sure to me, Fern thought bitterly. She gazed at Wanda's calm green eyes, willing the older girl to look back at her. She studied Wanda's elfin-cut brown hair and slightly sturdy body and knew that she still wanted to take her friend in her arms. Or to her bed, for Wanda's five-foot-eight-inch frame was somehow both masculine and feminine. She had the soft breasts of a woman, the harder flatter hips of a man.

She also suddenly had the honesty of an angel. What on earth had happened to change her so totally, Fern thought in despair?

'I think Fern didn't have the courage to make a full pass at me,' she was saying now. Fern shook her head slightly as if to shake the shameful truth away. 'So she suggested we go to the lingerie department just before closing and hide there. You know, to have our own underwear show after the staff had gone home for the night.'

The lawyer nodded: 'And you agreed to this?'

It was Wanda's turn to nod. 'I was curious, I guess. I'd never been with a woman. Part of me wanted to. The other part was scared.'

'But the curious part won?' the lawyer queried.

Wanda shrugged: 'I guess so. That is, I went to the store and hid with her behind some racks of satin housecoats. Then we crept out when we had the place to ourselves and started holding up bustiers and basques, dancing with the nighties. Things like that.'

'What was your physical state at the time, Miss Miles?' the lawyer asked.

'I was drunk. Very drunk,' Wanda admitted.

'And Miss Terris?'

169

'She was very drunk as well.'

'Go on,' the opposition said.

'Well, we kept drinking from our hip flasks and acting silly. It was like neither of us dared to make the first move, to start kissing. Finally we got tired and sat down, then fell asleep.'

'What happened when you awoke?' the lawyer asked.

'Fern was still asleep. I had a dry mouth and a sore head. I decided to go find the cafeteria and the pharmacy department. It was whilst I was on another floor that the flames broke out.'

'And do you smoke, Miss Miles?' the lawyer asked softly.

'No, sir – I never have.'

'So your only crime was staying in the department store after hours,' the judge butted in.

'My crimes include lethargy and lack of purpose, M'lord,' Wanda said clearly.

Fern stared at her – what the hell was this hair-shirt approach all about?

'I should add that my client has come forward of her own volition,' said the defence. 'Her conscience was troubling her. In fact she insisted we take a belt to her backside.'

'Did she now?' the judge queried, raising one eye. He turned to the witness. 'And what brought on this sudden full confession?'

Wanda faced him square on: 'I'm adopted sir, and recently I tracked down my real parents. After the incident in the store I fled the city and went to stay with them.' She lifted her chin. 'They're good people, honest hard-working people. They run a small stables and to pay for my keep I had to help out.' She cleared her throat. 'At first I felt resentful, too good for such work. But then I started to enjoy getting up early and breathing in the country air, gathering the new hay. I liked eating fresh vegetables and feeling my body become exercised and strong.'

The man nodded. 'Yet you gave all that up to come back here and confess to us.'

Wanda let her breath out in an extended sigh: 'I kept reliving the scene, hated the fact that Fern and I couldn't

170

be honest about what we wanted.' She looked at the ground. 'About what we wanted *then*.'

The judge peered over. 'You don't want this lesbian relationship now, Miss Miles?'

'No, sir. It would just have been another kick, something to hint at for the next few parties. I've met a man I admire – a man who breeds horses. I plan to continue our courtship when I'm released,' Wanda said.

The judge looked at his report book. 'I'm tempted to release you now, for you've obviously remade yourself in a better image. But I sense that you want to be punished for your earlier wrongdoing, so sentence you to one month here as a kitchen hand.'

'Yes, sir. Thank you, sir,' Wanda said. She took hold of the ra-ra skirt and curtseyed, then looked at Fern and smiled with relief.

Feeling rage and envy race through her, Fern looked away.

Wanda left. The judge beckoned to Fern: 'The prisoner will approach the bench.'

On suddenly locked knees, Fern walked stiltedly towards him.

'Lie over my lap, dear, whilst I pronounce sentence,' he said.

Tensing her bum cheeks and thighs, Fern did as she was told. She felt glad that she was wearing lacy pink panties, even if they only covered half of her helpless orbs.

'Why were you sent here in the first place?' the man asked, lifting her shirt dress and stroking her bottom through her briefs.

'To learn to be a better person, sir,' Fern muttered, breathing raggedly.

'And do good people lie about their motives and desires, my dear?' he continued.

'I . . . I guess not,' Fern said.

The judiciary continued to fondle her wriggling bum.

'Have you heard that this building comprises two parts, Miss Terris?'

Fern swallowed, recalling warnings made by various staff and inmates. 'Yes, sir,' she answered reluctantly.

The man ran a finger across the backs of her thighs: 'And what have you heard about the second part?'

'That it's a hidden part of *Compulsion* which visiting officials will never see, M'Lord,' the girl muttered.

She could hear the smile in the man's voice. 'It is indeed!'

The magistrate was obviously enjoying keeping her guessing about her fate as she wriggled across his knees. 'It's a building with stringent apparatus to hold sore bums,' he said eventually. 'A building where we can teach a naughty girl honesty and respect.' He pushed her from his lap, 'Strip, my dear, then kneel to have your collar fitted in place.'

Not looking at anyone, Fern obeyed him. Youths whistled from the public gallery as she unbuttoned her shirt dress, then unfastened her pink lace bra. Trying not to think of how hard the guards were going to whip her poor bum, she pulled down the matching lace pink panties, then stood, naked, her arms hanging awkwardly by her sides.

'Kneel,' the magistrate reminded her. She knelt. The carpet was thick and warm under her extremities. She looked up as Ms Lenn approached holding a studded slave collar in her slender right hand.

'I'm sorry I lied, Ms Lenn,' she murmured, meaning it.

'Be good in Building Two and don't give them a reason to make you even more sorry,' the admissions officer said.

'Will they thrash me really hard?' Fern whispered, wondering how many strokes of the cane she could bear on her naked bottom.

'They will – but I suspect it'll be the making of you,' the officer replied, then smiled. She looked more closely at the girl: 'You've been holding back all these lesbian desires, Fern. Now that they're starting to come out . . .'

'Less talking and more fastening of that collar,' the judge said sharply.

Ms Lenn looked over. 'I'll admit her to the second building myself, Your Honour. I'm just briefing her now on what to expect.'

'Tell her to expect no mercy,' said the man. 'She's had countless opportunities to admit her past misconduct. If Miss Miles hadn't come forward today . . .'

'Sorry, sir,' Fern said, looking at him through the dark lashes of her eyes. She felt afraid yet strangely relieved. She somehow felt closer to being cleansed.

She kept her neck still as Ms Lenn tightened the leather collar in place, though she winced as the older woman fastened a lead to it.

'Can't I just walk?' she asked tremulously.

The judge leaned forward. 'No, you've shown the morals of an alley cat so you have to move like one now.' He nodded to Ms Lenn. 'Fasten protective pads to her knees, though – she'll be crawling quite a distance. And it's only her arse we want to tan.'

Fern smiled gratefully as the admissions officer strapped the grey pads into place. Ms Lenn jerked on the lead and Fern put both arms then one knee out and started an awkward, shamed crawl up the busy court.

'Bye bye white bum, hello red one!' laughed a man from the front row, risking a sly slap at her bottom.

'You'll take two hot cheeks of your own for contempt of court,' the magistrate warned.

Hand. Hand. Knee. Knee. Fern found that crawling to Building Two took a tiringly long time. Ms Lenn let her stop for short rests, then pulled at the lead to urge her to crawl faster.

'Sooner you get this punishment over with the sooner you get back to us,' she said.

'How long will I be in this section?' Fern asked, her naked thighs and calves beginning to ache.

The admissions officer shrugged: 'Could be a day, a week, a month. It's unlikely to be longer.'

'Because of your internal rules?' Fern asked wearily.

'No, because after a few reddened bums in Building Two the inmates hasten to obey and are sent back cured!'

'This is the biggest corridor I've ever been in!' Fern added, hastily changing the subject from reddened bums.

'It's more like an under-the-cliffs road,' the admissions officer explained. 'We found some very large and high tunnels across the bay and turned them into the second building. We blocked off the original entrances, so this is the only approach.'

173

'Why bother when Building One's so large?' the girl queried.

'Penal Liaisons knows about Building One – though they don't all know about the corporal punishment we mete out here.' She pulled more firmly at Fern's lead as if to remind her of her lowly status. 'We need a second section we can put inmates with hot bums into if an impromptu inspectorate arrives.'

'Do they often arrive?' Fern asked.

'When we're miles from anywhere? No, we seldom see anyone official as they've got the option of nice short visits to establishments near London. But just in case . . .' She smiled sympathetically down at Fern as they approached a solid metal door. 'It also means the guards in Building Two can keep restraint equipment and punishment devices constantly on display and in use.'

Punishment devices that would hold her naughty nether orbs! Fern quivered as Ms Lenn spoke some muffled password into the intercom by the door. The pair of them were instantly admitted by a tall blond man dressed in a *Compulsion* guard's uniform. Some things didn't change, then, Fern mused, crawling obediently forward. What *would* be changing was the colour and tenderness of her poor arse.

As if to confirm her fears, the guard issued his first mocking orders. 'Let's get that wicked bare bum onto a punishment rack so that we can teach it obedience.'

'I'll be good – you don't have to chastise me!' Fern gasped. She could feel her heartbeat increasing its tempo throughout her naked body. It had been a long time since she'd felt so apprehensive – or so alive. Still she tried to pull away as Ms Lenn handed the lead to her new captor.

'Bad dog,' the man murmured, unclipping the leash from her collar. He hooked his thumb inside the neck restraint so that he held her in place. Before Fern could fathom out his plan, he'd doubled the leash and brought it down four times swiftly on her helpless rounded cheeks.

'Aaah!' Fern cried out, trying to squirm away from the stinging lash.

'That's just to remind you to come to heel when you're

called,' said the man, clipping the lead onto her collar again.

Fern scrabbled forward, anxious to avoid further transgressions as he started to march towards a second door.

'Be good,' she heard Ms Lenn mutter.

She tried to turn round and say something to the admissions officer but the guard jerked her head towards the front and continued relentlessly on his chosen journey.

'She means to be a good dog,' he called back, his enjoyment of the situation evident. 'When you finally come back for her I suspect she'll gladly give you a paw.'

Flushing, Fern stared at the ground as she crawled along in true canine fashion. She was just going to get through her time here as quickly and quietly as possible. She wouldn't respond to the man's humiliating jibes.

'Right, little pup, let's get you settled in your new home,' the guard continued as they walked into the next room and faced the seven foot square punishment rack.

Still holding her leash, he strode to the bolster in the middle of the rack, and patted its leather contours. 'Put your warm tummy here, little puppy, and stretch out these naughty arms and legs to their fullest extent.' He kept the leash taut as she moved, as if ready to pull her smartly forward if she dallied. But Fern was resigned to her whipping; she just wanted to make amends.

Dutifully she rested her belly on one twelve-inch high leather arc and let her arms and legs stretch out along the rack towards the ankle and wrist restraints. She watched nervously as the guard fastened the latter two in place. She tensed her tummy muscles as he walked back and reached for her left leg, pulling it out to one side of the rack and fastening it in place. Obediently she stretched out her right calf and let him bind it in place.

'We use two bigger straps here on the rack as well. They help us emphasise the girl's bare bottom,' the guard said conversationally, reaching to the side of the device and bringing up another restraint.

'Don't boys get thrashed here too, then?' Fern muttered, feeling her heartbeat speed.

The man nodded: 'If they've been very resistant, they get the judicial cane.'

'I've not been resistant!' Fern added, hugely aware that they could apply whatever whip or rod they liked to her helplessly displayed naked buttocks.

'No, you've been repressive and untruthful,' the guard said. 'And what happens to repressed and lying bums?' he added, tightening the latest strap over her waist and back.

'They get punished, sir,' Fern whispered sorrowfully.

'That's right,' said the man, pulling another strap across the back of her thighs and buckling it in place. 'They get their arses warmed really long and hard.' He stroked her trembling orbs, 'And after that their new master takes them walkies on their leads for the rest of the day.'

'Yes, sir. I'll walk real pretty, sir,' Fern muttered, forcing the words through clenched teeth. She wondered nervously who her new master would be. 'Can I ask who . . .?' she started.

'No. A good dog is a quiet dog,' the guard said.

He walked to the wall that Fern was facing, and selected an implement from one of the many martinets and paddles hanging there. Smiling he strolled back and held the punisher in front of her. 'Now, my pet, have you seen or felt a heavy strop before?'

'I . . . don't think so, sir,' Fern said. She stared fixedly at the black leather implement with its curved wooden handle. It was over two foot long and around two inches wide. Fern didn't want to even think about how thick it was!

'I'm going to raise it high and bring it down low to teach this bad little bum a long sore lesson,' said the man.

Fern held her breath as she heard his footsteps move towards her raised bare backside. It was a most vulnerable target. Her buttocks were small and tender, whilst the leather implement was wide and hard.

'Ready, sweetheart?' the guard asked.

Fern knew she'd never be ready. Mutely she shook her head.

'You should have thought of the consequences before

176

you lied,' said the man. 'You should have pictured the heavy strop coming down on your flinching bottom.'

Here they went again, Fern thought: the therapy before the thrashing. No pain no gain. 'I've apologised,' she forced out, 'I won't repeat my crimes, sir.'

'No, but you'll commit other misdemeanours unless we penalise your pretty young haunches,' her jailor said.

Fern sensed him drawing back the arm holding the strop, then its heat exploded across the centre of her bum cheeks. God, that hurt like blazes! She cried out and moved her limbs the little she could.

'Save the wounded sounds for later, love,' murmured the man.

Fern stiffened: the stripe across her bum was already a burning fire. She licked her lips: 'How much later?'

'Well, you're getting twenty of these,' the guard said matter of factly, 'I suggest you start howling round about lash ten.'

Twenty! She'd go mad with the pain, with the inability to rub at her punished buttocks. 'Please,' she whispered, 'I've reformed. Give me less.'

'Well, there is a way,' the guard admitted.

The change of air around her buttocks told her that he'd raised the strop again. 'I'll take the alternative,' Fern said quickly.

'We'll have a proper talk in a couple of minutes,' the guard said, 'you've got to take at least another three of these strokes.'

Fern yelled as the heavy strop brought the heat to the topmost backs of her thighs. Now she realised why the guard had fastened straps over her body. He only thrashed her within their dark confines, marking the fleshiest portions of her buttocks – but not her back or legs – inch by merciless inch. She was halfway there, assuming he agreed to let her have an alternative punishment. Fern closed her eyes and her teeth and waited for lash number three.

When it came, it tenderised the upper cheeks of her bum. She was still writhing from its effects when the lower more sensitive portion was lashed by the fourth stroke. Fern tried to push her belly flat against the bolster, tried to swing her hips from side to side. 'Please,' she whispered, writhing. 'Just let me touch my bum for a moment.'

'Sorry, we never allow an inmate to protect her punished bottom,' the guard said.

God, he was merciless, in word as well as in deed.

'You said I could do a different form of penance instead,' Fern said pleadingly. The man could put her over his knee or make her bend over the desk and submit to a caning. Anything other than this.

'This is the most severe thrashing a girl here's ever likely to receive,' admitted the man, 'so we have an alternative less physically painful option for those who can't bear it. It's much more shameful, though.' He started to unfasten the restraints from her wrists.

'I'll take it! I deserve to be shamed – I've done shameful things,' Fern said quickly. She thought that was the best ever line she'd come up with. Dr Marshall would be impressed if he could see her now. A sudden thought hit her brain and she put it into words. 'Oh God, you're not making Dr Marshall my temporary master?' She so wanted the psychiatrist to see her as someone who was functioning, healthy, cured.

'No way – he's kept busy in Building One,' the guard replied, continuing to unfasten her bindings. He freed her legs and body, then said, 'No more questions, angel. You're getting off lightly on the physical front so you can't expect to be told exactly what's in store.'

'But if you could just . . .' Fern continued, pushing for answers.

'Now I'm going to have to tell your new master that you've disobeyed me already, that you deserve chastising right away,' the guard said.

'No! Please . . .'

'Shut up and get onto the floor on your hands and knees,' ordered the man.

Not daring to risk a quick rub at her smarting bum, Fern did so. She bit her lip as he fastened the lead onto her dog collar again. He tied the end of the lead to a hook set high in the wall, then came back with two long bar-shaped devices which had hoops on them. 'These are spreaders,' he explained.

'What do they . . .? Fern tailed off, not sure that she wanted to know.

'They keep your ankles a certain distance from each other and do the same with your wrists,' the man said easily.

'But why do you want to?' she muttered.

The guard smiled. 'Your new master has suggested it.' He fingered the devices. 'Don't worry – he'll remove them every so often to limit your discomfort. Wearing them means you'll have to crawl slowly and can't run away.'

'I crawl slowly already,' Fern said, hardly able to believe that she was using such words with relative equanimity. 'And I'm committed to the regime here. I promise I won't escape.'

'You might change your mind when you see what he's got in store for you,' added the guard, bending to fasten the spreaders between her two sets of limbs. Fern swallowed hard when he was through: now she couldn't touch her bum or her clit, which was somehow wet and swollen with wanting. Yet her tormentor could do what he liked!

'Let's introduce you to your master, you naughty dog,' the man said mockingly. He pressed a buzzer on the wall, then removed the handle of the lead from its hook again. He pulled the strap through his hand till he had Fern on a very tight leash indeed. 'The bad pup's ready for walkies,' he said, as the connecting door between the rooms opened.

Fern looked up to see the man who was to bring her to heel for an indeterminate length of time. It was Rab! She stared up at the grinning oaf who'd driven the van that originally brought her to *Compulsion*; the man who'd tied her over a fence and spanked her disarmed bare bum. Dr Marshall had warned her that Rab loved to thrash wayward girls, that it was hard to get him to stop once he started.

'She opted for time with you rather than twenty of the heavy strop,' said the guard, handing her lead over to the driver.

'I've changed my mind!' Fern said through a half-formed breath.

Shame was rushing through every pore as Rab gleefully eyed her naked breasts and haunches. She couldn't bear it if he was allowed to get her on her own.

'As you can hear, the dog's been whining a lot,' the guard said over her head. 'As its new owner you'll have to give it a thrashing for being so noisy.'

'Aye, I'll warm the little pup's arse all right,' Rab replied.

Fern winced as he pulled on her lead, drawing her closer to his jean-clad right leg.

'I'll take her for a walk in the grounds then teach her obedience in my room,' he continued. 'Just give me a phone call when ye want her back.'

'Does Dr Marshall know I'm being trained like this?' Fern asked desperately, staring up at the guard. She daren't add *trained by this pig*, or a similar insult in case Rab took it out on her defenceless backside.

'Dr Marshall just said we were to be very strict with you because you'd had lesbian fantasies about which you'd consistently lied,' said the man.

'A lesbian puppy, is it?' Rab laughed.

Fern looked up at him to see that his already small eyes were going even more narrow, 'I'll soon take the doggie's mind off of other women,' he said.

It was awful to be spoken to like an animal in front of the guard. How she wished she'd told the truth about fancying Wanda! They'd have made her talk everything through which she found difficult, but they'd have understood.

'Exercise time!' Rab continued. He reined in Fern's lead till her nose was almost touching the back of his knee. Then he moved forward, forcing her to crawl behind him.

The spreaders ensured that she couldn't punch him over and thus try to escape. Not that she had the heart for a fight, Fern realised as she ambled along like a clumsy human sheepdog. If she could just get through the next few weeks at *Compulsion* she'd again be eligible for parole. And she'd hopefully spend most of the time leading up to her parole hearing back in Building One. If they let her back she'd become a model inmate! Surely Dr Marshall wouldn't leave her for long with the compassionless Rab?

'Give the nice man a paw,' he said now as a moustached man in his thirties approached them. Blushing, Fern held out her hand.

'Good girl,' the stranger said. He winked at Rab, 'I hope you've had her wormed?'

'Oh I'll be examining her tender parts all right. Don't worry,' Rab answered.

He walked up to a bank of fir trees and said, 'Right, doggie, it's time to raise your back leg.'

'But I don't need to,' Fern muttered. The stranger was still looking on, obviously keen to see her shamefully display her body functions.

'Well, you can use the litter tray in my room later on – I got it for you special, like,' Rab said.

God, he was a scheming hard-headed bastard! She'd make sure that she never fell into his gloating clutches again.

'I see you've let go of some liquid already,' Rab continued.

Fern tensed her thighs with shame as she felt the traitorous sex juice dripping from her labia. It made no sense for this humbled crawling posture to excite her. Yet little in her life had made sense.

She felt tired by the time he'd finished walking her down the paths and across the grass. The sun went behind a cloud and she shivered as a cooler wind caressed her naked breasts and buttocks.

'Don't fret, my bonny bitch – we'll soon warm these bits up,' Rab said. Obviously excited at the prospect of smacking her unprotected bottom, he quickened his step.

Crawling as quickly as she could on her leash, Fern was surprised when he went back into Building Two and along a corridor. Didn't he live in the first building like her, then? She wondered if it would bring prolonged painful censure to her helpless backside if she asked. There again, talking might get him on her side, might lessen his wrath a little.

He'd forget about the spoilt little bitch who'd snubbed him in the van, and would see her as a good girl who'd fully reformed!

'Do you live here all the time?' she asked as he pushed open the door to a large bedsitting room.

'Except when I'm on the road,' Rab said. 'You know, collecting a lad or lass from way down in England or from one of the islands.'

'Making a long journey. Right,' Fern clarified after a moments thought.

Rab used a mixture of local dialect and slangy expressions and Fern had to concentrate quite hard on each word he said. Unfortunately her new master seemed to realise this.

'See if I met the likes of you in a pub, you wouldn't give me the time of day,' he muttered sourly.

Fern realised it was true: once when a working man had asked her the time she'd told him to buy himself a Rolex watch. Christ, she'd been so snooty in those days!

'I'm not talking about you accepting a date or nothing,' Rab continued, 'I mean if I even asked you a civil question you'd have told me to shut my face.'

'Not now,' Fern said, meaning not now that I've spent time at *Compulsion*.

'No – not now when you're wearing your collar and lead and I'm your new owner,' Rab said.

Damn it – she hadn't meant to remind him of that fact! Fern trembled as he sat down on the edge of the bed and reined in the slack of the lead until her chin was resting on his calf side.

'Is the bad wee bitch going over my lap voluntarily, or do I have to put her there?' he said.

'I'll do what you want, master,' Fern muttered, snorting with shame. She half rose then let her spreader-held wrists bring her arms down on the other side of his knees. Then she stretched her spreader-held legs out behind her. Now she was reduced to the status of a bare bum lying defencelessly across his trousered lap.

'*Master* now, is it?' the man sneered.

Fern felt his rough workday hands on her smooth young bum, squeezing and releasing each portion.

'It's a while since I've lifted my palm to these cheeks,' he added, obviously thinking back to the first time they'd met.

'Yes, sir,' Fern said, trying to sound slavishly obsequious. Inside she felt disarmed and ashamed.

'This spanking's for talking when the guard told you to shut up,' Rab said. He raised his hand. 'If at any time I forget to tell you what your latest thrashing is for, you just remind me, right?'

'Yes sir,' Fern said quickly. She wondered just how many spankings she was going to get in the ensuing hours or days. 'What else are you going to do to me?' she whispered, tensing.

'To your hide, you mean? Not too much – that guard set limits. But I'm allowed to warm your arse as much as I want with my hand.'

Fern quivered over the man's strong knees at the thought of the number of times her bum was going to feel his hateful palm. She wondered again how on earth Wanda could have given herself voluntarily to the police and asked to be sent to *Compulsion*. Then Rab's hard hand came crashing down on her nude right buttock and she thought of nothing except her tender charms.

Christ, the man could spank! She cried out as he roasted her left cheek with an echoing severity. She wriggled as he slapped at the full curve of her heated rotundities before warming the tops of her thighs.

'Ah! Uh! Hm!' Fern grunted, driving her belly against his lap in a fruitless bid to make her bum a smaller target.

'You're not going anywhere, sweetheart,' Rab said, half-laughing, and pushed his knees up under her tummy in order to raise her bottom high in the air again.

Then he smacked that same bum for trying to evade his hand. He smacked it for not admitting to its lesbian desires. He smacked it for making too much noise and too few promises.

'I'm sorry I tried to wriggle away!' Fern gasped. 'Sorry I didn't tell the truth about fancying Wanda! Sorry I spoke back to the guard when he told me to be quiet!'

She allowed herself to relax slightly as Rab stopped spanking and started fondling her bum.

'I'm glad you've told the truth at last,' he said, moving his whole hand over her small red cheeks in a pincerlike gesture. 'Glad you're starting to be good.' He squeezed more firmly at first her right cheek then her left. Fern winced. 'Problem is,' he continued, 'when I've a snooty bum like this under my palms they just want to spank on.'

'But I've said I'm sorry,' Fern muttered, pulling ineffectually at the spreader holding her wrists. 'Dr Marshall and the others stop punishing me when I'm truly repentant.'

'Truly repentant, are you?' Rab repeated the phrase mimicking her well-modulated tones. 'Pity I've just gone deaf, ain't it, love?'

Worse and worse. Fern wished she hadn't been rude to him that day in the van. She wished she'd never been rude to anyone. Her character was becoming much nicer, yet this bastard was determined not to see!

'I'll tell the others if you keep spanking me when I've apologised,' she muttered.

Rab spanked both her cheeks again: 'By the time I've finished with you you'll just be begging the others to put cold cream on your roasting hot arse.'

'I'm supposed to get pleasure too!' Fern gasped between whimpers. The words felt as if they were being wrung from her. They were some of the last words she wanted to say – but her clitoris was a swollen nub of needing. And the shaven purse between her legs had been pulsing for ever so long.

'Want Master Rab up your hot little hole, do you, love?' the driver taunted, smacking the backs of her thighs despite her wriggles.

'Whatever,' Fern muttered, praying that he'd turn his attention to the glistening leaves between her legs.

'Tell you what,' said Rab, putting one of his fingertips lightly against her clitoris. 'I'll give you a choice of actions.'

'Anything!' Fern gasped out, pushing her pleasure bud against his unmoving digit. If he'd just stroke her lightly she'd climax in the shortest time.

'What I'm proposing,' Rab continued, 'is that you take part in a show for the inmates and staff here at Building Two, after which I'll give you an orgasm.'

'Or?' Fern prompted.

'Or,' Rab said, 'I'll go and watch the show alone and you can stay here tied to the bed so that you can't touch yourself.' He ran his fingertip lightly across the needful nub until Fern groaned.

'I'll take part in the show,' she muttered when Rab took his enchantment-giving hand away. She felt a mixture of relief and disappointment as the man helped her up off of his knees and down onto her knees. She was glad that he'd stopped spanking her, but was desolate at the loss of his sexy touch.

'Let's get these spreaders off,' Rab continued as she rested, doggy-fashion, on the floor. He removed both sets of the rigid bars. Fern flexed her wrists and ankles. 'Reckon you're ready,' the driver said.

Fern looked up at him, her eyes pleading: 'Master, aren't you going to take off my collar and lead?'

'Nah,' Rab said. He started to walk towards the door, pulling her behind him.

'But you said I was to take part in a show,' Fern continued, reluctantly crawling faster.

'Yeah – a dog show,' Rab said.

Eleven

A dog show, no less! Five minutes later Fern crawled on her collar and lead into a large well-lit room. Five other girls and two boys were already on leather leashes held by their owners. As she stared, one of the boys rolled over on command to have his bare tummy tickled.

'They've been to obedience classes,' Rab said.

'But I haven't!' muttered Fern, casting sideways glances at a girl in her twenties who was prancing fawningly round her trainer.

'Lets hope you learn fast then, sweetheart,' Rab said, 'else the man in charge'll take a rolled up newspaper to your lazy backside.'

She didn't doubt it. Fern looked up at the dog handler in the centre of the room and he stared back at her, unsmiling. His dark eyes raked her currently pendulous smooth young breasts. Fern longed to stand up so that her teats were round and firm; she longed to be free of this collar and lead.

But the alternative was a long day and night of sexual denial. Better to just get through this shameful showcase! The reward for behaving like a dog was to come like a bitch in heat under Rab's taunting hands. Okay, so she loathed the man, but her body somehow loved what he did to her. In an effort to speed her pleasure, Fern now nuzzled at the back of his leg.

'Don't go sex-crazed on me yet – you've hours of training to get through,' Rab said snidely.

Christ, she hated him. And she hated being here with this head dog handler who kept staring at her tits. 'What do I have to do?' she muttered, looking round the hall at the empty floorspace. There was a large tarpaulin arched over something in the centre. She wondered what was underneath.

'You listen to what you're told, then you follow the instructions,' Rab replied. 'Should make a change.'

'I've followed instructions for ages!' Fern said. 'Well, almost,' she added, realising it paid to be truthful. If this coarse bastard caught her lying she dreaded to think the colour he'd turn her already-tender spanked rear end.

'I see this dog's been especially bad,' the dog handler said, suddenly slapping at Fern's red bum.

Fern flinched, then tensed and stared at the ground. She hadn't heard him approach as she'd been studying the tarpaulin.

'Aye, she's certainly felt my hand against her backside,' Rab replied.

'We're putting the animals on the tables now so that we can examine them. She won't bite, will she?' the handler continued, staring down at Fern as he walked slowly round her naked frame.

'If she does I'll muzzle her!' Rab laughed. He tugged at the lead, 'Come on, my pretty. Time to display you to the world like a good wee doggy.'

The dog handler nodded to one of the guards at the door and called, 'You can let the audience in, now, Tom.'

To Fern's chagrin, inmate after inmate hurried through the side doors leading to the ringside circle. She hesitated, and Rab urged her on.

'Any resistance and we'll fit a choke chain, sweetheart.' Chastened, Fern limbered forward again.

The six girls and youths she'd watched at the onset were already clambering onto the high display tables. Tugging at her lead, Rab led her to a vacant one. Trying not to notice all the staring eyes and pointing fingers of the audience, Fern climbed onto the wooden surface and posed on her hands and knees.

She watched the dog handler touch and tease the other human dogs. Then it was her turn.

'Right little puppy,' the dark-eyed stranger said gloatingly, 'let's take a look at your teeth.'

188

He ran his fingers over Fern's lips, the gesture an oddly exciting one. Her lips seemed to part of their own volition. Then he traced the top surfaces of her teeth.

'And your ears,' he added.

He stroked the small pink lobes, then fingered the shell-like orifices inside. Again his touch was humiliatingly pleasing.

'Good dog,' he said, and patted her glossy head. He turned to Rab, who was still holding the end of her leash. 'Has she been mounted yet?' he queried.

'Nah, but I'm planning to take care of it,' Rab said with a wink and a grin.

'No pups?' the handler continued.

'She's nowt but a pup herself,' the driver replied contemptuously.

Fern felt another trickle of lust make its way down her inner thigh at their taunting, and had to admit that she was a very needy pup indeed.

'Better check the creature's rectum and vulva,' said the man in charge. Fern moaned as he circled her bottom hole with his fingers. 'Obviously in heat,' he continued, 'has been for some time.'

'She can wait a while yet,' Rab muttered.

'Mm? No, I like to see a young dog's sexual response before an audience,' the dog handler said thoughtfully. 'Don't worry, my man – we'll soon tease her into a sexual frenzy again.'

He called to the nearest guard to bring a finger bowl and medicated soap. Carefully he washed his hands. 'Just to make sure we don't transfer bacteria from her back passage to her front passage,' he said, as if thinking out loud.

'You what?' Rab asked.

The dog handler stared coldly at the driver: 'The human rectum is full of bacteria, so we can unwittingly give her cystitis if we transfer germs to her sex.'

He lifted his wet fingers from the bowl and began to dry them on a towel as he continued to stare: 'Looks like it's time you reread *Compulsion*'s manual, and learned all the safety guidelines. If you mistreat this little dog we'll have to take her away.'

'I've been doing all right – she's got wet enough under my fingers,' Rab said quickly.

'And now she'll have satisfaction under mine,' the dog handler replied. He stroked Fern's previously well-spanked rump. 'Let's get you lying across your doggie basket, sweetheart, with your little legs wide open.'

Oblivious to everything except her soaking heat-heavy crotch, Fern obeyed.

The stranger holding her leash now, she crawled over to the wicker canine bed and knelt before it. The man tugged gently at her collar, urging her forward till her soft belly settled in the central hollow, her arms and legs stretched out on either side.

'God, you need this, sweetheart,' he said sliding his right hand between the backs of her thighs and moving it towards her ecstasy button.

Everyone here called her patronising names like *sweetheart* or *pet* here, Fern thought sullenly. Then the man located the exact source of her pleasure and she decided he could call her whatever he liked.

'Such a hot little bitch,' he murmured. Further heat rushed to her groin. Fern whimpered. 'So desperate,' he added, stroking round and round and round.

His touch was gentle yet assured. He understood exactly how to please a lust-crazed clitoris. Knew that she needed to come soon, that she'd undergone enough taunting during her spanking and her walk in the grounds.

'Beg nicely for my fingers,' he said softly.

'I beg. Oh Christ, I beg!' Fern whispered. Then she made a low guttural sound that filled the hall and filtered through the roof and the many windows as her climax surged through.

When the last rapture-led contractions had passed, Fern slumped more fully into the basket.

'Curl up inside it. Rest. We'll continue your training after you've napped,' the dog handler said softly. He nodded to the guards, 'Bring the pup a nice warm blanket.'

Fern smiled at him gratefully. Then she slept.

When she awoke the clock on the wall showed that forty

minutes had passed. She sat up and stared dazedly around her. She saw immediately that the audience was still there, and that the other collar-led inmates were performing tricks. The tarpaulin had been removed to reveal a canine obstacle course. Both youths were slinking gallantly through the perspex tunnels whilst the girls crawled nimbly up a wooden slope and down the other side.

'Hey – she's with us again,' came Rab's hateful voice. Fern looked up at him warily.

'Ah, the sleepy young pup awakes!' the dog handler confirmed, walking over to stand next to him. He looked more closely at Fern. 'Are you thirsty, pet?'

'Yes, sir.' Orgasm always seemed to drain her body of its existing fluid. Fern's mouth and throat felt coppery and dry.

'Lets get the doggy a drink, then,' smiled the man, taking hold of her lead.

Fern crawled behind him till they came to a set of canine drinking bowls. The others were half empty.

'The rest of the pack has already been for drinkies,' the dog handler said.

'You mean I've to . . .' Fern looked dully at the bowl.

'That's the way a dog drinks, isn't it?' the man prompted.

Fern faltered: 'I . . . guess.'

They were doing this for her own good, but at that moment she truly detested them. Did they have to make her humiliation this prolonged? Doubtless they were going by the book: the inimitable Dr Marshall has probably worked out how many shamings and orgasms it took to turn a thoughtless party animal into a useful woman of the world.

'Lap your water all up now,' the handler said.

Fern bent her face to the liquid then dipped her tongue in it. Mm, that was refreshing! When she lifted her right hand to wipe her mouth, the man swatted it away.

'Drink like a *dog*,' he reminded her, 'no hands, love.'

'Sorry, I was brought up with good table manners,' Fern said.

She felt slightly stronger now that she'd climaxed and

rested and partaken of some much needed fluid. She felt ready to start sparring again.

'See what I mean? Dead lippy,' Rab said to the man, and she realised they'd been discussing her at some unknown time.

Had they just been making conversation whilst she slept, or had her part in this canine show been planned from the moment her latest crime was discovered? Fern wished she knew what had gone on before – and what was going to happen next. She didn't have to wait long.

'Sit up and beg real pretty for your supper now,' the dark-eyed handler coaxed. The audience laughed and a couple of the men in the front row whistled.

'Or what?' Fern countered.

'Or you'll feel my hand warming your rump again,' Rab cut in.

Flushing, Fern obediently curved her hands into an approximation of a dog's paws and held them out in a begging gesture.

'See, that wasn't so difficult,' the showman said, patting her head.

She'd like to see *him* try it, Fern thought, her face hot with shame.

'Now it's feeding time,' reminded the man.

Rab rubbed lewdly at his crotch: 'Want me to feed her?'

'I don't think even she deserves that level of chastisement,' the man said.

Fern watched as Rab's face tightened: 'I'll see about that!'

'She's being obedient. She's learning the ropes. You've no reason to demand oral,' the dog handler continued. He stared evenly at the less-educated man. 'I don't think that's what Dr Marshall wants.'

'Me neither,' Fern cut in.

The dog handler contemplated her coolly: 'When I want to talk to my dogs I let them know about it.'

'Yes, sir. Sorry, sir,' Fern muttered, as he pulled her closer to the alcove on the left. As she neared it, she could see the other human dogs on their hands and knees with their faces dipped towards their feeding bowls.

'It's salmon and asparagus with minted potatoes,' the man said. 'But if you prefer you can have meat or chicken or a vegetarian option.'

Fern sniffed hungrily at the tender-looking fillet: 'Salmon's fine.'

Shame coloured her face as she psyched herself up to put her mouth to the bowl. The familiar ache of arousal spread through her pubic patch and lower belly. Hugely aware of her raised naked haunches and swinging breasts, Fern lowered her face to the food. She grabbed at a slender spear of asparagus and lifted her head to swallow. She bent over the bowl again and took a piece of sizzling pink fish between her teeth. She'd been walked like a dog and had drunk like a dog. The pulse in her loins told her that she'd soon be ready to come like a dog again.

Sexual appetite took the place of her stomach's hunger halfway through the meal. Fern looked up from the bowl and focused on the eyes of the dog handler.

'Please,' she whispered, parting her thighs as wide as her crawling stance allowed. 'Oh *please!*'

'Wriggle over on your hot little tummy and ask again,' ordered the man, walking some distance away.

Gritting her teeth together, Fern pushed her arms out and stretched her legs back, the lino cool against her belly. Then she inhaled hard. It was easy to walk to him or even crawl, but to squirm over on her stomach made for a long slow journey. She kept her head dipped and tried to use her palms to pull her body forward, taking care not to scrape her knees. The familiar frantic urge permeated her pelvis, making her sex lips unbearably luscious. The collar around her neck tightened each time the leash caught under her body, making her feelings of bondaged eroticism soar.

At last she reached the dog handler, and lay naked at his feet.

'What were you saying, my pretty pup?' he asked, bending down to rub her behind the ears as if she was a canine.

'I wanted . . .' Too shamed to ask for an orgasm, Fern tailed off and shook her head.

'What did you want, doggy dear?' he prompted.

She looked up as she heard the scrape of wood on lino and saw him dragging a chair close to where she lay. Sitting down on it he resumed his taunting conversation.

'You said please, my sweet. Please what?'

Please my clit, my sex canal!

She couldn't say it. Yet she could act. Trying to keep her movements slow and stealthy, Fern slid her right hand under her tummy and began to feel for the satiation circle between her legs. She concentrated on keeping her breathing even. She knew she could come like lightning if she just gave a moment's clitoral attention to herself.

'Fern – what are you doing?' the dark-eyed man asked.

'Scratching my tummy,' she lied, finding the eroticised apex.

'I know all about the itch you've got,' the man replied.

Fern sensed rather than saw him lean forward. She felt the jerk on her leash and put her hands to her collar to halve the pressure.

'That's it, get over my knee for a stiff talking to,' the dog handler said.

'Is that all you're offering me?' Fern mumbled, feeling half-scared and half-excited. Maybe he'd be merciful. After all, he'd let her come before.

'In a moment your bum will be beneath my hands, then we'll see how much talking back you do,' continued the handler.

Rab stood behind him, jiggling his change in his pockets and grinning. 'Want me to teach her manners?' he asked, his voice thick with wanting.

'Soon,' the trainer said. 'You can take her back to your room and sort her out.'

Fern tensed as she was pulled over the dog handler's knees. She tensed some more as he fondled her helpless bum. She suspected she knew what was coming.

'This bum isn't very hot any more, is it Fern?' he said.

'No sir – but it still hurts,' she murmured, the last phrase a little white lie to protect her buttocks. Oh, her cheeks still felt tender, but they weren't actually aching. If only she could fool them all by obtaining a rouge that would make her white cheeks permanently red.

'So we have to punish you for being cheeky and for not telling us that you wanted to climax again,' the dominant party said, squeezing more demandingly at her squirming rotundities.

'Yes sir,' Fern muttered, blushing.

'What do you think we should punish you with?' the man said.

Fern breathed in and out, then in again, as she tried to summon up a suitable reply. She could say another spanking but that was probably too mild or too unimaginative and might earn her further censure. Yet she couldn't bear to ask for a taste of the whip or cane.

'I deserve the ruler, sir,' she said, as its wooden image filled her mind.

'On your palms or on your arse?' the man prompted, still fondling the latter.

'On my ar . . . on my bottom, sir,' Fern said reluctantly, deciding it was best to spare the tender surfaces of her palms. After all, she'd soon be living in Building One again and would need her hands to work in the gardens. She could hardly wait!

'Rab, get a ruler from the cupboard, will you?' the dog handler called casually.

'Coming up, mate!' Rab shouted.

Fern relaxed slightly as the leering driver walked away. Then she started to rise as she felt the dog handler's hand sliding under her armpits, coaxing her upwards. She pushed herself free of his body, then slid obediently to her knees, her sex throbbing its desire.

The man got up from his seat as Rab approached and handed him the ruler.

'All right, precious,' he said to Fern, 'grip the back of the chair and stick your bare bottom out to its fullest. Then thank me nicely after you count each of the four strokes out loud.'

'Only four?' Rab muttered, staring at Fern's breasts as they hung down towards the chair back.

'Trust me,' the dog handler replied. 'I know what I'm doing, and four will be enough.' He looked more closely at Rab. 'I'm beginning to think that you're not really a dominant man – you just don't like women. There's a big difference, and I'm surprised Dr Marshall wants you around.'

Fern glanced up at Rab, keen to see his reaction, but the driver just shrugged and looked away. For a second she dared to hope that the dog handler thought she was special, that he was on her side.

'Get that arse raised higher, Fern,' he said, and her hopes sank like leaden weights again.

The heavy feeling stayed between her breasts as she waited for her thrashing. Obediently she pushed her bottom out then leaned forwards almost on tiptoe so that it tilted further. She so wanted to please!

'Stroke one for false pride and for not admitting to your desires,' her captor continued.

Fern closed her eyes and clenched her shoulders. She sent messages to the twitching muscles of her bottom, willing them to stay smooth and relaxed. An unpuckered bum made for a more appealing target – and she wanted to appeal to this man a great deal. After all, he was saving her from the worst excesses of Rab.

Though she kept her lids downcast, she sensed the driver standing facing her. She knew that he was watching her full mouth, hoping to see it flinch with pain or submission. I'll take this like a big girl, she promised herself. I won't make a sound. Then the ruler strapped into her raised bare bottom and she yelled and let go of the chair.

Her hands flew to her bum, rubbing both cheeks with vigour. Rab laughed. Fern risked a quick glance back at the dog handler, who pointed back at the chair with the ruler.

'That bad bum's got to take three more like that,' he said matter of factly. 'And I'll double the number if it doesn't stay in place.'

'I wanted to obey,' Fern muttered, widening her eyes in an effort to appeal to his better nature, 'but it was so hard and sore.'

'It wouldn't be punishment if it wasn't painful, would it?' the man parried. 'Wouldn't make you better behaved.'

He stepped closer and tapped the ruler against the seat. 'Stop putting off the moment, my pretty dear. Get back into position now and lets see that bottom submit to a scarlet striping.'

Fern cast a last pleading look at him but his returning stare was coolly emphatic. Biting her lip, she bent forward and gripped the chair back then awaited the second lash.

When it came, it seared the flesh further down her cheeks, close to her thigh backs.

'Ah! Ah!' Fern yelped rearing back from the chair. Then she quickly recovered herself and gripped its back again, murmuring, 'Forgive me, master.' Still she couldn't help but wiggle her haunches from side to side as if to shake off the hateful sting.

'Control, Fern. Remember?' her tormentor said.

'Yes, master.' She'd do and say whatever he wanted now in order to end the pain and let the pleasure begin in earnest. Though for now she could just feel the burning strokes across her arse, she knew that the time would come when she'd again register the excitement between her legs. An excitement that would be evident a few moments after she endured the fourth ruler stroke.

But she had to get through ruler stroke three first! Fern pushed her poor hot bum obediently into the air though she longed to protect it with her fingers. She waited for the next instalment of her chastisement. It seemed to take a nerve-tauteningly long time. As she waited she felt the dog handler drawing the ruler across the two existing stripes.

One was close to the top of her firm backside, though he'd obviously avoided her spine. The other was low. There was a creamy trembling expanse in between them.

'I can fit two lashes in nicely there, can't I Fern?' the man teased, tracing the territory he was about to heat.

'Yes, master,' Fern said. She wished he'd just get it over with. She wished even more fervently that she'd never lied about Wanda in the first place, never ended up in this exacting Building Two. She'd started to love her gardening work in Building One. She'd started to . . . She gave a half-sob as the ruler bit into her vulnerable young spheres again.

Fern clenched her hands more tightly on the back of the chair. She tried to think of England, Scotland, Ireland. She tried to count the tiles on the far wall, tried to count imaginary sheep. Nothing worked. She'd been reduced to the status of a bare hot arse in a raised position, mutely begging for release.

'We'll make the last one a memorable one,' the dog handler said thoughtfully.

Rab sniggered and stepped closer to her flushed dipped head. At the same time she sensed the other man moving slightly away from her posterior. Damn him, he'd obviously decided to get in a good-sized swing!

He did. The ruler singed its way across the remaining unthrashed strip of flesh, roasting it and reddening it. Fern couldn't see the colour changes but she could feel the radiating heat.

'Christ, that's the rosiest bum I've seen for a day or two,' Rab said with a whistle, after hurrying round to see her beaten bottom. He reached out to finger her cheeks and Fern flinched.

'Submit to Rab's touch,' the man ordered.

Fern felt her tummy muscles contract. 'Don't leave me alone with him,' she begged. 'He hates me!'

She kept gripping the chair and looking straight ahead of her as she hadn't yet been given permission to move. Rab slapped lightly at both of her nether cheeks, bringing new warmth to the already overheated rotundities. Fern groaned.

'I think she's had a sufficiently sound thrashing for now, Rab,' the dog handler said, 'though you might like to train her for a little longer before you give her the ultimate satisfaction.'

'I know what I'd like to give her,' Rab muttered, playing with the zip of his jeans.

Fern glanced round in time to see the older man looking at Rab dispassionately.

'All in good time.' He turned to Fern. 'Let go of the chair and get down on your hands and knees. Rab – take hold of her lead again. Maybe you'd like to put her through the canine obstacle course?'

'Love to!' Rab said, brightening visibly. He tugged at Fern's leash till she started to crawl behind him again, wishing desperately that she'd been allowed even a few seconds to rub her punished bottom. The flesh felt hugely tender and scorched.

'Please, Rab,' she muttered obsequiously, 'just let me hold my bum for a moment.'

'Rab now, it it? I was master before,' Rab muttered, increasing his pace.

There was to be no relief, then, for her flaming orbs. Aware also of the sex juice on her thighs, Fern made her awkward way on her hands and knees, towards the climbing slope.

'Good dog – up you go!' Rab ordered, and, lead hanging down her back, she scrabbled up the wooden surface, then half-slid and half-jumped down the other side. She hesitated, then wriggled through the perspex tunnel on her soft little belly, her nipples brushing against the floor of the see-through tube.

The nipples were elongated, the breasts around them puffy with shamed new arousal. Her breasts ached to be caressed and held. If only the dog handler would take her in his arms, take her to his bed; take her anywhere! If only this tunnel had opaque walls and she could secretly slide two or three fingers up herself.

Excitement had put pressure on her bladder and she needed to urinate. Fern tried to catch the dog handler's attention as she crawled from the tube. He was busily stacking the dogs' feeding and drinking bowls in the cupboard at the far end of the hall. If he'd just look round.

He didn't. The low heavy weight of trapped water intensified in her belly as Rab led her to the next steep ascent. She'd have to tell him of her need to void before she disgraced herself.

'I've got to go to the ladies,' she mumbled, forcing herself to meet his sardonic gaze.

'You're on a lead like a *dog*,' the driver grinned, 'You're not a *lady*.'

'Please – it's urgent!' Fern muttered, cupping a hand between her legs.

'Maybe a wee walk'll take your mind off it,' Rab continued, increasing his pace till the leash stretched taut between them and exerted its harsh pull on her collar and the neck beneath it.

Helplessly Fern crawled behind him. She whimpered with frustration as he marched her round and round. 'I've got to urinate!' she gasped to the dog handler as he strolled over.

'Let her do it, Rab,' the older man replied.

'She's my bitch till she learns to do what she's told. I'm supposed to be teaching her obedience,' Rab muttered disconsolately.

The man nodded, looking from one to the other: 'I've read the reports. I know the dog needs firm handling. I'm just worried you'll get carried away.'

'I've only spanked her so far,' Rab muttered. 'I've not even slid inside her.'

'Plenty of time yet. Just wait till she asks for your cock nicely,' the other man said.

Fern quivered as she crouched on her hands and knees between them with her poor distended bladder. Did they have to talk about her as if she wasn't there?

'Please – the ladies!' she pleaded, looking up at both her trainers and tightening her groin muscles to keep the yellow fluid inside her.

The dog handler stared down at her swollen nipples and full belly, then he smiled coolly: 'Little pup, we're going to watch you use your litter tray.' He pointed to the plastic recess in the corner that was filled with a sweet-scented soil.

Rab pulled her over, still on her collar and lead. Fern looked at the tray. She looked at the two men. She couldn't do it!

'Please show me to a real loo,' she said, pressing her thighs inwards even more tightly. Her bladder pulsed its increasing need. The girl quivered: she was already naked,

200

displayed on a collar and lead like a mindless puppy. Surely they wouldn't make her urinate in public as well?

'You essentially pissed on us all with your lies and half-truths and caused us pain. Now you can piss in front of us for our pleasure,' the dog handler said.

The audience that was nearest whistled and clapped in agreement, and spread the shameful word.

'Rab, help the doggy by massaging its tum,' the man continued.

Rab obviously didn't need a second invitation. He squatted down in front of Fern, his eyes searching hers. Meanwhile his hands had located her belly and started their devilish caresses. Fern groaned as he manipulated the water-filled sack.

'Stop,' she whispered brokenly, 'I'll do anything. I can't bear it!'

'You could suck me real pretty and I'd consider being nice to you,' Rab said.

She would do it, if that was what it took to be granted toilet privacy. Driven beyond endurance, Fern reached blindly for his zip. She tugged his jeans and underpants down and immediately his leaking hardness sprung free. The fluid smelt reassuringly of coal-tar soap and tasted like burnt salt and looked like glycerine. Fern took the first inch of wet manhood in her mouth and Rab tried to push the other five inches in. Fearing she might choke but wanting to please, Fern wrapped her fingers round his shaft holding it in place whilst she tongued the shiny glans over and over. She put her left hand beneath his balls and brushed them with butterfly lightness till he muttered 'Jesus!' and screwed his eyes shut tight.

Fluid suddenly spurted out in several jerking spasms. Fern swallowed it quickly. Surely now he'd let her use the loo? She stayed crouched in place for a moment as Rab recovered enough to put his shrinking rod back in his underpants and rezip himself.

'Christ, girlie,' he said. 'You've got a velvet tongue.'

'And do girlies get to go to the ladies?' Fern murmured sweetly figuring she was winning.

'Not when they've used their sexuality to get what they want,' the dog handler said.

Damn and blast it – she'd forgotten about that rule! It was one of the first things she'd been thrashed for here at *Compulsion*. Lately she'd been so much less flirtatious; had been doing so well. But in a moment of pressure she'd reverted to her old ways in front of witnesses. That didn't bode well for her arse. Or for her bladder.

'You're right – she's a scheming wee minx,' Rab said, and pulled her closer by a couple of inches till she was again positioned with her pubis above the litter tray. He turned the persuasion of his right hand to the tender walls of her urine-heavy belly again.

'Oh please! No more! Can't take it!' Fern gasped in short little sentences as he palpated the hugely sensitive area.

'You'll take every squeeze and thank me nicely,' Rab said. As if to emphasise his power, he pressed his fingers round the perimeter with increasing insistence. Fern sensed some mental or physical limit give way and felt the thick heavy stream of her own ammonia begin.

It seemed to go on and on, splashing over the soil of the litter tray, a spray of moisture lightly beading her inner thighs. When the last few yellow drops had left her she felt hollow and spent and beyond thought.

'Shower,' said the dog handler, pointing the way. He nudged Rab. 'She's a randy little bitch so go with her to make sure she doesn't touch her more sensitive bits.'

'Aye, aye, sir,' Rab replied, saluting and grinning broadly. He urged Fern to crawl in front of him doubtless admiring her ruler-striped bum as she slunk to the nearby showers.

When they got there, Rab started to unbutton his shirt.

'Reckon I'll keep you company, sweetheart,' he murmured.

'Oh. Right.'

That was all she needed! Fern ignored his lewd wink. Quickly she switched on the hot spray and stepped under it. She watched anxiously as he bared his chest.

It was a nice chest, she realised with a dart of surprise.

202

It was toned but not too muscular. He was endearingly hirsute without having the appearance of an ape. She shivered despite the warm water. The man's personality was the only animalistic part of him; was the part to fear.

What was he going to do now? He was staring at her breasts, at her naked juice-slicked loins, at her slender thigh fronts. Fern stayed facing him. With her bottom bare and reddened, she daren't turn round! He'd been angry when the dog handler took over much of her training and might make the most of the next few minutes with her wet bum and his wide belt. God knows how much he could hurt her tender cheeks.

She cast a hesitant glance through her eyelashes as the driver pulled down his own jeans and underpants. It seemed a long time since she'd sucked him. But then the minutes passed slowly when you were naked and displayed on a leash.

'Like what you see, babe?' the man jeered.

Ordinarily she would – but she hated this bastard. She played it safe by shrugging and looking away. She looked back when she sensed movement and noted with slight alarm that Rab was fully stripped now and moving towards the shower.

'Gotta clean the doggy up after it pissed itself,' he said tauntingly.

Fern closed her eyes as the shameful lust rushed through. She shut her mouth into a tight line to hold back the whimpers of reluctant desire as Rab grabbed the woodland gel and started to soap her smooth young breasts.

'Let's make these teats bonny,' he muttered, staring challengingly into her eyes as he worked the frothy lather round her globes. His words and deeds sent traitorous tremors through her. 'And we mustn't neglect this wee soft tummy,' the driver added, soaping the womanly curves.

'Yes, sir,' Fern said. She was flattered yet anxious to see his manhood starting to twitch again. She wanted him to find her attractive, for that boded better for her poor bare bottom, but she didn't want him using his new hardness in some punitive way that would have her writhing on its tip for torturous hours.

She liked being touched, even if she hated the toucher. Fern groaned softly as her uncouth tormentor turned his attentions to the dark divide of her recently punished bum. He ran his thumb lightly down the cleft, stimulating each of the tiny hairs within it. He traced the sensitive weals which ended where buttock meets thigh.

'Time for your final walkies,' he muttered thickly, pulling her out of the warm spray and reaching for a towel. He wrapped them both in its thick lemon expanse, grinning into her eyes as he patted her bottom through the cloth. More quickly now, he blotted the rest of her bare flesh and his own, then threw the patchily wet towel on the changing room lino.

'Right, puppy, let's have you on your hands and knees,' he murmured, 'and we'll go and see your handler for a minute.'

Anxious to stay in his good books, Fern got into the doggy position and obediently began to crawl.

The dog handler was now pulling the tarpaulin back over the canine obstacle course. The audience had gone home, Fern noted. She wondered when she'd get to do likewise. She realised with a start that when she thought of home she was thinking of Building One. Mentally she gave herself a thorough shake. What a ridiculous concept! The whole point of these past few weeks had been to earn parole then win her ultimate freedom back to the outside world!

'You said I could fuck her when she was ready to beg,' Rab told the other man.

Fern stiffened. Was Rab going to lie about her words? He'd managed to turn her on in the shower but she sure as hell hadn't done any begging.

'I don't hear her saying anything,' the dog handler said evenly.

So he was at least partly on her side!

'She was desperate for it a minute ago. Quivering like anything when I soaped her bum,' Rab continued. 'Can I just show you with those parallel bars?'

Fern looked at the bars. Two were fastened to the floor

and ran half the length of the hall. The idea was for the dog to run fast in between them without touching their surfaces. If he inadvertently touched either bar a light glowed to warn the judges that the dog had failed. High above the bars was an arched metal bridge with steps leading up and down on either side of it. Other dogs were supposed to create a potential diversion by racing along its overhead breadth. But where did she, Fern, fit into all of this?

'Let's get you fastened,' said Rab. He pulled her over to the floor-based bars and got her to take up the doggy position between them. Then he went to the cupboard and returned with four sets of cuffs. 'Just to keep you from wriggling about too much,' he grinned, clicking the restraints to her wrists and her ankles, then locking the other side onto the bars.

Now she was held in the canine stance without access to her hands or feet, Fern realised, pulling impotently at her bound extremities. She was wondering what further indignities Rab had planned for her when she felt something soft caress her clit.

'Aaah!' she cried, pushing her body forward as far as she could, but knowing that the cuffs ensured she wasn't going anywhere. She looked back to see Rab holding up his middle finger, which was covered in a feather fingerstool. He was looking very pleased with himself.

'I'm going to tease your private parts with this for a while,' he said. 'But I'll not let you come because you've not been a good enough wee puppy.'

Fern moaned softly as he caressed her clitoris with the feathers again. God, that was so soft and sure and sexually exquisite. But he wasn't keeping the rhythm or pressure up, so she couldn't go over the edge.

'Oh, that wee bud's peeking out of its cage. Oh, it's a horny wee bud. It's awfully wet. You should see it!'

She could *feel* it, Fern thought, writhing against the erotic torment again. She looked up to see the dog handler standing in front and staring at her heaving tits and straining nipples, just as Rab must be staring at her twitching bum.

Screw them, she wouldn't beg. She just wouldn't! She'd

have to concentrate her mind on other things. She could think about .... Fern cried out as the feather devilishly stimulated her sex source again. And again. The teasing continued. She knew her pubis couldn't bear much more.

'Please let me come,' she mumbled, the words unwillingly formed by her whimpering vocal chords.

'Beg me to fuck you nice and hard,' Rab said.

Damn him, she couldn't – and she wouldn't. He was such an all-out misogynistic pig! Fern closed her mouth. The misogynist stroked the feather down her desperate bud. He repeated the gesture, and Fern's lubricants leaked. She writhed and groaned low in her throat.

If only she could increase the feathery pleasure, or just evade its wicked teasing for even a few moments! But the bars held her arms and legs unerringly in place. She could arch her tummy and back a little way, but was otherwise helpless – and Rab was making the very most of that fact.

'Och, the feather wants to play here. And here,' he continued, caressing each surface of her clitoris in sexy succession. He taunted the base, he teased over the tip, he traced round the sides. Sensation was throbbing through her, a pulsing plea for satisfaction.

'Please fuck me. I beg you to fuck me!' Fern said.

'So the bitch on heat wants me to fuck her. What do you think?' Rab said.

He was obviously looking at the dog handler, for it was he that shrugged and then replied, 'That's up to you, Rab. Suppose you could treat her to an inch or two. You know, a reward for walking close to heel and for remembering to use her litter tray.'

Fern blushed at his words and stared at the lino. She heard a zip go down behind her and stuck out her bum hopefully. She tried to make the back way into her front as open and tempting as possible, whilst praying Rab wouldn't try to take her anal virginity instead.

'Can I shove it up her arse?' he asked, putting her worst fears into words.

The girl tensed. The dog handler shook his head: 'Even masochistic women don't always like that.'

'You'd like it, wouldn't you, sweetheart?' Rab prompted, reaching for the hellish power of the feather again.

'Please no,' Fern muttered, 'I beg!'

'Her front passage is more than oiled for you, Rab,' her trainer said.

Fern parted her thighs the little she could given the ankle cuffs. She was waiting for some much needed vaginal relief. Instead, she sensed Rab was standing up.

'If I'm not getting in the back I'll at least make sure you don't wriggle while I'm in the front,' he said with his usual coarse cynicism.

He hurried off to the cupboard again. Fern heard clumping noises some distance behind her as he obviously discarded unwanted restraints from some of the shelves.

When he returned he was breathing hard. Fern felt something brush against her back as he moved forward. She breathed in the pleasing scent of new leather, then looked distractedly through her bound arms as Rab fastened a harness round her back. He buckled it beneath her tummy, then handed some leather strips to the dog-handling man. 'Hand them up to me in a moment,' he said, and hurried towards the steps of the bridge.

Fern watched Rab's ascent. He stopped when he was directly above her waist. Meanwhile her trainer was tying two strips of leather to hoops in the harness round her back, whistling as he did so. He handed the ends up to Rab, who immediately exerted a cruel tug on them. As he pulled on the ties, Fern felt her tummy start to arch and her back follow. When she was fully extended, Rab tied the free ends of the leather to the bridge's bars.

Fern swallowed hard and helplessly awaited his return. She was now stretched to capacity in both arms, legs, back and tummy. Her openings were flagrantly apparent and vulnerably displayed. She licked her lips as Rab came back and put his large hands on her bum, teasing the tender ruler marks. He could now do anything he liked! She tried to flex even the smallest of leg muscles, and failed to do so. She realised that her mouth and tongue were the only parts of her body that she could move.

207

Should she offer to suck Rab again, or would that be presumptuous? Should she try to win him round by letting him slide just the tip of his shaft into her unsullied anal hole? The trainer had said she could have sex as a reward, but she daren't ask for it. She could only wait in her ungiving bonds till the two men decided what happened to her next. She didn't have to wait long.

'Still want shafting, do you?' Rab asked.

She heard his zip going down and knew that her erotic tunnel needed active service. 'Uh huh,' she muttered, hoping that such an encouraging sound would suffice.

'C'mon, sweetheart – you can do better than that!' her tormentor jibed.

'I . . . please.'

Fern's flesh was totally captive now, but she still squirmed inside at the ignominy. It was awful to have to ask your enemy to fuck you, terrible to be held in bondage just pleading for his cock like this. It was worse, though, to be left without satisfaction at all. 'Please put it in me,' she managed, her opening glistening.

'I've heard you weren't this shy in the glasshouse with some poser,' Rab said. 'I've heard you showed him a really good time.'

He was kneeling by her bum, so she couldn't see him but she could hear the glee and laughter in his voice.

'What do you want me to say?' she whimpered, her brain trying to limit her indignity whilst her craving crotch promised absolutely anything.

'Say, "Master, I ken I dinnae deserve it, but please put even an inch of your wonderful cock up my horny wet wee hole",' Rab prompted, sliding a teasing digit inside her labial lips.

Beyond caring what the man himself or the watchful dog handler thought of her, Fern repeated Rab's words. She used her own precise English, then wondered belatedly if she should have echoed his actual dialect, then decided that might have sounded as if she was imitating him.

'You may have a posh voice, but you've still got a hot cunt,' Rab sneered, then he slid his thick hardness right up her.

Fern winced at his tone then sighed with gratitude and relief as he gave her his rod. God, she needed this! Her conduit had been empty for ever so long, had felt achingly hollow. Now every pulsating millimetre was delightfully filled.

'Just make sure you let her come, Rab – she deserves it,' the dog handler said in his matter-of-fact way.

'You not staying to watch?' Rab muttered, starting to thrust in and out.

'Got to make a couple of phone calls in the office,' the handler told him. Then he patted Fern's head and joked, 'Be a good little dog.'

She'd be great if Rab let her climax soon! Fern hardly saw the other man leave the hall, she was concentrating so fully on her quim's inward sensation. If Rab would only put his right hand to her clit.

'Don't get too hopeful, pal. I can keep you like this all night,' he said, circling his cock round and round rather than thrusting. If only he'd push completely in! He was keeping her right on the edge, now – stirred but not shaken. He was a bastard, but one that was very much in charge.

'After this, I'm gonna take you home and tie you to the four corners of my bed,' Rab muttered.

Fern tensed inside as she pictured the scene – the reality scared her. But the shameful words sent a sudden rush of heat to her pubes.

'Then,' Rab said with obvious deliberation, 'I'll take off my belt.' He thrust in harder. 'And do you know what I'll do then?'

'Surprise me!' Fern muttered. He'd already decided to warm her arse so she'd gain nothing by being obsequious.

'I'll thrash the living daylights out of you,' Rab said.

Fern shuddered, yet her breast tops tingled with excitement. She could envisage her helpless nether cheeks.

'Can you imagine how red it's gonna be?' Rab taunted, pushing in and out, deeper into her crevice.

'I'm sure you'll fetch me a mirror!' Fern said.

She was close to coming now, her spirited words quickly

209

fading as nirvana grew near. The approach of orgasm always heightened her sense of submission.

'I'll put a mirror before your face so that you can look in it and see how angry I am with you,' Rab replied. He increased his shafting speed. 'An I'll put another mirror at the foot of the bed so that you can see your warmed backside. Darling, I'm telling you, it's gonna be roasting! You're gonna beg so sweet.'

He stopped the delicious friction of his rod and held it half out of her. 'Talking of begging, I'm not hearing you ask nicely for my cock.'

God, he couldn't stop now when she was so close to coming! 'I beg for it,' Fern forced out, waiting frenziedly in her bondage for release.

'Yet not pleading quite sweet enough. Say "I'll do anything, master",' her tormentor said.

'I'll do anything and everything!' Fern gasped urgently, then added, 'I beg, master. I truly beg!'

'Oh well, if you're as desperate as all that,' said Rab and began to slide slowly up her aroused wet ravine.

The action was exquisite. He felt so thick.

'You're squealing now with pleasure,' Rab continued, 'but once you've had three dozen of the belt you'll be crying with pain.'

'Aaaah! Aaaah! Aaaah! Aaaah! Aaaah!' Fern's orgasm raced through her and she tilted her head and let loose five deep wolverine howls. Sensation spread and peaked and stayed there. Every nerve seemed filled with sexual ecstasy. Her belly and her pubis pulsed with internal fire, and she was only vaguely aware of Rab leaning forward and reaching for her nipples as his own climax began.

'You've a nice tight grip between your legs, but you need not think that'll get you off with anything,' he warned, grunting his orgasm then withdrawing from her quickly.

Fern whimpered at the sudden sense of loss. She watched as Rab waddled across to the cupboard, a black rubber sheath still clinging to his diminishing member. She wondered what he was going to do next. How she wished that she could be untied and could revisit the showers. She wanted to eat and rest awhile. Okay, she'd deserved much of this punishment for her earlier lies and evasions but she needed some human comfort too!

Rab waddled back, his left fingers cupping his obviously sensitive testes. In his right hand he held a heavy-looking willow birch. Was he going to use it here and now, with her arms and legs bound to the bars and her naked haunches cruelly exposed? Fern stared at the implement and trembled.

'Let's get you back to my room for a taste of the belt and a long session with this beauty,' Rab said.

'*You will not!*'

Fern flinched the little she could as the warning words ricocheted round the hall. They were the dog handler's words. She realised belatedly that he'd silently entered through the open door again.

'I've got to punish her,' Rab muttered, flushing and moving the birch from hand to hand as if it was electrified.

'She's had sufficient correction today. She's already been spanked, dog-trained and rulered,' the trainer replied.

He knelt and started to uncuff Fern, rubbing gently at each limb as he set it free. 'There's a difference between strict discipline and sadism, Rab. A difference between controlling a wayward girl and half-killing her. You have to exercise caution as well as administer a caning. You sometimes have to give a cooling balm to a bottom after it's writhed under the belt.' He looked up at the other man. 'I've been on the phone to Dr Marshall suggesting that you're going beyond *Compulsion*'s training guidelines, that it's getting personal. Suffice to say that the inmate is to be recalled.'

Did that mean what she thought it meant? Fern felt new hope spark through her as she squatted, now untied, on the lino.

'Permission to speak, sir,' she whispered to the trainer, looking up at him through her eyelashes' dark veil.

The man's features softened: 'Permission granted, Fern,' he replied.

'You said I was being recalled. Does that mean I'm

211

going back to Building One, to Ms Lenn or Dr Marshall?' she murmured hopefully.

'It means you're returning to Building One,' the handler confirmed. 'That's right.' He unbuckled her collar and lead then scooped her gently up into his arms. 'I understand it's a Sonia Shendon who's to continue your instruction,' he told her.

'Sonia? She's the sports coach,' Fern said, yawning. Sleepily she leaned her head against the man's broad chest. Then she smiled inwardly as he carried her from the hall. Sonia had helped Fern get her own back after she'd been hurt by Melissa during a netball game. Sonia seemed to be the mild and unassuming kind. With the gym teacher as her new trainer, the next few days of her supposed punishment should be laughable. Surely this somewhat passive woman wouldn't hurt Fern's backside?

Twelve

'I'm going to have to leather your bum,' Sonia murmured in the sweetly reasonable tone she was increasingly adopting.

She walked round the bottom in question, tapping the two-tailed tawse against its bare expanse. For such a slim implement it left an impressive red mark.

Not that she'd used it on the nude backside that was bent over the punishment stool now, the backside of a youth in his early twenties. But she'd warmed Clarissa's arse with it on the football pitch the other day.

Sonia grimaced, remembering Clarissa's faux pas. The girl had foolishly insisted that it was sexist to expect her to run around chasing a ball, that participant sports were only for the male gender. When her attempts to be excused the exercise had failed, she'd even tried to get the other female footballers to stop playing. It was this very rigidity of attitude that had led to her initial crime. Sonia knew all the details, for she'd sent for Clarissa's case file before punishing her. It told how the girl was obsessed with being a Scarlet O'Hara style heroine; how she'd turned to fraud when her soprano singing career failed. Clarissa had seen fraud as a completely viable option – after all, a lady shouldn't ever get her hands dirty by doing a nine-to-five job.

She had robbed other people rather than examining the more masculine part of herself. Sonia had felt no guilt in turning the tables by upturning the young woman's bottom. She had pulled back the tawse then brought it forward over Clarissa's plump expanse. Sonia smiled, remembering how the girl had squealed as she was tied firmly over the football pitch fence.

She was becoming good at restraining disobedient delinquents and meting out discipline, Sonia realised. She was enjoying herself. The regime here had tapped in to some previously unexplored part of her psyche. It felt right. She particularly savoured punishing the naughty girls, something which surprised her. She'd always been heterosexual in her fantasies and deeds before. But then the only female bums she'd seen had been in the movies! Having two creamy pert cheeks bent over submissively before you was quite different to seeing an actress's bottom on the screen. Now she could walk round the bum in question, could tell it what she was going to do to it and make it tremble as she took her time sizing up the cane.

Bad girls got very good when they imagined that long thin rod coming down on their bare backsides. Sonia had found that four well-placed strokes would reduce them to a grovelling subservience. She'd tried the rattan out on her own buttocks in the privacy of her bedroom and knew how deeply it stung. As such, she modified each stroke, making it very sore but not overwhelmingly agonising. She made sure that the girl wanted to remain on her tummy for a while afterwards but did not give so severe a caning that she couldn't sit down for a week.

'Ten of the tawse for threatening to punch another player,' she said now, turning her attention back to the small boyish bottom before her.

'He was asking for it!' the youth muttered, tugging futilely at the rubber restraints she had used to fasten his wrists to his knees. The bonds ensured he stayed nicely doubled over and had made it easy for her to pull down his gym shorts and underpants.

'Let's have fewer excuses and more forethought,' Sonia said now, raising the two-tailed leather strap.

She swung the tawse in a sideways movement so that its length seared the youth's muscular hips. The boy grunted and jerked slightly, but kept his untethered feet in position.

'There's another nine like that to go. I want you to count them and ask me politely for the next one,' Sonia said. She was starting to know what to say and do – she'd picked up some tips from watching Ms Lenn and the other guards in action. And Dr Marshall had lent her his thesis and several explanatory books.

Humiliation and a hot bum led to succour for these particular inmates. Oh, this youth was wincing and grunting at the pain of the lash now, but afterwards he'd orgasm and find a measure of peace.

'You like this really,' she whispered, looking at the half-hard shaft moving in inches up his tummy. She used the tawse again and again.

'Ten!' she said finally with the satisfaction of a job well done. 'I'm going to send you to the boy you threatened now,' she continued, 'he's to bring you off in the public lecture hall. His actions will be accompanied by Dr Marshall's lecture on Male Violence and its Homo-Erotic Subtext.'

The boy's phallus strengthened but his voice sounded weak as he groaned.

'Don't fight it,' Sonia advised, kneeling to unfasten his wrists from his knees. She was halfway through unbuckling one of the restraints when her mobile phone buzzed insistently. She looked over to the bench in the far corner where it lay. Then she shrugged and turned back to what she was doing. No way was she going to leave this boy in bondage whilst she indulged in a chat with her penal liaisons boss! Sure, Robert was important, but it was even more vital not to leave a submissive helplessly trussed.

After all, she'd have to turn her back to him to have a whispered conversation with Robert. And if the boy suddenly felt faint he wouldn't be able to move himself into a comfortable position.

'Don't you want to answer that, miss?' he asked now as the buzzing continued.

'It can wait,' Sonia told him. 'Your wellbeing comes first.'

The youth rewarded her with a surprised start then an eye-reaching smile. His wellbeing had probably seldom come first throughout his twenty years on the planet. Now he needed a knowing fusion of love and discipline to see him through.

'Right, that's you sorted. Get yourself off to the lecture hall for a quick release,' Sonia finished as the phone at last stopped beckoning.

'At Gary's hands? Probably still be there tonight!' the youth grinned.

He left with the guard, his limbs swinging and no longer full of anger. Sonia walked slowly to the phone, and pressed out Robert's number, wondering what to say. So far she'd played safe merely admitting that the place was well-disciplined. Robert had pressed for further details. 'Well, they have lots of rules,' she'd added, 'and everyone works for a modest fee.'

Plus they get caned and spanked if they misbehave! She hadn't yet told of that part – though she'd intended to. Problem was, she'd now participated in those thrashings herself. She had intended just to dole out a few light buttock slaps so that she looked suitably dominant, to fool the other staff members. She had, however, found her hand coming down harder and harder on these spoilt bare bums. In the few weeks that she'd been here she'd made the inmates writhe under the tawse, cane and ferula. Her arm had risen and fallen for real rather than in pretence.

'Robert – sorry I couldn't answer a moment ago.' she said into the receiver now.

'Staff meeting, was it?' he asked.

Buttock-based beating more like! She pushed away the erotic image. 'Just a bit of unfinished business,' she said quickly. 'Anyway, how are you?'

'Fine, fine,' Robert said testily.

Had he always been so impatient? She'd never noticed. There again, she hadn't spent most of her working hours listening to his dulcet tones. Instead she'd been admiring his strong sure features and wondering how to lure him into her bed!

'This investigation of yours is taking much too long,' her boss continued, his voice unusually flat and low. 'Your temporary replacement is hopeless at fending off unwanted callers. Sonia – I need you back!'

Sonia felt a spreading satisfaction warm her chest. Still,

she didn't want to leave just yet. It was . . . interesting here. It was important. Despite their unorthodox approach, the staff at *Compulsion* were doing well.

'So, is anything improper going on?' Robert continued.

Sonia hesitated, then sucked in her breath. If she hinted she was close to the truth he'd hopefully let her stay on for a few weeks longer. She'd have to choose her words with care. 'I've . . . heard rumours,' she told him. 'But then many of the inmates are liars. If there is any physical chastisement being administered it goes on behind closed doors after hours.'

Robert's sigh was evident even down the phone line: 'Can't you plant a tape recorder or something, then?'

'I'm working on that,' Sonia lied. 'I have to be careful not to blow my cover.'

Blow her cover with her boss, more like!

Sonia thought the thought then stilled with surprise. How ridiculous. For a moment she had thought of Robert Greene as being the enemy! She loved him – didn't she? She'd only gone on this lengthy assignment in the hope of awakening his feelings for her. Suddenly tired and confused, Sonia put her lips closer to the receiver! 'Robert – I have to go,' She strove to end on a cheerful note. 'Give my best to Mrs Greene.'

'If she can make the time to see me between her oil-painting classes!' Robert muttered heavily.

For once uninterested in the details of her boss's marriage, Sonia said her goodbyes then disabled the phone.

Thirteen

'. . . and he really laid the ruler on!' Fern finished. She lay on her tummy along the kitchen work surface chatting to Wanda.

'Can't blame him!' the older girl said wearily, reaching over Fern's waist for the wall-hanging ladle and the slatted spoon.

She pushed Fern's arms out of the way, moving them closer to her chest, 'Fern, how can I make vegetable soup for a hundred inmates if you keep taking up all my work space?'

Fern grinned at her former friend: 'Just open a few tins of minestrone instead!'

She felt nonchalant now, the ignominy of being treated like a dog far behind her. That episode felt as if it had taken place over a week ago, though it was only two days. Two days since the dog handler had carried her back to this building and personally bathed and fed her. He had covered her tenderly with the duvet and given the guards instructions that she was to be excused punishment training and work duties until Wednesday.

So here she was with one day of freedom left! Fern searched round for a new topic of conversation as she tried yet again to win the diffident Wanda's attention. If only the girl would stop chopping potatoes and grating carrots and simply relax.

'You could just use a stock cube,' she murmured as Wanda added fresh basil and parsley and chives to the bubbling cauldron.

'No, they're full of additives,' her old party pal answered, grating some black pepper into the mixture. 'Dr Marshall likes to offer wholesome food.'

219

Wholesome food cooked by wholesome young women, Fern thought angrily, starting to drum her slippered toes against the work station. Wanda hadn't just decided that she was heterosexual rather than bisexual – she had also decided to become a first-class bore! Was this really the same girl who had once lived off liquid lunches in smoke-filled bars?

'So, what are we going to do once you've finished this bloody soup?' Fern tried again.

Wanda looked briefly over from her task of shredding six home-grown leeks: 'I'm going to sit in the sunshine and write to my fiancé.'

'I'll tag along,' Fern said, her spirits lifting. She'd been wondering how to get through her unexpected time off work.

Wanda took a spoonful of the soup, blew on it then sipped tentatively. 'Needs more seasoning,' she said. She turned towards the rosemary and oregano which grew in pottery containers on the inner window sill.

'Oh for Christ's sake just add a dash of salt or we'll still be here at teatime!' Fern muttered. She grabbed the rock salt carton, and slithered along the worktop till she reached the soup. She shook the carton impatiently, then watched with shock and alarm as its top flew into the liquid and half the contents poured swiftly in.

'Oh God, I didn't mean to!' she gasped, wriggling hastily backwards again.

'You never *mean* to do anything, Fern, but you still create chaos,' Wanda said, her mouth tightening into a firm line.

Fern stared at her. This wasn't the first time she'd heard these words. Dr Marshall had said something similar. Every time she felt she was improving some silly action like this got in the way.

'I'll help you make more soup,' she promised, flipping herself on to her back before moving into a sitting position on the kitchen surface. She was relieved to find that her bottom didn't hurt any more.

'Forget it!' Wanda said, turning towards the overflowing vegetable rack.

'You won't tell on me, will you?' Fern murmured, feeling suddenly nervous.

'I should tell Dr Marshall. I should tell the parole board!' Wanda said darkly, looking at the ruined lunch. Fern jumped down from the work station and took a step towards her erstwhile companion.

'Tell them what?' a new voice said.

Fern gasped and moved her hindquarters nearer to the wall, as if to protect them. Then she remembered she'd been promised another day without a thrashing, and she relaxed. She looked over to the open door to see that the question had come from Sonia – a slightly grim-faced Sonia.

'I . . . oversalted the soup by mistake,' she admitted, restlessly pleating her short lilac skirt.

'So I see,' Sonia commented drily, striding into the room and picking up the half-empty carton. 'Was it really a mistake?' she asked Wanda, her voice steely and determined.

'I think so. She was bored and was trying to rush the cooking process,' Wanda said.

The sports teacher shook her head as she turned to Fern: 'Good citizens don't get bored, do they, dearest?'

Fern's head raced with answers that might save her hide, but she quickly discarded them as being flip, and she shook her head forlornly.

'Good citizens do self-help style reading and evening classes in their spare time don't they, Fern?' the sports coach continued, 'and some of them assist other people or raise money for charity.' She looked the twenty-four-year old up and down. 'You could have watched an educational film, Fern, if you were at a loose end. You could have done voluntary work in the grounds. You could have familiarised yourself with our library and borrowed some books that would add to your personal growth. Instead you've got in another person's way and ruined their morning's work.'

'I know. I'm really sorry,' Fern muttered, actually meaning it.

Sonia took a step closer: 'The part of you I'm going to make sorry is your backside.'

'You can't – I've been granted an amnesty!' Fern gasped, her fingers going swiftly round to protect her skirted and pantied bottom.

'It's true. She's got one day's grace left,' Wanda chipped in.

'I know that. I came to make the arrangements for to-morrow when she starts under my tutelage,' Sonia said.

'Rab lifted his hand to me and the dog trainer used his ruler,' Fern got out with difficulty. She still hated to discuss each humiliating punishment. 'Haven't I been through enough?' she asked, looking up into the teacher's neutral face.

'I initially thought so when I saw the film of what you'd experienced,' Sonia said, her tone thoughtful and steady.

So the bastards had been filming her! Fern flinched at the thought.

'I just planned to train your body for the next few days,' the sports coach continued. 'You know – get you doing cross-country running, create a healthy body to house your increasingly healthy mind.' She sighed and ran her thumbs along her waist-outlining belt. 'Now I realise that your mind isn't as sound as I'd imagined. Oh, we've installed some of the work ethic in you and you no longer balk at manual labour. But left to your own devices you still don't know what to do.'

'I could learn,' Fern offered, not liking the look of the thick strap the woman kept fingering.

'And you learn best dancing at the end of a belt,' the sports teacher said.

She treated the younger girl to a smile completely lacking in warmth before turning towards the kitchen door-way: 'Be at the main gym for 9 a.m., Fern, wearing the cheerleading outfit I'll have supplied you.' She rubbed her palms together, obviously anticipating the meeting, 'And don't bother to cover that pretty bum with a pair of pants.'

The next morning Fern listlessly nibbled at the sugar-free muesli the guard had brought her. Uncertainty had taken away much of her appetite, yet when she thought of her forthcoming day – or days – in the gym she suspected she would need this food to give her succour. Valiantly she sipped her decaffeinated coffee then drank the milk straight from the jug to settle her nervous tum.

Now her bottom was about to be taught a lesson! With her accusatory words and the way she'd fingered her thick belt, Sonia had made Fern's fate abundantly clear to her. As she lathered her hair and limbs under the ensuite shower, she wondered how many lashes she'd receive for tipping a carton of rock salt into the home-made soup. She felt a momentary sarcastic rush – she was surprised they hadn't ordered an internal trial for her wrongdoing! Then the sarcasm subsided to be replaced by uncertainty and mild fear.

Wrapping herself in a towel, Fern walked towards the clothes laid out on the armchair. A guard had arrived at her door and handed them to her last night, saying, 'Don't know why they bothered with the skirt – it'll not be covering anything!'

Now, as she pulled it up and fastened it at the waist, Fern could see that the pleated blue cotton just skimmed the top of her pubis and left the lower portion of her bottom cheeks quite naked. Hastily she put on the white bra top to find that it lifted up her breasts but left her midriff bare. The only other items she'd been handed was a pair of white ankle socks and blue canvas slip-on shoes.

Weren't cheerleaders supposed to have a blazer? Sonia had conveniently forgotten that particular item, the heartless bitch! Grimacing, Fern fetched her own long-look beige cardigan and buttoned it over the revealing costume. then, clothed and shod to the best of her ability, she walked extremely slowly to the gym.

She reached its double doors at five past nine to find Sonia sitting on a bench and tapping her plimsolled feet on the floorboards.

'Five minutes late, Fern,' she said. 'That's not a good start, is it? In fact it's earned you five whacks with the sole of my shoe.'

She seemed to take her time pulling off her shoe and

Fern watched each controlled firm movement with a mixture of uncertainty and curiosity. She wondered how hard the sports coach would administer each stroke.

'Bend over and touch your toes, dear,' the older woman continued, 'but first take that cardigan off. You'll be punished later for wearing it without permission.'

I was using my initiative, Fern thought, but she kept the words to herself. She didn't yet know how much a plimsoll would hurt a girl's bare bottom. She wasn't sure how merciless an enemy Sonia would make!

The answer was a surprisingly mild one. Fern removed the cardigan and bent fully from the waist, using her hands to grasp her ankles. She gave a little gasp as the plimsoll hit home. She gasped again as the shoe slapped against her other cheek with the same firm pressure. Oh, the implement connected firmly with its target, but this was nothing to the thrashings she'd had in the past! Fern smiled inside as she accepted the other three whacks, but she made sure to give little grunts of pretend pain and discomfort. Sonia couldn't have tried the implement on herself; she obviously had no idea how little it really hurt!

'I'm sorry I was late, Sonia,' she said in a mock-obsequious voice at the end. She'd felt genuinely contrite for her actions whilst the dog handler and Rab were leading her around on her leash but now her earlier cheekiness was returning. 'Can I go to my room and recover?' she asked with a lopsided grin.

'Recover from what?' Sonia queried putting her plimsoll back on.

'From this beating,' Fern said pitifully.

'My dear girl, that was hardly even a spanking!' the teacher said contemptuously.

Fern licked her lips at the woman's dismissive words.

'Did you think I was just going to give you a few whacks and send you to your room?' the sports coach continued. 'Silly thing, I've hardly started yet. You're to spend the entire day here at the very least doing circuit training, maybe lifting weights.'

'And I'll be . . . *chastened* if I don't put the effort in?'

Fern prompted, anxious to know exactly what was in store for her disarmed buttocks.

'You'll be chastened anyway. Those five whacks were for being five minutes late. You still have to be disciplined for wasting Wanda's time and for ruining lunch for a hundred hungry inmates,' the taller woman murmured.

'Oh. I see,' Fern said.

Her words sounded inadequate and flat even to her own ears. She decided it was because she didn't know quite what to make of Sonia yet. Was she truly dominant or just pretending? Was she really capable of doling out significant pain?

'You've been slouching around the place these past few days,' the sports teacher said, 'so your bottom's doubtless in need of a proper firming up. Let's get you moving up and down on a step.'

'Aren't step classes supposed to be exhausting?' Fern queried.

Sonia pursed her lips as she obviously searched for the most realistic answer. 'They're demanding for the leg muscles if you're not used to it.' She smiled, 'But we'll start you off with the most simple moves on just one level.'

She pointed to the plastic steps and the bases which slotted in at each side to raise the equipment higher from the floor.

Dutifully Fern brought her step and its accoutrements into the centre of the room. She put the plastic rectangle over its plastic foundations. She stepped up and down experimentally, then smiled at Sonia. Hell, this was a cinch!

'I'll spend five minutes showing you the various steps, then I've to go see Dr Marshall about the parolee's reports,' the sports coach said.

'No problem!' Fern grinned. 'I'll just keep going!' She speeded up her rhythm to match the rap music Sonia had switched on. This was great!

Matching each other with move for agile move, the two women stepped up, down, faced the corners, hopped over the sides, did a basic step and a wide-legged step. Carefully copying the older woman, Fern stepped smartly up and down.

'When you tire, Fern, don't just stop,' the sports teacher warned. 'As with any aerobic exercise just ceasing to move can be dangerous. Instead, walk smartly on the spot to bring the heartbeat down gradually or march round and round.'

'Right. Okay,' Fern answered. Her calves were starting to feel somewhat stretched and heated now. Her arm muscles ached as she swung them. She was glad when Sonia looked grimacingly at her watch and started to walk towards the door.

'Remember, Fern – just go at your own pace,' she called back over her shoulder.

'Yeah, yeah, yeah!' Fern muttered under her breath.

She was bored with the exercise now, bored with supposedly being trained by the seemingly indifferent Sonia. Why, the woman didn't know how to dominate, just didn't have a clue!

Fern moved off of the plastic step and stayed off it. After a moments hesitation she flopped down on one of the big beanbag cushions near the gym door. It was nice here – soft and warm and soundless. Fern stretched each limb.

She could only have slept for a couple of minutes: leastways the hands of the clock had hardly moved forward when she opened her eyes again. One thing was different though – Sylvie stood in front of her clutching a cane.

'I heard you'd be here,' she said with a hellish quiet certainty. 'I knew that the sports coach couldn't possibly keep her eye on you for the entire day.'

She raised the rattan, obviously aiming it at the side of Fern's bare thigh, for the tiny skirt offered little or no protection.

'Don't touch me!' Fern yelled, scrabbling backwards. Then she turned and rushed out of the door – and straight into the arms of her coach.

'Not trying to escape Fern, were we? That's bad. That's very bad,' Sonia said, holding her firmly by the shoulders and sounding as if she meant it.

'This girl, Sylvie, was threatening me!' Fern said.

'Not as much as I'm about to start threatening you,'

226

Sonia confirmed. 'Or, to be more precise, threatening your poor bare bottom.'

'But I didn't do anything wrong!' Fern said.

'Talk me through the events,' Sonia continued, taking a firm grip on Fern's arm and marching her back into the hall. Fern looked around. There was no sign of the threatening Sylvie. She could have left through one of the side doors or gone up onto the dais and out through the entrance at the back.

'I was just dozing on the cushions when I looked up and . . .' She trailed off as she realised her mistake.

'So we have to warm that arse for sneaking off to have a nap,' Sonia said, giving the small bum in question a warning tap. She paused. 'As you're so partial to wandering about I think we'll have to tie you into position.' She looked round the vast hall and the upper level dais, her gaze seeming to settle on the latter. 'Yes, let's get you up there on the stage tied over that nice big administrative desk.'

Knowing that to argue might earn her further whacks, Fern walked before the teacher to the stage. She told herself that the woman was probably only capable of doling out a mild spanking. She could even lessen the punishment's length by pretending that it hurt like hell. Sure that she could handle the situation, Fern stretched out over the piece of furniture, turning her bottom into a vulnerable nude target. She shivered slightly as the sports coach took the straps attached to hoops in the desk lid and used them to fasten Fern down by the waist.

'Miss Shendon, I forgot to ask you about Inmate Ten's attitude to competitive sports,' called a familiar voice from further down the hall.

Fern clenched her bum cheeks. Damn it, it was Dr Marshall!

'I see you're fully occupied,' the man continued, his words growing nearer. Knowing that he was approaching her helpless posterior, Fern closed her eyes.

'She ignored my safety instructions for her aerobic exercise,' Sonia said, 'so I'm showing her little cheeks the consequence of foolhardy actions.'

'Good idea. What are you going to tan them with?' the psychiatrist replied.

'I've used my plimsoll so far – seemed appropriate!' Sonia laughed.

Fern closed her eyes more tightly still. It was awful being held down by the strap across her waist while they discussed her thrashing.

'Failure to exercise? An appropriate punisher might be a whipping with one of these heavy exercise bands,' Dr Marshall said.

'It'll have to be a double flogging,' Sonia said, 'because she also needs disciplining for slacking off and having an unscheduled sleep.'

'Sleep, did she?' Dr Marshall echoed.

Christ, Fern thought, it was like being in the presence of two parrots. She wished they'd just choose their implement of anguish and get it over with!

'I like to use a hard slipper on a sleepy bottom,' the psychiatrist said.

Fern quivered as she felt his hands palm her arse from spine to thigh crease.

'I could get one of hers from her room and bring it to you now.'

'That seems fitting,' Sonia admitted, sounding happy at the thought. 'Should I bind her wrists before her in the meantime?'

Fern tensed her tummy at the psychiatrist's reply: 'No, need, I'll hold her hands.'

He seemed to leave the hall for a long, long time. Fern lay there, every part of her being concentrated on her naked buttocks. She didn't think that Sonia had the desire to punish her mercilessly – but Dr Marshall certainly did! Why that spanking he'd given her in the van and the birching in the bottom garden had left her bum on fire. The slaps had gone on and on and on.

'Don't let him hurt my bum too much, Miss. I'll behave,' Fern whispered, twisting round to look pleadingly at Sonia.

'You're only this good when you've a thrashing due,' the sports teacher said.

It was true. Why were they always right? Fern lay tethered across the desk as the psychiatrist re-entered the gym. She heard his footsteps cross the floorboards then mount the steps to the dais.

'Look Fern – your own slipper to be used on your lazy backside,' he said, coming round to her face to hold the hard-soled footwear before her. Then he disappeared in the direction of her trembling arse.

'I'll do it,' Sonia said.

Fern relaxed a little against the polished wood. Then she jerked as heat exploded across the centre of her naked bottom. God, that whack had had real force behind it!

'I let you off lightly for unpunctuality, Fern,' Sonia said calmly, 'but you didn't show me any respect.'

'I'll be respectful, Miss Shendon!' Fern blurted out, starting to twist her head back. Then the slipper's sole crashed mercilessly into her nether cheeks again.

Fern's hands left the sides of the desk and moved automatically to protect her rear, but Dr Marshall stepped forward and grabbed her shoulders.

'Dear me, girl, all this moving about. Time we held these naughty hands in place.' He took hold of her wrists, holding them in front of her and staring into her face, his dark eyes fathomless.

Unable to meet his gaze for a second longer, Fern put her own face down against the desk. Sonia had obviously picked up the slipper again. Leastways Fern felt a third flush of heat exploding across one previously cool buttock. It was swiftly followed by a fourth, fifth and sixth. 'I won't be a bad girl ever again!' Fern pleaded, 'I swear I won't, Miss!'

'Auntie Sonia will thrash you till you're very good,' Sonia said, stopping to stroke Fern's exposed sore buttocks. 'Remember you're currently being slippered for laziness. We'll talk about your little escape attempt later on.'

Fern shuddered: 'I won't run away again! I'll do what I'm told? I'll . . .' Her promises turned into an impassioned wail as Sonia brought the slipper's sole across her sensitive buttock crease.

Cool leather met hot tenderness. After every two strokes the older woman stopped the discipline to palm the vulnerable globes.

'Think of this next time you're causing chaos in the kitchens, Fern,' she said smoothly.

The younger girl was shameless now: 'I will! I swear, Miss – anything!'

'Oh don't swear – bad language has always upset your Auntie Sonia. Don't do anything that might cause me to dole out a further lashing lesson to your arse.'

Fern moaned. Dr Marshall tightened his grip on her hands presumably lest she try to get up, but she was exhausted now, slumped over the desk with her red orbs sticking out for target practice.

'Please,' she whispered, 'no more strokes.'

'Just another four,' Sonia confirmed, fondling the quivering flesh. 'Then we'll have a little talk about your actions.'

Fern licked her lips: 'Thank you, ma'am,' she whispered. She looked dazedly up at Dr Marshall. 'And thank you, sir.'

One stroke. Two strokes. Three. Sonia put her slippering hand into action again, and Fern flattened her tummy against the desk and wailed as each spank hit home, then relaxed her buttocks for a few seconds until the next slippering fell.

'Four!' said Sonia with some satisfaction. 'Now lie there quietly like a good girl and think about the lessons we've taught your wicked bottom.'

'Yes, ma'am,' Fern whimpered, flushing further. She wondered if her face was as well-warmed as her arse.

'No touching your punished rump,' Dr Marshall added firmly, letting go of her hands. He walked over to join Sonia.

From this point in the room, Fern realised, the two of them had the best view of her chastened backside.

For long moments they left her lying there, then Dr Marshall came back and undid the strap from her waist. Fern stood up shakily to see Sonia had seated herself on the highest of the six sports benches.

'Come over here, my dear,' she said.

Fern walked slowly over till she stood facing the sports coach.

'That's it. You're not too big to go over my knee and bare your bottom,' the older woman smiled.

Fern felt her body still. 'But you promised . . .'

'Oh I know your punishment has ended for today, but I just want to make sure you understand who's in charge here.'

Looking at the ground, skirt hitched up round her waist to show her flaming extremities, Fern did as she was told.

'Yes, this bum has had enough for this morning,' Sonia continued, hoisting the twin spheres over her lap and stroking the heated contours.

'Thank you, ma'am,' Fern whimpered, writhing in humiliation and pain.

'But what about her clitoris?' Dr Marshall cut in teasingly.

'It's fine . . .' Fern muttered, her brave words turning into a gasp as the man's knowing fingers touched the throbbing bud.

'Pity I've to sit on the parole board in five minutes,' Dr Marshall said, withdrawing his pleasure-giving hand. Obviously addressing the sports coach, he added, 'Perhaps you'd like to frig her?'

Fern wriggled over Sonia's knee as the older woman replied: 'I've never . . . you know.'

'Call someone else in to do it, if you like,' the psychiatrist continued. 'You'll find that after an orgasm Fern's much more malleable.'

'Point taken, Dr Marshall. I'll organise something. See you later,' the sports coach said.

Fern tilted her head up to watch the man leave. Maybe now her life would get easier. But the teacher's next words suggested otherwise.

'I'm going to tether you in place whilst I search for a girl to bring you sexual relief,' she said, fondling Fern's sore bottom. 'Just to make sure you don't run away again.'

'I only took off because Sylvie was threatening to cane me!' Fern muttered.

231

Sonia slapped first one hot buttock then the other: 'Don't you dare start making excuses for your misconduct again!'

The spanks reawakened the slipper pain. Fern yelped then firmly shut her mouth. Then yelped again as Sonia dumped her unceremoniously on the floor and crossed the room towards the many chairs and stools stacked up beside the cupboard. She looked closely at several before dragging an armchair-sized four-legged stool into the centre of the floor. The stool had a wide surface to provide support for a bad girl's tummy. It had stocky legs on which to bind her flinching arms and legs.

'Bend over it and stick your bum out, Fern,' the sports coach said.

Fern stayed crouched on the floor, but put her hands back to cup her punished bottom: 'You said that you were through with thrashing me,' she whimpered, scrabbling back a little.

'I am. I just want to stop you escaping whilst I fetch another girl.'

'You could just tie one of my wrists to the desk,' Fern suggested, looking hopefully in the direction of the dais and its large administrative table.

'I could,' Sonia agreed mildly, 'but if you fell over you'd wrench your arm from the socket. I want you fully supported by this piece of furniture whilst I'm away.' She grinned over at Fern, 'Anyway, it'll be easier for some stranger to find your clit and rub it if your legs are bound far apart.'

Damn the woman, she was proving to be formidable after all! Reluctantly Fern rose to her feet and walked over to the stocky stool. Each movement reminded her that her labia and inner thighs were salaciously wet. She did want to come – Dr Marshall was right about that fact. If only he'd been the one to pleasure her, rather than suggesting she be touched by another female inmate. It felt somehow shameful to think of a strange girl touching her inner sanctum. It felt exciting yet dirty and wrong.

'I was right, wasn't I, telling you to leave off your pants?' Sonia smiled.

Fern blushed and looked at the stool then let the weight of her head and hands take her over it. She was aware of the tiny cheerleader's skirt sticking up even further away from her helpless bottom. Then Sonia knelt and bound her arms and legs in place.

'Just reflect on the fact that you could have been having pleasure rather than pleasure after pain if you'd behaved yourself yesterday in the kitchens, Fern,' she said.

Fern listened to the soft slap of the sports coach's plimsolls on the wooden floorboards as she left the hall. She tugged at her wrists and ankles, but the woman was surprisingly skilled at restraining a bent-over body. After a moment of panic the twenty-four-year old gave herself up to the sensation of being firmly bound. She'd just accept the clitoral stimuli this new girl was to give – she had to! Maybe she could enjoy the lesbian overtures without guilt, knowing she had no choice.

Two sets of footsteps sounded in the hall. That was quick!

'Hope you didn't miss me, Fern,' Sonia said with a petty half-sneer. 'I knew we'd have to tend to your hungry clit in a hurry.'

Fern tensed her thighs the little she could at the woman's shaming words. She raised her eyes, trying to see the body or face of the girl who was about to pleasure her. She realised that the girl and teacher were standing next to her behind.

God, she must look vulnerable with her reddened cheeks sticking out under the silly skirt and her sex-lips dripping! A finger touched her entrance lightly and she moaned.

'It won't take long,' came the teacher's voice. 'She started to glisten halfway through her slippering and by the time I turned her cheeks scarlet she was dripping.'

The touch came again, equally tenuous. If it was to remain this teasing she wouldn't be able to peak for a very long time.

'This isn't a prolonged punishment arousal,' Sonia said, obviously realising that the stranger was making Fern wait for it. 'Just bring her satisfaction so that I can get on with teaching her how to exercise again.'

'You got it!' muttered the girl, and Fern pushed back the few millimetres she could against the more firmly rubbing fingers. The touch brought her much closer to the edge.

'God yes, like that!' she groaned, not caring now that the sex act was a lesbian one. She just wanted the wondrous rush of her climax. She strove towards it with every sentient cell.

'She's a horny little bitch, isn't she?' came Sonia's voice, and the girl presumably nodded. Nodded and fondled and felt.

'Ah,' Fern heard her own voice give the last warning sound it made before the crescendo into a lengthy orgasm. Then the sensation rushed through her mons and lower belly and she cried out.

The girl kept rubbing even after Fern's rapture had faded. Too tender now, Fern tried hopelessly to squirm away.

'You did well,' came the teacher's voice, but Fern couldn't tell if she was addressing her or talking to the other inmate.

'Can you untie me now?' she muttered peevishly.

'I was about to, Fern,' Sonia answered, 'but I don't like your tone.'

Fern tensed her bottom. Drat it! Surely she hadn't earned herself a further whacking? She just wanted to get free. She didn't like being tied over the stool like this with some unknown girl standing at her naked bottom. Something about the situation made her feel uneasy, even scared.

'I think, Fern, that I'll leave you like this whilst I go and make us both a packed lunch,' the sports coach said. 'Leave you for twenty minutes or so to reflect on your sins.'

Her next words indicated that she was addressing the other girl. 'You don't mind keeping an eye on her, do you? I don't like leaving her alone when she's tied up for extended periods. And if I free her she may try to escape.'

'My pleasure,' said the girl.

Fern strained to hear more. That voice sounded vaguely

familiar. Had she been taunted by this particular inmate before?

She listened as Sonia left the room. She hoped the packed lunch would be good. That earlier slippering had made her feel increasingly hungry!

'I think we have a little unfinished business,' the stranger's voice said. She walked round till she crouched by Fern's face.

Fern raised her eyes – to find them staring at Sylvie! So it was Sylvie who had brought her off and Sylvie with whom she'd now been left alone.

'Handy that, wasn't it, my hanging around outside when Miss Shendon came looking for a girl?' the blonde female said.

Fern's mouth and tongue dried and she found she couldn't answer.

'I had to hide my cane behind the radiator of course, so that she wouldn't suspect anything,' her enemy said. 'I'll just fetch it now. Back in a tick.'

She had to get out of here or her bottom was in trouble! Fern tugged again at her bonds, but just succeeded in chafing her wrists and ankles. Within seconds Sylvie reappeared.

'Kiss the cane,' she ordered, holding it before Fern's mouth.

Fern flushed, but put her lips slackly to it.

'At least I'm showing you what's about to happen to your bare arse,' Sylvie continued. 'When you thrashed me that day in the bottom garden the first I knew of it was when the cane lashed into my backside.'

Fern trembled. What on earth had made her use the rod on the girl's tethered posterior? More importantly, how had she been so stupid as to get herself caught doing so? Now she was tied over a wide stool with her already-crimson arse sticking up like a beacon whilst her arch enemy stood behind her wielding the bendy rattan.

'You don't have the right to whip me!' Fern muttered, pushing her nude little tummy further against the ungiving stool.

'You're not supposed to make the rules,' came Sylvie's reply. 'You have to accept that I'm in charge now. I'm going to have to teach a lesson to your wilful little backside.'

Fern wished she could put her palms over her slippered globes: 'God, no!'

'Yes, yes,' Sylvie said tauntingly. 'What do I have to say to you to make you learn obedience?'

'I'll be obedient, Sylvie,' Fern said as she heard the blonde girl whipping the rattan experimentally through the air. Then a hot stripe burned its way across the centre of her reddened bottom and she yelled and tried to jerk her feet.

'The tip of this cane's dirty,' Sylvie murmured, stroking the first cane mark with the end of the rattan. 'But not as dirty as a girl who likes her clitoris rubbed by another girl,' she taunted.

'I know, I'm filthy,' Fern muttered, anxious to keep the other girl talking in order to keep her from laying on the cane.

'In fact, I think you should address me as Mistress,' continued the other girl.

'Yes, Mistress,' Fern said quickly.

The blonde girl's tone became increasingly mocking: 'You need your mistress to beat all the bad thoughts out of you, you wicked slave.'

Helplessly Fern shook her head.

'How many strokes does a dirty girl get?' Sylvie queried.

'Two . . .' Fern started, then realised her mistake. 'That's for my mistress to decide.'

'Mmm, it is – and she's angry that you didn't remember that right away,' the blonde girl replied.

She would doubtless take her rage out on Fern's bare behind. Fern could foresee the pattern. Her backside twitched as Sylvie traced the rod down its bent-over expanse. Any second now it would come whistling down, sending its lasting torment through her arse.

When it did she almost went over the footstool.

'Ask nicely for the next,' Sylvie warned.

Fern wriggled around, gasping for breath. The footstool

felt cool against her belly. Her arse, though, was two swollen orbs of fire marked with two stinging lines.

'Please give me the next stroke of the cane, Mistress,' she whimpered, afraid to say it yet terrified not to lest Sylvie caned her more firmly.

'It's what you need,' the blonde girl said, bringing the rod smartly down.

This time it hit the underswell, and Fern drove her thighs forward and twitched her stinging bum and howled.

'Ask nicely for another stroke,' Sylvie said.

Fern shook her head, and, obviously enraged, her mistress laid on three more strokes of discipline.

'No more! I can't take any more!' Fern begged. She squirmed helplessly against the stool, her abused bottom writhing. She felt very close to tears.

'You'll take what I give you,' Sylvie warned.

Fern wept as the cane fell again and again. At last her new mistress walked over to her head and pulled at the top of Fern's hair till she was forced to look up at her.

'Sonia will be back in a moment,' she explained, 'so I'm going to free you and say that when I went to the ladies you cut your bonds and tried to escape.' She took out a pair of scissors and quickly snipped through Fern's bonds.

Snivelling, Fern wriggled free of the punishment stool and got onto her knees, both hands cupping her burning rear end.

'I'll tell her I had to thrash you to keep you from running away,' Sylvie continued. She sounded slightly nervous now.

Fern knelt, clutching her fevered arse, and said nothing. I'll be good from now on, she thought over and over again, I'll be so good. She was vaguely aware of voices, of Sylvie making up lies, of Sonia believing them. She watched dully as the blonde girl left and the sports coach approached.

'I'll do whatever you want!' Fern muttered. She threw herself forward, her lips going under the older woman's short skirt to press against her panties. She felt the sports coach's vaginal folds through the close thin briefs.

'You really shouldn't . . .' Sonia started, then tailed off

as Fern tugged her pants down and put her mouth directly to the teacher's pouting flesh.

'Uh! Ah!' Sonia muttered.

Fern ran her tongue over the musky bud.

'If we're really doing this at least let me lie down,' the teacher added gutturally. Even as she spoke the words she was sliding to the floor and spreading her legs.

Aware only of her roasting bum and this woman's hot clit, Fern tongued and tongued, making the wet flesh wetter. She pushed Sonia's firm thighs further apart to gain greater access to her sex.

'Ah, ah, ah, ah, aaaaaaaaaaah,' the sports teacher groaned. They were cries from heaven or hell, a strange mix of pleasure and joy and confusion.

Fern kept licking, licking, licking, knowing that whilst her tongue was on this woman's clitoris there couldn't be a belt licking at her poor arse. Only when Sonia started to clamp her thighs together in post-orgasmic rigor did Fern pull her head away.

'God, you're a little beauty!' the teacher murmured.

Fern's heart swelled with pride at the words. Hesitantly she curled against the older woman's side, half-expecting a rebuff.

'To think that I could have been having orgasms like that for years and years!' the woman sighed.

Fern felt wearily pleased as the woman kissed her lightly on the nose. Then she stiffened as Sonia's mobile phone started buzzing.

'Ignore it,' Sonia murmured.

Ten minutes later, as they lay entangled in each other's arms the phone buzzed again. Fern watched as Sonia stood up and walked to the window. She opened it then dropped the telephone out.

'Now where were we?' she asked, squatting down next to Fern and beginning to unbutton her own polo-top.

Fern looked up to see that the woman's eyes were full of lust and love.

Fourteen

God, that orgasm had been exquisite! Sonia lay on the floor still trembling with sensation. Fern had licked her till the ecstasy rushed through every exuberant pore.

'You're a horny little bitch, aren't you, Fern?' she murmured tenderly, then smiled as the younger woman blushed and buried her face under Sonia's arm.

The sports teacher propped herself up on one elbow to read the clock. Her gaze focused on Fern's bare bum. It was a sore-looking scarlet. Darker glowing marks stood out against the background red. Had she really laid on the slipper that hard? She'd certainly put a lot of energy into the thrashing because Fern had been rude after receiving the lighter plimsoll strokes.

'Let's have a closer inspection of that bad little backside,' she murmured, pulling Fern over her knee.

Fern seemed to be in a world of her own: 'Please, don't leave me tied up in here again,' she whispered. 'Don't use the cane. Don't . . .'

'You know that providing you do what you're told you don't get disciplined,' Sonia said. She laid her cool palms over the girl's sore globes and watched Fern quiver. She realised that Fern had licked her so insistently to avoid earning herself an even hotter arse.

So punishment was the key to a relationship with this deliciously curved submissive girl! Sonia's mind searched for ways that might further exploit the power differential between them. 'I think,' she said finally, 'that you should come here for exercise training every day.'

Fern's shoulders tensed slightly, then she turned her head to look up into the sports coach's face: 'But my work in the gardens, Miss? Bill Stark the head gardener will be angry if I fail in my duties!'

'And *I'll* be angry if you fail to achieve a fitter body, Fern,' Sonia said. She stroked the nervous hot bum, enjoying the way it wriggled under her palms. 'But I'm sure we can find a compromise, my angel. Just report to me here every morning at 7 a.m. and I'll train you for an hour. You can then bathe and breakfast and still be at work in the gardens for nine.'

'An hour of step class or running?' Fern queried, letting her weight relax across Sonia's lap.

'Both – with extra time put aside at night for stringent punishment if you fail any of the morning tasks I set you,' Sonia replied.

She felt the lust slake through her loins as the bottom across her knees twitched at the mention of stringent punishment. She slid a cautious finger between the girl's taut thighs to find that she was lusciously hot and wet. That blonde girl had made Fern come earlier though, so the teacher decided that her new lover had had enough satisfaction for today.

Sonia smiled as she pushed Fern from her lap. If the girl was aroused when she attended the exercise classes she'd be distracted and likely to forget the routines she'd been taught; to lose her concentration. And such failures would give Sonia an excuse to thrash those exquisitely smooth little cheeks.

Three days later she had a genuine reason to tan the girl's lethargic arse. Sonia was about to supervise Fern's six lengths of the pool when one of the guides told her that she was needed in the staff room.

'Just start without me, Fern. Remember to concentrate on your breathing,' the sports coach ordered, hurrying away. She looked back at the door to see Fern still splashing about playfully at the shallow end.

'Can this *tête à tête* wait for five minutes?' she asked the man.

'I guess so, Miss Shendon.' The other staff member's eyes widened with curiosity.

Sonia put her middle finger to her lips to indicate that they should keep their voices down: 'Only I think my little charge is about to disobey.'

Quickly the two of them climbed the stairs to the observer's gallery and knelt behind the balcony wall, just peeping over the top of it. They watched Fern jump up and down in the water then turn on her back and float. The white raw silk of her costume clung to her breasts and waist and belly. Sonia longed to caress them all with her satiating hands.

But first the girl had to suffer, had to learn obedience.

'Make a noise as you walk to the poolside,' she told the other staff member, 'then tell her I'll be gone some time.' She stayed at her overhead perch and watched Fern start to swim the required lengths as she heard someone approaching. She saw her start floating aimlessly in the water again after the guard delivered his message and went away. Loins starting to tingle, Sonia went to the discussion she'd been called for and sorted out the problem.

'Now I'm going to teach my young student compliance,' she told the guard who'd originally fetched her. 'Like to watch?'

'I'll help if you like!' said the man, but Sonia shook her head. She didn't want any more male cocks up Fern, she needed to have the girl to herself, as her submissive.

'No, it'll be shame enough to have you watch her baring her bottom,' Sonia said.

They reached the poolside and Sonia called Fern over, ordering her to leave the chlorinated water.

'I'll get cold!' Fern muttered, clambering onto the poolside and hopping from foot to foot as she rubbed her arms.

'Don't worry, darling,' Sonia said sweetly, 'I'm going to warm that lazy bottom for a very long time.'

She picked up one of the coils of rope in the corner and handed it to the guard. 'Loop it through the balcony spars and throw me down both ends.' Grinning, the guard did so. Sonia turned her attention back to her fidgeting lover: 'Fern, pull down your shoulder straps then hold your arms together above your head.'

'Haven't done anything wrong!' Fern muttered, her eyes widening.

'You didn't complete six laps of the pool,' the sports teacher said.

She watched as Fern reluctantly dislodged her swimming costume straps then let her hands sneak round to cover her costumed buttocks.

'I could do the laps now,' she offered. 'Sonia – please?'

'The only lapping I want is your tongue against my clit after I've thrashed you into submission,' Sonia replied softly. She bound the younger girl's wrists together then ordered the guard to pull on the rope from his balcony position. She smiled with satisfaction as the cord exerted a steady pull on Fern's lifted arms.

A moment later the guard joined Sonia and they looked at Fern's costumed back and bum.

'Lets get this nasty wet costume all the way off, love,' the man murmured, looking to Sonia for approval.

Sonia nodded: 'Yes, you go ahead and bare her naughty bottom. We're going to have to make it very red indeed.'

'Do you have to let him paw me? I'm sorry I didn't swim the lengths!' Fern muttered as the man took his time pulling the costume free of her backside and edging it down to her knees.

Sonia touched the younger girl's bum. It was smooth and slightly clammy. 'What do you think we should warm this with?' she asked her fellow staff member, fondling the helpless nether cheeks.

'They've got some new martinets in the punishment supplies hall,' the man said eagerly. 'You know, those leather-thonged French whips which leave lots of marks with each lashing?'

Sonia nodded, looking at the suddenly-twitching bum: 'That sounds ideal.'

'The domestic martinet will probably be enough for a naughty girl's bottom,' said the guard thoughtfully, 'given that her arse is bare and wet.'

He strolled away whistling and came back a few minutes later with an eight-thonged lightweight whip. Not that it would feel light when lashed into defenceless naked buttocks, Sonia thought gloatingly. Buttocks that were so tautly held that they could do little more than flinch.

'Six strokes for six unswum lengths,' she said, and stood well to one side so that she could swing the martinet smartly forward.

The thongs whipped into Fern's smooth posterior and the girl snorted hard and shuffled her bare feet. The strong pull on her arms kept her from going very far.

Sonia traced the heated pattern of lines with her middle finger, then stood back again. 'I'm going to aim this one lower down,' she warned. 'Where the rump is much more tender, my unfortunate dear.'

She followed up her threat with action and Fern flinched and grunted and did a little dance that made her bare thighs jiggle.

'You should have thought of how the whip would feel before you were naughty,' Sonia said evenly. 'Maybe then you'd have done what you were told.'

'I'll do it now!' Fern muttered, tensing and untensing her poor red-and-white bum. 'I'll swim for hours!'

Sonia lined up the martinet with its sorry target. 'No,' she said, 'for the next hour you'll just dance on the end of my whip.'

Not that it was going to take that long to mete out this discipline – but the ensuing sexual teasing could take ages. And Sonia really loved that bit. She doled out the third stroke, watching the little rump helplessly twitch, watching the myriad lines appear and stay there. She knew that Fern would be sexually open by the time she'd whimpered under lash number six. The whip, paddle or the cane seemed to break down the girl's resistance to her own lesbian sexuality, made her give in to her Sapphic needs.

Smiling, Sonia stepped closer and fondled Fern's hot-and-cold writhing cheeks. The girl squirmed further.

'Please don't whip me any more, Miss,' she pleaded, trying to look back over her shoulder even as she tried to move her bum away.

'I have to, love. I have to make this wicked little bottom sore and scarlet,' Sonia answered. 'It's for its own good.'

'Then you could lay the strokes on further up,' Fern haggled.

Sonia fondled the sensitive buttocks some more: 'You mean nearer the fleshy tops of your poor hot arse cheeks?'

The girl nodded vigorously.

'But I so love heating the tender lower globes,' Sonia said.

Knowing that to take her lover to her limit would result in a better sexual end, she lined up the martinet with the juicy undercurves and whipped them firmly. She murmured, 'Oh I enjoyed laying on that last stroke so much that I'm going to have to do it all again!'

Fern quivered. 'Please,' she whispered. 'Anything! Please!'

'Please lay the last two on extra hard? Please give me the sorest bum?' Sonia taunted, getting ready to inflict the multi-thonged punishment.

Fern breathed hard and fast as Sonia flogged the crease at the top of her tender thighs.

Sonia watched assessingly as Fern's feet jerked on the wet floor, her arms pulling uselessly at the thick soft ropes and her bottom jiggling. She redoubled the girl's frantic flinching by laying on the sixth and most authoritative stroke. It landed halfway up the helpless arse, leaving blurred, sore lines over the other sore lines that already reddened the girl's bottom. Lines that would sting and glow fiercely. Lines that would remind the twenty-four year old that the sports coach was in charge. Lines that would excite – even as they pained the tethered young woman.

'Rub against my fingers, Fern,' Sonia said, putting the middle digits of her right hand to the restrained girl's clitoris. 'Want to come?' she continued sweetly.

Fern groaned and nodded, pushing her labia down faster and harder.

'Then you have to please your mistress with your tongue,' Sonia said.

She ordered the guard to remove the rope end from the balcony. 'Tie her hands behind her back this time,' she said, 'I don't want her touching herself.'

244

She squeezed Fern's bum as the man expertly replaced one set of wrist bondage with another, keeping the girl as a willing sexual slave.

'You're just to lick really nicely and subserviently, sweetheart. Understand?' she continued.

Fern nodded: her cheeks were flushed with shame and her eyes were bright with need; her clitoris obviously craving.

Sonia lowered herself down to the poolside and spread her thighs as wide as she was able. She thought that Fern had never looked so incredibly alluring. It would be so easy to fall in love.

Fern licked. Sonia came. It took about thirty seconds – she'd become so aroused when whipping the girl's helpless bottom.

'Your turn, my sweet,' Sonia said, determined to make her lover's ecstatic peak take longer than her own. 'As you failed to complete your swimming task I'll have to make you swim now on the poolside.'

Fern squatted on the ground, her face hectic with desire as Sonia untied her slender wrists: 'Mistress,' she whimpered, 'I swear I'm paying attention but I don't know what you mean by swimming on the poolside.'

'Lie on your tummy,' Sonia ordered, 'and you'll see.' She watched the younger girl scrabble to obey. 'No – kick that costume from around your ankles first!' She nodded as the girl pulled off the wet material. Obediently Fern got down on the tiles on her tender tummy. She was now completely nude, her arse a glowing twitching red.

'Don't punish me any more, Sonia,' she pleaded.

'I won't have to if you do as you're told,' Sonia said. She curved her palm under Fern's pubis. The pubis in question immediately bore down upon her hand. 'You can keep doing that as long as you make swimming motions,' the sports coach murmured.

Fern twisted her head around, a new flush starting: 'You want me to pretend to swim here on the floor?'

'Got it in one,' Sonia grinned. She looked at the girl's stripped form. 'I think we'll have five minutes of breast

stroke. That'll provide some exercise for those sagging titties!'

In truth the girl's breasts were firm and high and pert-
nippled, but Sonia knew the shaming words would arouse
them both to greater heights.

'I feel stupid,' Fern muttered.

'That's because you are stupid,' Sonia said. 'You've
brought this chastisement on yourself rather than doing a
few laps of the pool for your mistress. You deserve to
squirm on your belly for a while.' She slid her thumb
across the girl's clitoris, then added, 'There'll be no more
pleasure like that if you don't start swimming right now!'

Snivelling with obvious shame and unsatisfied desire,
Fern pushed her arms to the front, then moved them com-
pliantly into a wide circle.

'I think we need a few cushions under her tummy so that
we can see each limb moving fully,' Sonia said.

'I'm with you there, Guv!' the guard half-laughed,
marching towards the cupboard. He came back with three
bolsters and slid them under the quivering Fern's tum.

'Squat at her face and make sure she's doing the breathing exercises right,' Sonia said to the man, who
immediately hurried to do so.

He hunkered down and stared hungrily at Fern's hanging tits.

'Swim, sweetheart, swim!' Sonia prompted, rubbing her
hand against the girl's mound of Venus, knowing the guard
was seeing the girl's pink nipples harden and enlarge.

As she made Fern squirm and beg she was barely aware
of her mobile phone ringing and ringing from the bushes
outside where she'd thrown it. Then Fern moaned with joy
and pushed rapturously against Sonia's fingers and Sonia
could think of nothing except their mingled desires.

Where on earth had that woman gone now? Robert Greene
listened to the tone ring out as he waited for Sonia to pick
up the mobile. Was she in danger at that bloody reformatory? Didn't she know that he cared? He'd always cared,
of course, but with Mrs Greene around he'd been unable

to prove it. But now that she'd gone to live with her sister for good – he was suddenly wifeless. He was suddenly free. Free to love again, to have sex with – and even marry – the sexy Sonia. He was also free to spend even more time making Penal Liaisons the best organisation in the world. An organisation free of rumour and scandal. An organisation above reproach.

Carefully Robert stocked the passenger seat of his car with fruit and sandwiches and a flask of coffee. He'd stop overnight at a hotel, of course, but would still need sustenance for this long drive across the border. He'd take his mobile phone with him and keep buzzing Sonia. He'd make it his business to find out the truth.

Maybe his personal assistant had been so overawed by what she'd seen that she only wanted to tell him in person. Maybe she'd even been threatened to keep the peace. He should have listened to the subtext of her conversation instead of snapping at her all the time during their few rushed phone calls. He should have had the place bugged at the very least.

Getting behind the wheel of his gleaming Daimler, Robert set off for Scotland and its experimental reformatory. If he found anything untoward there he was going to close the place down.

Fifteen

'Fern's going before another parole board?' Sonia repeated tonelessly.

Dr Marshall nodded. 'She's been doing splendid work in the gardens – and with you in the mornings, I hear, Sonia. Plus she's shown a marked improvement in her attitude to other people, and usually thinks now before she acts.'

Sonia cleared her throat: 'So you ... uh ... think she'll get a weekend pass for good behaviour?'

Dr Marshall studied Fern's case notes then smiled with obvious satisfaction. 'I think she may even be set free.'

Sonia's heart seemed to shrink and immobilise. She felt the sensation she always got in her chest when she heard news that was disappointing or frustrating. She knew that she wanted to keep being tongued by Fern for a very long time. Why, just staring at the girl's obediently bent head made her libido start to quicken. Just watching Fern pull down her own pants made Sonia's liquid lashings start. She must say something to stop the girl getting a parole date! She must act.

After a full day spent supervising the netball, hockey and rounders games, Sonia went off to her room and sat on her bed wondering what she could do to blot Fern's copybook. Fern worked in the gardens and her original crime had been arson, so if Sonia could burn some of the grounds Fern would be blamed.

For two days she alternately accepted and discarded various saboteuring activities. She desperately tried to think of ways to keep her lover with her, without resorting to lying. Finally lust and love won over goodness and common sense and Sonia went in search of a can of petrol.

After a thorough search she found one in the largest out-house.

Now to find Fern's vegetable plot! Sonia traipsed across the fields carefully clutching the can. It was growing dark so most of the other inmates had retired. She was startled when a youth stepped out from behind a glasshouse.

'Having a bonfire, Miss, are you?' he asked, smiling lop-sidedly.

'No, but *you* are,' Sonia replied, an alibi suddenly presenting itself. She went on to offer the boy fifty pounds and two bottles of sloe gin if he poured the petrol over Fern's vegetables and plants.

'Bill Stark does a late-night inspection to make sure deer haven't got over the fence,' the youth said, 'but I could get up at 5 a.m. and start the blaze for you. It would be eight or nine till they discovered it.'

'I'll set an alarm clock and watch!' Sonia murmured, her mood lifting. She patted the youth's arm. 'If you're caught you don't admit it was my idea, all right?'

'Scouts Honour!' the boy said.

Sonia left, went back to her room and eventually slept. She got up at a quarter to five and showered away the grit-tiness from her eyes, splashing her face until the skin tingled. Dressed in a pair of loose white trousers and a white belted top, she walked to the window and looked out. She could see the reddish glow in the distance, the grey smoke spiralling and the darker puffs dispersing into the clouds like Indian messages. Now she must breakfast and meet Fern at the gym and act as normal. She must wait.

She was halfway through teaching the younger girl how to trampoline when there was a knock on the gym hall door. *This must be it!*

Sonia fixed her features into a mask of nonchalance and got ready to look startled. She realised that surprise was a difficult emotion to fake. She opened the door to find Ms Lenn and Robert Greene standing there. Suddenly the shock was real!

'Robert! What on earth . . .' Sonia started to speak then realised her mistake. She was supposed to be a gym teacher, for God's sake, not the personal assistant of Robert Greene from Penal Liaisons.

She watched the man's mouth tense, then he said smoothly, 'I had no idea you were working here, Sonia. I've come to inspect the premises and Ms Lenn here is kindly showing me around.'

'Well, don't let me keep you,' Sonia murmured, wishing she could wring the high pitch from her voice. She smiled stiffly at Ms Lenn. 'As you'll have gathered I know Robert from . . . em from before,' she finished vaguely.

'It's a small world, isn't it?' Ms Lenn said.

The two of them turned to go. Robert turned back as if by an afterthought: 'Sonia, perhaps we can have lunch here, catch up on old times?'

Still thrown by this new turn of events, the sports coach nodded dumbly. 'See you in the dining room at twelve then,' Robert confirmed.

He was there. For the first time Sonia saw him as being a tiny bit square. He seemed to weigh each word in his head before giving birth to it. And his suit was the grey serge beloved of older politicians; his cobalt blue tie lacked verve.

'Mrs Greene not with you this time?' she asked cautiously as she brought her tray of prawn and egg salad over to his table.

'Mrs Greene and I are officially separated as of last week,' her boss said. 'So, what's been going on here?' he continued, spearing a sauce-coated pasta shell.

More than you could imagine in your wettest dreams, Sonia thought.

The idea expanded in her mind. Maybe she could organise a wet-dream-style scenario! Perhaps she could rekindle the passion she'd felt for Robert by dominating him in the sack. The last few months had shown her that therein was where true excitement lay – in dominance and submission. She just had to make her boss see it that way too.

'I'll tell you about what's been going on here after I've shown you my bedroom,' she promised, putting the emphasis on *bed*.

'Lead the way!' Robert smiled, his mouth curving into a sensuous promise.

Maybe they'd be good together after all, Sonia thought, her heartbeat starting to speed. Hands brushing, they hurried up the stairs till they reached her quarters. They went in, locking the door behind them. Then Robert turned to her and took her in his arms.

Hold me more firmly, Sonia thought as she sank down onto the duvet with Robert on top.

She had a sudden desire for the man to take charge of the next lust-filled hour. She wanted him to untie the cotton belt of her trousers and pull down her pants. When he didn't, Sonia decided to lead the way.

'Now you're my prisoner!' she teased, rolling over till her body weighed down on his as fully as she was able. She trapped his wrists above his head in one of her hands then unbuttoned his shirt and used her teeth to gently graze his hirsute chest. 'You've been bad, staying with your wife for so long,' she murmured with mock firmness and rage. 'I should put you over my knee and spank your bottom.'

'You'll do what?' Robert muttered, opening his eyes and warily searching hers.

'I'll warm your arse for being presumptuous,' Sonia said.

Aroused by her own plans, she tried to roll the man onto his belly, planning to thrash him with his own leather belt.

'No way! Not my scene,' the head of Penal Liaisons said, holding onto the quilt and staying firmly on his sturdy back and bottom.

Sonia stilled for a moment. Christ, she'd read the situation all wrong. She thought some more – if it stayed wrong then Robert would go back to London and arrange for *Compulsion* to be closed down, and she couldn't bear that.

'Just kidding!' she laughed, rescuing the situation. 'After all, you're the one who's imagining there's corporal punishment everywhere!'

She watched the little lines in his face smooth out as he realised she was only joking. She felt his manhood harden beneath her palm. The thoughts of tying him up and reddening his bum had made her inner core sufficiently sex-slicked. Manufacturing a smile for her boss's benefit, Sonia lowered herself onto his man-pole and was soon riding it fast and hard.

'God, you're so unrestrained!' Robert gasped, spasming into his condom. 'Mrs Greene never did it like that!'

Did Mrs Greene never fake orgasm either? Sonia opened her lungs and tensed her legs and gave an Oscar-winning performance.

'Darling, you loved that!' Robert Greene murmured triumphantly. Then he slept.

Sonia stayed awake. She was still awake when someone pushed a notice under her door giving details of the fire.

The accused will be tried at 11 a.m. tomorrow, the information sheet continued. Sonia felt a cold prickle of guilt, then her heart swelled with renewed hope and happiness. Fern would be found guilty and be forced to stay.

At last Robert gave a final three-part grunt and opened one cautious grey eye. Once she'd loved these same eyes, but now she loved brown eyes and long brown hair and breasts that were as soft as cushions.

He treated her to a smirk that said I've-really-got-you-by-the-groin-now. 'So, do I have cause for concern about this reformatory?' he asked amicably.

'None at all! It's run by the best psychiatrists and nurses. They've a clear behaviour modification agenda. They're doing sterling work,' Sonia said.

Robert sat up. Sonia noticed he'd kept on his socks.

'But these rumours we heard about people being whipped?' he pressed.

'Just new inmates causing trouble,' Sonia reassured him, keeping her tone light and even. 'It's a mentally rigorous and very sports-based regime which isn't immediately to everyone's taste.' She shrugged. 'Those of them who would rather have a soft option leak information that they're being ill-treated in the hope that they'll get a reprieve.'

'So you'd recommend this place for certain miscreants?' Robert queried, reaching for one of his Hush Puppies.

'I would indeed,' Sonia confirmed. She took a deep breath. 'In fact I like it so much here that I'm staying on.'

Life wouldn't be the same without her. There was always a place as his PA if she got bored with being a sports coach.

Sonia listened with a mixture of pleasure and cynicism to the kind of platitudes employers usually make when an employee is leaving.

'Maybe I could come down here every few weeks to take you out?' Robert asked, looking covetously at her breasts.

'No, long-distance relationships seldom last – best to make a clean break and avoid undue heartache,' Sonia said.

With the smile of a man who thinks he's given a woman the orgasm of her life, Robert left the room. Then he left *Compulsion*.

Soon, Sonia knew, he'd be actually leaving Scotland and driving out of her life. She smiled both inside and out as she realised that she was free of her infatuation with him. Free to punish and pleasure the luscious young Fern.

Sixteen

'Fern Terris, you are accused of setting fire to the crops in field three. How do you plead?' the balding judge thundered.

'Not guilty,' Fern said emphatically from the dock. She'd learned so many lessons these past few months that she couldn't believe this was happening! She'd been so good.

She didn't deserve to be standing in the dock as she was now, wearing only a halter top that served to further emphasise her vulnerable bare bottom. She didn't deserve to have been marched like this through the corridors as an example to others who might misbehave. 'M'Lord, I shouldn't be forced to dress without pants while I'm still regarded as innocent,' she protested during a lull in the procedure.

'It's my newest practice for custodial prisoners,' the judge said.

'But that doesn't make it right!' Fern continued. Since arriving here she'd learned to think for herself, to apply the rules of logic.

'How dare you contradict my dictates!' the judge, who looked to be in his mid-seventies, yelled.

Fern stared at the man with distaste. He'd been unreasonable since the moment she was led into court, and she suspected that he was nursing a hangover or a headache. Leastways, his right eye continually watered and he kept misplacing the handkerchief he used to dab it with.

'All I'm saying is that . . .' Fern started quietly.

'I sentence you to an immediate spanking for contempt of court,' the judiciary said.

God, no – she couldn't bear it! It had been many weeks since she'd been publicly humiliated in this way: she'd recently just been punished by the innovative Sonia. Fern backed off till she came up against the rails. Two guards entered from both sides of the dock and grabbed her shoulders.

'Time to go before the bench!' one murmured, grinning.

Kicking and squealing she was half-dragged and half-carried to the waiting judge's knee.

'Tie her hands behind her back to keep her in check,' he ordered, and one of the guards took the leather thongs that hung from his belt and immediately complied.

'It's not fair!' Fern muttered as she was held firmly over the waiting black-cloaked lap. Then the first spank radiated heat across her curving left cheek. It wasn't the gentle early slaps of a prolonged erotic spanking. Rather it was a mercilessly vicious spank that was purely designed to cause pain. Fern grunted at its harsh impact and jerked her body, the movement increasing the pull on her tied-back arms. She relaxed again, only to repeat the flinching movement as the judge doled out the second spank.

He hadn't sentenced her to a specific number of buttock slaps, Fern realised miserably as the hot smarting punishment continued. Damn it, the mood he was in he might warm her arse all day!

'This is to teach you not to answer back, to teach you humility,' the judge grunted, a hard spank accentuating every fourth word with cruel precision. 'By the time I've finished toasting this little rump you'll be grateful for the chance to obey!'

She'd be grateful for that chance now, Fern thought, pushing her belly as hard as she could against his judicial robes in the hope of making her bum a less raised target.

'Sorry I answered back, sir!' she whimpered, aiming for an expedient answer whilst secretly believing she'd been in the right.

'Sorry enough to parade your reddened arse around this court room?' the judge asked, doling out another four stinging spanks.

At the mention of a humiliating parade Fern felt her

bare bottom twitch, and one of the observers shouted, 'Keep wriggling it real pretty, sweetheart!'

There was laughter from the front row. Fern hung her head.

'It's that or another fifty spanks,' warned the judge, fondling her hot sore cheeks.

'I'll parade, sir,' Fern muttered, trying not to make eye contact with anyone as the man helped her to her feet.

With her wrists still tied behind her, she walked to the first row and turned so that each youth and young woman had access to her punished posterior. She winced with shame as fingers traced the crease between her cheeks then felt her entire rump. She let out a whimper as a harder hand rimmed its way around her rectum. She moved slowly on to the second row to have her sore buttocks further felt.

At last she reached the row where Sonia and several of the other staff members sat.

'I didn't do it, Sonia, I swear!' she whispered to her formidable lover.

'I believe you, Fern,' the teacher said, then looked away.

Did Sonia feel sorry for her? Or did she want to see her stripped and spanked like this? Fern was still trying to fathom out the older woman. She knew only that they gave each other immense pleasure with their mobile tongues and limbs.

The punishment parade completed, Fern was ordered back to the dock.

'Call the witness for the defence, Dr Brett Marshall,' the judge commanded.

Dr Marshall entered the court. On the way to the stand he glanced at Fern, then frowned as he noticed her crimson buttocks.

Inordinately glad to see her bearded mentor, Fern managed a wan smile.

'State your case,' said the judge.

'I don't believe the prisoner committed this arson attack,' the psychiatrist began. 'She's shown herself to be hard working and an increasingly thoughtful individual . . .'

257

'An individual who in the past has set fire to a department store,' the judiciary cut in.

'Yes, Your Honour – but the relevant words are "in the past",' Dr Marshall claimed. 'Fern Terris is a reformed character. In fact, we are getting close to releasing her on parole.'

'She had the means. She has no alibi,' continued the judge.

'That applies to half of the inmates at *Compulsion*, sir!' Dr Marshall demurred. 'Fern Terris had no particular motive.'

'I believe her motive was pure malice, and nothing I've seen or heard today leads me to believe otherwise,' the judiciary said. He banged his gavel. 'I'm forced to make an example of this girl who has let the system down. I sentence her to an hour-long taste of the master whip to be applied intensively to her tied bare buttocks.'

'I demand an appeal!' Dr Marshall said.

'The punishment is to be carried out immediately,' the man continued, ignoring him. 'Guard, usher the prisoner and the observers outside.' He looked stonily at Fern, though his words were meant for the guards. 'Tie the prisoner to the whipping post and fetch the nine-thonged leather whip.'

Fern stood in the dock and felt as if someone had thrown freezing water over her face and breasts. Though she'd railed against this reformatory at the beginning, she'd come to recognise that there was justice and fairness here in its luxurious confines. Now they were going to destroy her belief in the philosophy, which would leave her without a framework that was worthy of respect.

Mutely she shook her head and stared wildly around as she was marched towards the post. She trembled as the guards freed her wrists from behind her back only to tie them higher above her head to the post's short handles. She quivered as they bound her ankles directly to the foot of the pole, thus immobilising her body and her feet.

This was to be punishment without pleasure – and such a punishment! Fern twisted her head back to view the whip

258

as the muscular guard approached. It was long and thick and multi-thonged with a thick dark handle. A handle on which the whipper could take a merciless grip. She looked away as the man pulled his arm over his shoulder, and then tensed her bare bottom. She screamed into the daylight as the thongs branded her tethered arse.

The audience gasped. Fern bit back a sob. She heard the judge say, 'Keep thrashing her, man. She's due a full hour's whipping.'

She whimpered with fear as she sensed the master whip being pulled back again. Then she heard Sonia's voice shouting: 'Stop the thrashing at once – Fern's innocent! I forced a male inmate to start the fire.'

Fern sagged with relief as she was untied and carried to the medical bay. She quivered with pleasure as Nurse Bryson stroked a cooling lotion into her heated bottom. Then they helped her to her room where she slept.

When she awoke Dr Marshall was sitting by her bedside.

'We've put that judge to work at our trout farm where he can't do any more damage,' he said heavily. 'His health hasn't been good for months and he's been showing increasingly irrational behaviour. Can you forgive us for that travesty of a trial?'

Fern nodded: she suspected she could forgive the wonderful Dr Marshall absolutely anything. If only she could learn from him for the rest of her life!

Thinking of her life reminded her of her sports coach lover.

'Will Sonia be punished?' she whispered. 'I think she lied about arranging the fire to save me from a whipping, sir.'

'That's what we thought at first,' said the man, 'but it seems she really organised the flames to keep you here with her.' He sighed, 'The boy she paid to ignite the petrol has admitted it.'

Again Fern felt that drenched by cold water sensation: 'But I thought . . .'

'Thought she was your lover? She is,' the psychiatrist said. He leaned closer. 'She did it for love of you, Fern. It was a crime of passion.'

Fern sat up on the pillows: 'But because of her I was spanked in court and had to let strangers stroke my sore bottom. Then I was tethered and whipped!'

'Oh, I agree she did wrong, and she'll have to be severely punished,' the doctor continued. 'I'm sure we can think of a way . . .'

The next morning he called Fern into his study.

'As you've probably gathered,' he said, 'I was about to recommend you for our parole board.' Fern waited for the rush of excitement to come. Instead she felt suddenly root-less and sad.

'I'm still happy to do that, of course,' Dr Marshall con-tinued, 'but there's another road you can choose instead.'

'Tell me more!' Fern sang out, striving for her old flip-pancy. Then she realised that with this man she didn't need an alter ego.

'You can stay on here and become our new sports coach. There's an immediate vacancy,' the psychiatrist said.

The twenty-four-year old felt her chest lighten at the thought of staying at *Compulsion* for as long as she wished. Then she realised that the ensuing years would be without Sonia, and the lightness darkened a little. Okay, so she wanted to thrash the older woman until she begged for mercy, but she hated the thought of never making love to her again.

'If I'm to be made sports teacher that means Sonia's been sacked,' she said, swallowing heavily.

'No, she's just been demoted to the position of a naughty gardening inmate,' Dr Marshall said.

'An inmate!' Fern stared at him: this couldn't be hap-pening. 'But she hasn't been tried first in the outside world or undergone the masochistic test!'

The doctor nodded: 'She agreed to be tried by our inter-nal court and accept their jurisdiction. She's been sentenced to an indeterminate time here and has signed a disclaimer just like you.' He grinned as widely as a playful porpoise, 'As for her having a masochistic side? Let's just say we've checked!'

Fern looked at him friskily. 'I suspect the woman will need regular cross-country runs in the mornings to teach her self-discipline.' She stared at the psychiatrist's broad belt, 'And as she's taking over my job in the gardens I'd like to spend the first fortnight showing her the ropes.'

Showing Sonia the ropes in a literal sense! The following Monday Fern strolled into the vegetable plot to find Sonia trying to dig out the burnt plants, sweat beading her forehead. Her tall thirty-year-old body was inadequately clothed in the silvery top and stiffened ra-ra skirt. Her bare bottom stuck out as she bent over to reach each cabbage. Bill Stark stood watching her, slapping his right hand against his side.

'For a sports coach she's not so fit – she's failed to meet her morning quota!' he said to Fern sourly.

Fern smiled: 'Sadly, she spends most of her time just supervising. *Tells* rather than *shows* in the gym.' She walked up to her suddenly tensing lover. 'Isn't it lucky, darling, that I'm here to thrash you into shape?'

She stroked the woman's bent bum, then turned to Bill Stark. 'How many more cabbages ought she to have extracted from the soil by now?'

The man smiled coldly. 'Oh, at least thirty.'

Fern nodded. 'Then I'll give her bum thirty strokes of the birch throughout the day.' She squeezed Sonia's bare cheeks, 'Go and cut twelve willow rods from that tree over there, sweetheart, and use this nice strip of leather to bind them together. It's fitting that you make a rod for your own deceitful arse.'

Ten minutes later Sonia approached holding the whippy birch in both outstretched hands. 'I'm sorry, Fern,' she muttered, eyes bright with shame and fear and anticipation.

Fern kissed her lovingly on the lips, then whispered: 'I'm going to make you very sorry indeed.' Firmly she led Sonia over to the fence and bent her over it. She used soft ropes to bind her hands and legs in place against the wood. 'I'll give you fifteen of the birch now, and dole out the other fifteen when your sore cheeks have had a chance to recover,' she said mildly.

'Thank you, Fern,' came the muttered words from Sonia's hanging head.

'I think you should refer to me as *Mistress* from now on,' Fern corrected, looking at the bare bottom in front of her and realising that she could make it red and hot and squirming. She realised that she could take this woman to her limits and win her respect. Slowly she traced the willow -formed rods over the helplessly tensing pale globes. She knew that she could make them quiver and beg.

She swung the birch. Sonia tried to swing her hips from side to side but the fence and the ropes kept her from escaping.

'Less movement if you please, sweetheart, or we may have to double the punishment,' Fern said, already enjoying herself. She studied the pink marks she'd already made and aimed the swishy willow twigs beneath them. Then she applied the implement to the squealing Sonia again. 'I think I'm going to find job satisfaction here,' she laughed, stroking the girl's bum and keeping her waiting for the rest of her thrashing. 'I think I'm going to find this work has a lot of perks.'

'I could suck your toes, Mistress. Lick your clit,' Sonia suggested her voice thick with apprehension and the submission that would lead to a heavy hot arousal.

'I think I'd like you to tongue my arsehole,' Fern said. She swung the birch at the woman's lower buttock curve then repeated the whacking: 'I'm not hearing you answer in the affirmative, slave!'

Sonia flinched and whimpered as she tasted the birch: 'Please, Mistress, anything but licking inside your arse!' She wriggled her bum, obviously hugely shamed by the debasing image. 'But I could kiss your bottom cheeks for hour after hour.'

'You could stick your tongue inside my arse and thank me nicely for allowing you to do so,' Fern cut in. She knew from Sonia's slightly defiant silence that she'd have to apply the birch again and again. Fern smiled to herself as she contemplated the helpless reddening globes. She was going to love life at *Compulsion* now that Sonia was the one serving time.

262

NEXUS BACKLIST

This information is correct at time of printing. For up-to-date information, please visit our website at www.nexus-books.co.uk

All books are priced at £6.99 unless another price is given.

THE ACADEMY	Arabella Knight 0 352 33806 7	☐
AMANDA IN THE PRIVATE HOUSE	Esme Ombreux 0 352 33705 2	☐
ANGEL £5.99	Lindsay Gordon 0 352 33590 4	☐
BAD PENNY £5.99	Penny Birch 0 352 33661 7	☐
BARE BEHIND	Penny Birch 0 352 33721 4	☐
BEAST £5.99	Wendy Swanscombe 0 352 33649 8	☐
BELLE SUBMISSION	Yolanda Celbridge 0 352 33728 1	☐
BENCH-MARKS	Tara Black 0 352 33797 4	☐
BRAT	Penny Birch 0 352 33674 9	☐
BROUGHT TO HEEL £5.99	Arabella Knight 0 352 33508 4	☐
CAGED! £5.99	Yolanda Celbridge 0 352 33650 1	☐
CAPTIVE £5.99	Aishling Morgan 0 352 33585 8	☐
CAPTIVES OF THE PRIVATE HOUSE £5.99	Esme Ombreux 0 352 33619 6	☐
CHALLENGED TO SERVE	Jacqueline Bellevois 0 352 33748 6	☐

- - - - - - ✂ -

Please send me the books I have ticked above.

Name ....

Address ....

....

....

.... Post code....................

Send to: **Virgin Books Cash Sales, Thames Wharf Studios, Rainville Road, London W6 9HA**

US customers: for prices and details of how to order books for delivery by mail, call 1-800-343-4499.

Please enclose a cheque or postal order, made payable to **Nexus Books Ltd**, to the value of the books you have ordered plus postage and packing costs as follows:

UK and BFPO – £1.00 for the first book, 50p for each subsequent book.

Overseas (including Republic of Ireland) – £2.00 for the first book, £1.00 for each subsequent book.

If you would prefer to pay by VISA, ACCESS/MASTERCARD, AMEX, DINERS CLUB or SWITCH, please write your card number and expiry date here:

....

Please allow up to 28 days for delivery.

Signature ....

Our privacy policy

We will not disclose information you supply us to any other parties. We will not disclose any information which identifies you personally to any person without your express consent.

From time to time we may send out information about Nexus books and special offers. Please tick here if you do *not* wish to receive Nexus information. ☐

- - - - - - ✂ -